T3-BIK-433

"Aren't you going to get in trouble over my skunks?"

"You shouldn't think of them as your skunks, Emma, or you'll hate letting them go even more. Yes, I can get into trouble, but I can ask forgiveness."

"As opposed to permission?"

He rinsed out the sink and hung the dish towel on its hook. And yawned. "Sorry."

"Go home. Go to bed."

She followed him to the front door.

He turned, took one step, swung back and reached for her.

It might have started out as a meet-the-new-neighbor kiss, but it got out of hand—fast. She wasn't used to being lifted off her feet. When he wrapped his arms around her, she felt as if she was being hugged by that bear in the honey tree.

He set her down, let her go, wheeled around and almost ran across the street.

Dear Reader,

City girl Emma French gets fired from her job and dumps her unfaithful fiancé the same day. She moves to the country to recover, but instead, she finds herself rearing three orphaned baby skunks. Although it is illegal in Tennessee to foster skunks, she persuades her neighbor, Seth Logan—a tough, by-the-book game warden—to help her.

Emma knows nothing about animals, and she doesn't plan to stay in Tennessee—and certainly not with a game warden, even one as sexy as Seth. Although she rocks his world the first time he meets her, Seth realizes she absolutely cannot fit into his life.

They've both suffered pain and loss, but with the help of three cuddly baby skunks, they may find their way to one another and to the love that is waiting for them.

I hope you enjoy Emma and Seth's story and will look for the next book in the series. This is a work of fiction. I hope I got things right, but if I made mistakes, they are my fault.

Carolyn

CAROLYN McSPARREN

Tennessee Rescue

HARLEQUIN® SUPERROMANCE®

If you purchased this book without a cover you should be aware that this book is stolen property. It was reported as "unsold and destroyed" to the publisher, and neither the author nor the publisher has received any payment for this "stripped book."

Recycling programs for this product may not exist in your area.

ISBN-13: 978-1-335-44923-8

Tennessee Rescue

Copyright © 2018 by Carolyn McSparren

All rights reserved. Except for use in any review, the reproduction or utilization of this work in whole or in part in any form by any electronic, mechanical or other means, now known or hereafter invented, including xerography, photocopying and recording, or in any information storage or retrieval system, is forbidden without the written permission of the publisher, Harlequin Enterprises Limited, 22 Adelaide St. West, 40th Floor, Toronto, Ontario M5H 4E3, Canada.

This is a work of fiction. Names, characters, places and incidents are either the product of the author's imagination or are used fictitiously, and any resemblance to actual persons, living or dead, business establishments, events or locales is entirely coincidental.

This edition published by arrangement with Harlequin Books S.A.

For questions and comments about the quality of this book, please contact us at CustomerService@Harlequin.com.

® and TM are trademarks of Harlequin Enterprises Limited or its corporate affiliates. Trademarks indicated with ® are registered in the United States Patent and Trademark Office, the Canadian Intellectual Property Office and in other countries.

Printed in U.S.A.

HARLEQUIN®
™ www.Harlequin.com

RITA® Award nominee and Maggie Award winner **Carolyn McSparren** has lived in Germany, France, Italy and "too many cities in the US to count." She's sailed boats, raised horses, rides dressage and drives a carriage with her Shire-cross mare. She teaches writing seminars to romance and mystery writers, and writes mystery and women's fiction as well as romance books. Carolyn lives in the country outside Memphis, Tennessee, in an old house with three cats, three horses and one husband.

Books by Carolyn McSparren

HARLEQUIN SUPERROMANCE

The Wrong Wife
Safe at Home
The Money Man
The Payback Man
House of Strangers
Listen to the Child
Over His Head
His Only Defense
Bachelor Cop

Visit the Author Profile page at Harlequin.com for more titles.

This book is dedicated to that remarkable group of volunteers called animal rehabilitators who spend a lot of time and money looking after wounded, abandoned and displaced animals. There is even a specially trained group that works with wounded raptors—eagles, owls and hawks.

Each state has its own licensing requirements, but all require that these hardworking folks know what they are doing. The animal doesn't have to be cute. Turkey buzzard or baby bunny—if it's in trouble, they help.

Good for them!

CHAPTER ONE

"I HAVE SKUNKS in my pantry," Emma French said.

The man who opened his front door to her wore the green uniform of a Tennessee Wildlife officer. At least according to the emblem on his mailbox down by the road. Skunks were wildlife, so he should be able to deal with the three in her pantry. She had no intention of touching them. He, on the other hand, looked as though he wrestled moose on weekends—not that there were moose in Tennessee. Skunks should be only a small distraction.

She had obviously interrupted him in the middle of his dinner. He still held a napkin. But this was an emergency, drat it. She expected him to grab a cage or gloves or a net and follow her out into the downpour at once. Instead, he lifted one eyebrow and said, "Interesting. And you are?"

"I'm Emma French, the one who inherited Martha's house across the street. I just moved in this afternoon and found them."

He stuck out a hand. "I'm Seth Logan. Moved

in here after Miss Martha had to go into assisted living, so I never knew her, but I've heard good things about her. Since the last renters left six months ago, everyone in the neighborhood figured the property was up for sale."

"My rental agent hasn't located any new renters for me way out here. Can you come get the skunks? Isn't that your job?"

"Not precisely, no. How big are the skunks? How old?"

"I have no idea how old they are." She held her thumb and middle fingers apart. "They're about this size, I guess. Little bitty."

"Excellent. At that age, they can't 'skunk' you. Their scent glands don't function."

"Great. Then you'll be safe when you pick them up."

He didn't move or even ask her in out of the rain. Good grief! The last thing she needed was a useless muscle-bound stud in a snappy uniform living across the road. Judging by that lifted eyebrow and the quirk at the corner of his mouth, she'd bet he had to beat women off with a stick. Assuming he wanted to.

The man was laughing at her! "Sir, I am formally requesting your assistance in getting the wildlife—" she pointed to the insignia on his khaki shirt "—out of my house and back into the wild. Thank you in advance for your assistance."

Then he really did laugh. Well, more of a snort, but he obviously considered her amusing. She was *not* amusing. She was a serious executive—okay, a currently unemployed executive—moving into the shambles of a house she'd inherited in the middle of nowhere. She'd expected grime and peeling paint. She hadn't expected live creatures inside. Definitely not skunks.

As long as *they* were in residence, she didn't plan to be. Either they'd have to go or she would. But where? She couldn't afford to live in a motel for very long, even the rent-by-the-hour place close to the interstate. She had to shepherd her savings and severance pay, in case she didn't get a new job right away. She'd rather die than ask her father and stepmother for money to tide her over, although they'd gladly help her out if she was desperate. She didn't plan to ask them unless or until she *was* desperate.

She'd expected that after three years of renters and six months standing empty, Aunt Martha's house—her house now—would have problems, but skunks? Ridiculous.

It might take months to find another job as good as the one she'd just been fired from. Until then, she needed to live as frugally as possible. It made no sense to live in a motel while she owned a three-bedroom house on five acres; she'd inherited the place from her aunt Martha with taxes paid and no mortgage. It was empty and urgently needed renovation, but it had a roof and working plumbing. Good enough. She was a stranger here. She wouldn't have to deal with personal questions.

Aunt Martha's inheritance was the only thing that did belong to her free and clear at the moment. She still owed money on her SUV, and her little town house in Memphis still carried a hefty mortgage. She didn't want to sell it. She'd told her agent to try to rent it furnished on a short-term lease.

Okay, so she was escaping. She simply had to get away from all the damned sympathy! Who loses both a job and a fiancé in twenty-four hours?

Living in the boondocks near the Tennessee River was strictly a stopgap. She was a city girl. Period. She'd loved her childhood summers up here with her aunt, but Martha was gone and Emma wasn't a child anymore. In those long-ago summers she'd come here to a place and a person she loved, someone who'd cared about her, too. Now she wanted sanctuary. She was lucky she had this sanctuary.

"Does your pantry have a door?" Mr. Wild-life asked. Finally, he stood aside to let her in.

She stayed under the porch overhang. No

sense in dripping all over his living room floor. "Yes, why?"

"Shut the door on the skunks and forget them. Either they have a way out and will leave on their own, or you can let them out tomorrow morning in the daylight."

"With all this rain? They'll freeze."

"Probably not."

"Then they'll starve! Will they find their mother?"

He sighed. "Wish I could say yes, but skunk mothers don't abandon kits. I suspect she's road-kill."

"Oh, no! Then I'll have to look after them!"

He shook his head. "Not in Tennessee you don't. It's illegal to foster abandoned skunks."

"Why on earth?"

"In east Tennessee they can be rabid. Here in west Tennessee we haven't had a rabid skunk in a hundred and fifty years."

"But the law still applies throughout the whole state? So you're just going to let them starve or get eaten by coyotes? No way!" She turned on her heel. "Thank you, Mr. Officer, sir. Go enjoy your dinner. I've got this."

She could feel his eyes on her back as she stalked down his front path, across the road and through her front door. She didn't exactly slam it behind her, but she gave it a hard shove. She'd left all the lights on, so she could see her way among the boxes she'd brought with her. She brushed the rain off her short hair, tiptoed through the kitchen and stuck her head in the pantry.

Toss them out to die? Not in this lifetime! The heck with the laws of Tennessee. She'd find a vet to give them rabies shots, then she'd hide them from Mr. Big Lawman if she had to. But what on earth did baby skunks eat?

Inside the pantry, she found the three babies cuddled on the fluffy towel she'd folded up for them and stuffed in a corner. For a second they were so still she was terrified they'd died. Then she saw three furry little tummies rise and fall gently and blew out a breath in relief.

She got a shallow bowl from a kitchen cupboard, half filled it with water and set it carefully beside the towel. One tiny paw waggled at her, almost like a greeting. She had to admit they were about the cutest babies she'd ever seen. Skunks. Who knew?

How long had they been without their mother? Was she dead or trying desperately to get into the house to to reach them? How had they gotten inside in the first place? And, more important, as their foster parent, how was she going to keep them alive and teach them to live in the wild?

She had no intention of living with three skunks with functioning scent glands, but they seemed to have no scent yet. When she finally turned them loose, she wanted to release three skunks proficient in survival skills. Not pets. She'd never owned a pet, and she wasn't about to start with skunks.

SETH LOGAN STOOD by his front door and watched his new neighbor march from his house back to hers, then disappear inside. The last thing he needed was a crazy city neighbor with a do-gooder mentality and the practical knowledge of a newt.

At least she wasn't beautiful. Shoot. On reflection, he decided that when she dried off she might well be beautiful. Not many women reached his six-foot-four-inch height, but she didn't miss six feet by much, and he suspected she spent hours of city time in a fancy gym to keep what, even in jeans, he could tell was a sleek body.

She might find some yoga classes at one of the churches in the neighborhood, but the closest gym was twenty miles away.

She'd probably brought a treadmill or a stair-climber in the back of that big SUV. Clare had filled his guest room with expensive exercise equipment, but she'd taken it all with her when she walked out on him. He certainly didn't need it. He got plenty of exercise chasing down poachers and rescuing lost hikers.

He had a sudden vision of his new neighbor in bicycle shorts and a tank top. He felt his face flush and an immediate reaction from other parts of his body that had been underutilized lately.

It had been too long. Much too long. He'd worried last week that Wanda Joe at the DQ was starting to look good to him, even though he and Earl had gone to high school with her children.

What had possessed him to be borderline rude to his new neighbor? She was right to be annoyed. She had no way of knowing that her skunk problem had capped a god-awful day that began at three in the morning with a couple of idiots jacklighting deer on posted property. He'd caught one of them after the guy put a couple of slugs into the stuffed decoy deer, but he'd lost the second one.

Not the woman's fault, and yet he'd still taken it out on her.

She had no way of knowing what a can of worms she'd stepped into with the skunks. He didn't want to toss the orphaned kits into the wide world any more than she did. He could stretch the rules for a bit, but rules were made for a reason and he obeyed them. Rules saved lives.

"Heck," he said, sliding his dishes into the dishwasher. He changed into old jeans and an even older sweatshirt, filled a clean jelly jar with milk, found a couple of cans of dog food left over from before Rambler died, and headed across the road to do what he should've done in the first place. Help the woman. He'd worry about a practical solution to her skunk problem tomorrow.

He felt instinctively that having her as a neighbor meant his peaceful life was sliding back down into chaos. Shoot, he was just getting used to peace.

CHAPTER TWO

EMMA JUMPED A foot when she heard the knock. She turned on her front porch light and peered through the antique oval glass set in the door. Ah, Mr. Wildlife himself. He swept off his wide-brimmed hat and shook streams of water off it. So she'd recognize him? Not necessary. She didn't know anyone else within a hundred miles in any direction, much less a giant in a dripping poncho.

Had he come to arrest her for harboring her three orphans? Just let him try. She opened the door and said, "Yes?" in her coolest executive-of-the-month voice.

"You wanted help." He held out a small jar full of white stuff that sloshed. "I have an old kitten syringe. You can squirt some milk down their throats. How many, by the way?"

This was more like it. She morphed from uppity to Scarlet O'Hara helpless in one breath, flashed him what she hoped was a killer smile and stood aside so he could come in. "Three. Two girls and a boy."

"Tell me you haven't named them." He hung his dripping poncho and hat on the old hat rack and slipped out of his sodden muckers. He was wearing a khaki sock and a red one.

Big, tough government official couldn't even match his socks. Probably meant there was no woman living with him. If there was, she didn't take very good care of him. Trip would no more wear mismatched socks than he'd wear bunny ears to an international conference.

But it was kind of endearing in a goofy way. She smiled at him. He didn't smile back. "I had to call them something to tell them apart."

He sighed. "Not a good idea. Keep them depersonalized. Makes it easier afterward. So what did you call them?"

"I thought maybe Chanel, Arpege and Brut, but then I decided that might get me in trouble with copyrights," she joked. "So at this point they're Rose, Peony and Sycamore."

He just shut his eyes and shook his head. "Okay, let me see them."

He handed her the jar of milk and the syringe, followed her to the pantry and dropped onto his haunches beside their makeshift bed. "They're cold. You got a heating pad?"

"No, I don't."

He glanced up at her. "Well, I do. Let's get them fed and I'll go get it. Give me the stuff."

She handed the jar to him carefully. She didn't want it to slip out of her hands and break on the pantry floor. No worry there. He enveloped the jar with a paw that would make Bigfoot feel inadequate.

For a moment he simply gazed down at the babies. "Cute little buggers," he said. He went up a good ten points in her estimation.

He took two pairs of rubber gloves from his pocket, handed the second set to her.

"Come here, critter," he whispered and picked up the nearest baby. There was a comic strip in her local newspaper in which one of the characters was so huge that he could hold his baby in the palm of his hand. This little one was cradled just as effectively.

"Here, fill the syringe with milk," he said, "then lift the corner of its mouth and slip it in. Do not, I repeat *not*, jab it in and shoot it down the throat. The milk'll wind up going into the lungs. They've got enough troubles without pneumonia."

She gulped. Great way to make her feel competent. She lifted the corner of the tiny mouth with her index finger, then with her other hand inserted the syringe and pushed the plunger so that a drop of milk went into the baby's mouth.

Wonder of wonders, its little throat moved and the milk disappeared. After a dozen further drops, the baby seemed to get the idea.

"Okay, now try the center of the mouth. Easy!" he said. A moment later she actually held a suckling baby—a very hungry baby. The others were stirring, making mewling noises and swimming toward her the way puppies supposedly did when they were just born. They must smell the milk.

"Whoa," he said and took the syringe. "Don't you have any brothers or sisters? You can't let the baby drink down to the last drop. It'll get a stomach full of air. Besides, it's had enough." He set the complaining baby back on the towel and picked up the second. "Okay, this is one of your girls."

"That's Rose. She's the one with the two broad stripes on her head. Peony's are narrower. Sycamore has two all the way down his back." This time the nursing went better, and Emma felt she was getting the hang of it. The third baby had problems, but eventually managed a few sips. When she set her down, the towel had begun to smell and felt damp. "I thought they didn't have any scent yet," she said.

He grinned up at her. "They don't. That's baby poop. In the wild, Momma would take care of it. Since you've elected yourself their foster mother, it's your responsibility. Incidentally, they'll have to be fed every four hours around the clock and stimulated to go to the bathroom."

"How do I do that?"

"I'll show you. Welcome to the world of foster parenthood." He surged to his feet in one easy motion.

He reached down and offered a hand to pull her up.

She took it and found herself lifted against him as though she'd been shot out of a cannon. He smelled male—no fancy aftershave, just good, basic male.

Oh, boy, talk about pheromones! The hair on her arms stood straight up. She stepped back to get out of his zone, which, at this point, felt as though it might extend all the way to Memphis. "Um," she said. "Heating pad?"

He dropped her hand. "Be right back. In the meantime, find a clean towel to replace this one, then soak the dirty one in the sink with some bleach if you have it."

"I have it, but I don't know where it is." She waved a hand at the boxes on the kitchen floor. "I'll wash it by hand. The washer and dryer are hooked up, but I'm not about to do a load to wash one poopy towel."

After the front door closed behind him, she sank into the closest dining room chair. Some introduction to her new home. Her new lifestyle. Quite a comedown from assistant marketing manager for one of the largest public relations firms in Tennessee. From a town house in Mud

Island on the Mississippi River to a hovel in the middle of nowhere, complete with skunks. From having her picture taken at the symphony ball to scrubbing skunk poop.

She'd never really cared how often she and Trip made the society pages of *The Commercial Appeal* for attending some party or concert or art exhibit in Memphis or Nashville. Trip cared, though. He wanted them to be the Golden Couple, and their upcoming marriage to be the event of the season. She wondered how long it would take him to replace her with another princess bride. And how long before he'd betray his new fiancée the way he'd betrayed Emma.

This time Seth Logan didn't bother to ring the bell or knock, but opened the door and came in. Again he shed his dripping poncho and slipped his feet out of his muckers before he stepped from the tiled area to the wooden floor. Somebody had taught him manners. Or maybe that was standard procedure in the country when it rained.

"Here you go," he said and handed her a plush-covered heating pad. "You'll have to wrap it in a towel and keep it on the lowest setting…" He glanced at the boxes. "You find the other towels yet?"

"I just sat down for a second." Suddenly she felt as though she couldn't get up again.

"Always take care of your animals first." He peered at the boxes. "Here we go. This box says 'towels.'" He set the heating pad on the kitchen counter and opened one of the boxes.

She clambered to her feet when she caught sight of the brocade edging on the coral towels. "Not those! Those are for company."

"Then find me some for skunks."

She wanted to yell that he should find them himself. Wrong. He was probably as tired as she was, but at least he was *here*. That counted for a lot.

She had to tear open only two other boxes to find the everyday towels. She arranged one under the babies, which were now fast asleep.

He wrapped the heating pad in another towel, plugged it in and set it up under the makeshift nest. "We don't want them to overheat."

"I should keep them at mother temperature, right?"

He actually smiled. "You got it. Happen to know what skunk-mother temperature is? I don't, so just keep it on the lowest setting. The next time you feed them, kick it up a notch if they're shaking. Otherwise, I think we're good to go." He narrowed his eyes at her. "Look, have you had anything to eat?"

Glory, she must look really terrible. "I vaguely remember a cheeseburger sometime around the year 2003. I'm not hungry, which is a miracle. But I could murder a cup of tea."

"Any idea where the teapot might be?"

"First thing I found." She pulled herself upright by an effort of will, took the snazzy imported electric pot out of the cabinet, filled it and plugged it in. "That'll take five minutes to heat and another five to steep. Gives us ten minutes to find the mugs."

Ten minutes later, she handed him his mug of tea, which, thank goodness, he said he drank with lemon, no sugar and no milk. She had lemon, but the only milk was for the babies, not their caregivers. The sugar was hidden somewhere.

"You said you were tired, too. I'm grateful you came, but you don't have to stay," she said, hoping he would. Between exhaustion and skunks, she was starting to feel panicky-lonely. She'd never been lonely, damn it, but then she'd lived in a city house with lights and neighbors and traffic. She could drive to her family's place in Memphis for dinner with her father, her stepmother, Andrea, and both her brother and sister in twenty minutes. When she was there, she knew where she belonged and who she was.

Now, not so much. Sitting here in this living room she might as well be on the far side of Alpha Centauri.

"Nice sofa," he said as he drank his tea and relaxed into its depths.

Well, yeah. It had cost a month's salary; it *should* be comfortable.

"This doesn't solve the problem," he said and set his empty mug on the coffee table. "You cannot keep the skunks."

"Now, wait…"

"Can't foster bats either, because of possible rabies. If you'd discovered a cache of raccoons, I could hook you up with one of the local animal rehabilitators."

"There is such a thing?"

"Absolutely. There are people who specialize in raptors or abandoned fawns. Sometimes a momma possum will get hit by a car and killed, but the babies in her pouch survive and have to be tended. There's a lady outside Collierville who takes in orphan foxes…"

She felt the tears threaten to spill over. "You say there's no rabies in our skunks, yet you'd just let them die?"

"Can't take the chance."

"Nonsense!" She slammed her mug down on the table so hard the edge of the cup cracked.

"You saw we wore gloves when you fed them?" he said. "And you'd better continue to do that. At the moment they have no teeth, but their little milk teeth will be sharp."

"Fine. So vaccinate them against rabies. Heck, vaccinate me, too. Problem solved." She sat down again.

"That's not the way the rules read."

That did it. "Then arrest me." She got to her feet again and held out her wrists. "I'll have a public relations campaign set up for 'Save the Skunks' before the cell door shuts on me. You and your rules will feel as if you've run into a buzz saw. Every animal rights organization in the Western Hemisphere will be knocking on your door and marching with signs. This is what I do—did—for a living. Coordinating the message to spread across all possible outlets. One picture of my babies snuggled up on Facebook, one podcast, and even the governor won't call your name blessed."

"You can't do that."

"Watch me."

"Sit down before you fall down. I have no intention of arresting you, nor do I intend to starve, freeze or euthanize your trio of illegal aliens."

"So I can keep them?"

"No, dammit! I've got to figure out how to handle this without getting me fired and you fined." He ran a big hand down his face. "Right now I can't think straight, and you're starting to get on my last nerve." He stood and closed his eyes, swaying on his feet for a moment. "Just for tonight I've never met you, I do not know that you have skunks, but that can't go on. I'm going to get some sleep, assuming I can with all this hanging over my head. I'll call you tomorrow. You do have a phone?"

She nodded, took a piece of paper out of the pocket of her jeans, wrote her cell number on it and passed it to him. "I'm sorry I've been such a pain."

He reached into his pants pocket. "Here's my card with both my numbers. If you need me, call."

She followed him to the door, helped him on with the damp poncho, and watched him stuff his feet in their mismatched socks into his muckers and go back out in the rain, which showed no signs of letting up. She handed him his hat and watched him trudge out to the road and across until he disappeared into his own house.

Only then did she sit on the sofa and burst into tears. Why did he have to be gorgeous and kind? He was still her enemy, with the entire state of Tennessee backing him up.

CHAPTER THREE

SETH NOTICED WHEN he stripped off his wet clothes that his socks didn't match. That woman—he'd better learn to call her Emma, since they were way beyond Ms. French—probably figured he was either color-blind or incompetent. Which was how he felt at the moment.

Emma was a nice old-fashioned name. Not that she was a nice old-fashioned girl. Far from it. Probably never bought a pair of jeans from a discount store in her life. Heck, the way hers fit, they were worth the investment.

He poured himself a small Scotch and sank onto his saggy leather sofa with his feet on the slab of hundred-year-old oak he'd salvaged from a downed tree. One of the few pieces Clare had left when she'd walked out. And which was now covered with dust like everything else in this house.

He leaned his head back and laid his hand on the sofa where he was used to feeling Rambler's deep furry pelt. Now that Rambler had died of old age, Seth needed another dog. Dogs didn't present insoluble problems with beautiful women. They didn't care whether a woman was beautiful or a clone of the Wicked Witch as long as she petted and fed him.

Why did he invariably get involved with women who complicated his life and didn't belong to his world? He'd tried to convert Clare to country living, but in the end she'd moved to Nashville and married a dentist. A rich dentist. She really had tried to put up with living in the back of beyond—her words—with a man who frequently stank of blood or fish and came home covered in mud or dirt. At least she'd tried for a while. He knew now that she'd assumed he'd quickly be promoted to a desk job so they could buy a suburban house and have a country club membership. Meanwhile, he'd assumed she'd loved the country as much as he did. Talk about a lack of communication.

Thinking back, the water moccasin marked the true end of their relationship. He'd tried to teach her about good snakes and bad snakes, but she never understood. Snake was snake to Clare. He wasn't thrilled to meet copperheads or rattlers or water moccasins either, but he was fond of the king snakes. Keep a big king snake around, you never saw a poisonous snake. Well, mostly. Didn't have to worry about rats or mice either. A good king snake would beat a barn cat every time when it came to killing mice. And a king snake sucked down the whole mouse—didn't nibble the edges like a cat did and leave you to clean up the remains.

That moccasin she'd nearly stepped on wasn't even coiled. Just stretched out across the front porch steps sunning itself. Couldn't have struck Clare if it had tried—not without coiling first.

When he'd been with the department less than six months, he'd had to deliver a baby for a woman who couldn't make it to Jackson to the hospital. He'd never heard screams like that before, and he'd prayed he never would again.

Clare's screams when she saw that snake as she started up the porch step put that other woman to shame. Who was that comic book character that could move so fast? Clare would've beaten that guy back to the car. She dived in the passenger side, screaming, "Shoot him! Shoot him!"

When he explained to her that snakes are protected in Tennessee, she hit him so hard he'd had a bruised shoulder for a week. He'd walked over and checked, then reported back that the snake had removed itself from the porch, no doubt annoyed that its nap was interrupted. She refused to get out of the car. Ever.

They'd spent that night in the local motel. Not exactly the Peabody. She'd been upset about that, as well. It was clean, and the Patels were nice people, but the towels were thin. Clare hated thin towels. He'd finally convinced her to come back to the house, after he spent a couple of hours patrolling the yard and shed for the snake, but that was the beginning of the end. A week later, she moved out. A week after that, she served him with divorce papers. He never saw the snake again; Mother Nature might say that snake had done its job by getting rid of her. Took him a long time to admit that, even to himself.

He'd give Emma French about three days before she moved out and back to the city. At that point, the skunks would become his problem. Hell, they already were.

He checked his watch and was surprised it was only a little after nine. He dug out his cell phone and hit his speed dial.

He got the clinic's voice mail. "This is Dr. Barbara Carew. The clinic office hours are eight thirty till six, Monday through Friday. Saturday eight thirty till one. If this is an emergency, please call our emergency service at…"

He waited to leave a message, then said, "Barbara, it's me, Seth. I need some advice. Please meet me at seven tomorrow morning at the café. I'll buy you breakfast. If I don't hear from you, I'll assume you'll be there. This is important." He hung up. She'd pick up her messages before she went to bed. If she wasn't out working on a colicky horse or birthing a calf, she'd meet him. He let his head fall back against the sofa. He could feel that Scotch down to his toenails. Or maybe he was feeling simple exhaustion. He was too damned tired to feel lust.

Whom was he kidding? A man would have to be dead and buried not to lust after Emma French. But in his present state of weariness, he might not be capable of doing much about it.

ACROSS THE STREET Emma called her father to tell him she had a roof over her head that didn't leak and a dry, if lumpy, bed to sleep in. She got his answering machine. Of course. She could call her stepmother Andrea's cell phone instead, but decided she was too tired for explanations.

She didn't mention her invaders on her message to her father. He would be horrified. He was already haranguing her about moving to the country instead of coming home to stay until she found a new job. Which he would no doubt find for her with one of his cronies regardless of whether they needed her.

Not happening. At least, not yet. She had enough savings to survive for a bit. If she rented out her town house, she'd be able to hold out quite a while.

She got ready for bed, set her alarm for midnight—four hours since the babies were last fed.

She hadn't answered any of Trip's calls on her cell phone. Sooner or later she'd talk to him, but not yet. He'd sworn he still loved her, wanted to make things right between them. As if. He'd even fooled David French. Her father had welcomed him as her fiancé. Although in this case his usual mantra—that the man wasn't good enough for her—was accurate.

She was always afraid men would realize she wasn't good enough for *them*.

THE MIDNIGHT FEEDING went okay, but at four, Emma hated slipping out of her warm bed and into the cold house to heat up…whoa, she should've asked Seth how warm the jar of milk that presently resided in her refrigerator should be. She put her hand on her cell phone to call him, then set it back on the kitchen counter. The man was exhausted. She couldn't repay his kindness by waking him from a sleep he obviously needed.

She ran the jar under hot water in the sink to take the chill off, but not enough to heat it up. That should be safe.

As she cradled Sycamore, who already had this nursing business down pat, she wondered whether her semiconscious state was what human mothers felt during the late-night feedings. Remembering her half brother and half sister as newborns, she decided that these skunk babies were a bunch cuter than their human counterparts and didn't scream blue murder between feedings.

Would she ever have that mother feeling with her own newborn? Didn't look like it at the moment. She wanted a man she could count on, who believed in fidelity. Trip obviously did not. If he could cheat on his fiancée, what would he do to his wife?

The whole situation had looked so perfect at the start. Even her father had finally agreed that marrying Trip would be a good choice. Well— *goodish*. Daddy's take was that no man who'd ever lived was good enough for his Emma, but Trip would keep her safe and happy.

Now, she'd come to the realization that even if Trip wanted her back, she did not now or ever want to marry him. Whatever she'd thought she felt for him, she knew it was never love. Convenience? Appropriateness? Timing? She wasn't sure she'd recognize real love if she ran into it like a brick wall.

Maybe she'd move to Montana or Alaska or somewhere there were more men than women. The pool of eligible bachelors in west Tennessee that she hadn't already crossed off her list was getting smaller and smaller.

Okay, she'd been raised to be picky. Even in high school her father had second-guessed her crushes.

He'd guessed wrong on Trip. Daddy simply couldn't understand why she'd broken her engagement. If she had her way, he'd never know.

Actually, losing her job working for Nathan was worse than losing Trip. Maybe she should take up fostering abandoned baby *scapegoats*. She'd be right at home being the mother of *that* herd. Accepting blame for something that was her fault was one thing. Being fired because of someone else's screwup made her angry. She hadn't even had a chance to plead her case before Nathan fired her.

She settled Rose next to Sycamore and picked up Peony. She could already tell them apart not by their looks—although their stripes were different—but by their personalities. Sycamore was a bit of a bully and certainly greedy. Rose was gentle and liked to be cuddled. Peony was sweet, but Emma decided she didn't have a brain in her soft little head. The poor baby tried to figure out the nursing thing, but the practical aspects simply eluded her.

Eventually Emma managed to get enough milk down Peony's throat, rather than on her fur, that she felt comfortable returning her to the nest. She put the remaining milk back in the refrigerator and realized she'd have to make a run to the grocery for another gallon or so come morning. She had enough for only one more feeding.

Seth had left a couple of cans of dog food on the kitchen counter, but she'd better do some internet research on how to feed her charges before she offered them dog food. She'd ask Seth tomorrow, as well. Maybe just a tiny bit mashed up in the milk. But how would she get the solid food into their mouths through that syringe?

Relishing the still-warm bed, she snuggled down again. This time sleep eluded her. The whole country-life thing had turned into a major fiasco. She ought to pack her duffel bag and go home. What did she know about living in the country? Rehabbing a run-down house? Feeding skunks?

A niggling voice in the back of her mind whispered, "But Seth knows how to help me."

Another niggling voice followed. "Yeah, but I'll bet he won't."

BARBARA CAREW'S MOBILE vet van was already sitting in the parking lot at the Forked Deer Café when Seth pulled in beside it. She was reading the *Marquette County Gazette* in the back booth of the café and cradling a giant mug of coffee.

"You ever sleep?" he asked as he slid into the banquette across from her.

"When the animals let me," she said. She

folded the paper, put it down on the patched leatherette bench and took a swig of her coffee. "This helps. Good morning, Seth."

A brawny arm and hand carrying a mug of coffee the size of Barbara's reached across his shoulder and set the cup on the table in front of him. "Hey, Seth," a gravelly voice said. "The usual?"

"Thanks, Velma."

"You have bags under your eyes," Barbara told him.

"Those bags probably have bags," Seth muttered.

"Rough day yesterday?"

"No worse than usual. At least not until last night. Then things got complicated." He laid out the entire scenario, from Emma's knock on his front door until he left her with her black-and-white invaders.

"Here ya go, sweet thing." Velma set the plate with sausage, hash browns, eggs and grits on the table, then added a large glass of orange juice.

"If I ate like that, I'd be even fatter than I am," Barbara said. "Here I've got one country ham biscuit. Life is not fair."

"You are not fat," Seth said. "Just not skeletal."

"Way I work, I should be—skeletal, that is."

Seth cut into his eggs. "So, what should I do?"

"About what? The woman or the skunks?"

"Take your pick. I doubt the woman will stick

around for long, but if she does, what should I do about the rules on skunks?"

Barbara got up, went behind the counter and brought back the coffee carafe. She refilled both their cups, then returned the carafe to the hot plate. "Okay. I'm going to give you a bit of motherly advice." She scowled at him. "I *am* a mother, you know, even if mine are both semigrown. This, however, is advice from *my* mother. When Patrick hit the terrible twos, John and I had just taken over my practice and were trying to keep from throttling him. Seemed he was into something every minute. River otters are said to have two states—asleep or in trouble. I swear that kid has river otter genes instead of human. Anyway, one day when I was absolutely at my wit's end, and my mother was visiting, she said, 'Barbara, dear, do not *see* so much.'"

"What if he's hanging off a precipice by his fingernails?" Seth asked.

"That, of course, you do see. But if it's nondangerous stuff that you don't know how to handle, simply don't see it. In most instances, the problem resolves itself without you or the kid going to jail for first-degree murder. If this Emma is doing something that's against the rules—rules you say you don't believe are appropriate in the first place—is she doing it under your nose? Can you see or hear those skunks from inside your house or your car?"

"No, but I know they're there."

"Can you see them?"

"Of course not. But I need to check on her, make sure she's managing."

"Can you see the skunks from her living room?"

"They're in the pantry."

"Stay out of the pantry."

"I'm sworn to uphold the regulations."

"You are sworn to protect wildlife." Barbara reached across the table and laid her hand on his. "If you get caught, I had nothing to do with this."

"Oh, thanks, I appreciate that."

"We need to get those babies up and weaned as quickly and quietly as possible. Return them to the wild far enough away so they can't show up back on this woman's doorstep, and in the meantime, you forget they exist."

"I can't do that."

"The alternative is to come down on her like a ton of bricks, take those babies away from her and abandon them to the coyotes and the foxes before they even have their scent glands functioning. Can you do *that*?"

"No, but—"

"I'll stop by her place on my way back to the clinic to introduce myself. I'm the only vet in her neighborhood, and she's a new neighbor. Does she have any pets?"

He shook his head. "Not as far as I know."

"Okay, then I'll do the neighborly thing. I'll help her with those babies. First of all, rabies shots all around. It's early, but not dangerously early to give them the shot. You go on to work and put it all out of your mind." She shoved her plate away. "I'll go check on Skunk Lady. Velma, honey, fix me a couple of sausage biscuits and a small orange juice to go, please." She turned to Seth. "Vets bearing gifts. Good ploy. You pay for breakfast."

As he watched her van drive out of the parking lot, Seth thought, *The skunks are one thing, but no way can I put Emma French out of my mind. I'm already stuck with her. Heck, I may be stuck with her for the rest of my life. I can't get her out of my head. I don't even know whether that's good or bad.*

CHAPTER FOUR

THE HOVEL—EMMA'S new nickname for her house—had a good hot water heater and plenty of water pressure from her well, so as soon as she'd finished the eight o'clock feeding, she was able to stay under the shower until she turned pruney. She washed her hair, threw on clean clothes and actually put on some makeup. Once the babies were settled, she picked up her purse and started for the front door, only to see someone looming outside the glass.

The babies! That man had set the cops on her! She'd never felt like a fugitive before. Should she try to hide them? Would they search?

"Hey!" called a female voice. "I'm Barbara Carew, the local veterinarian. Seth sent me to give you a hand."

Emma didn't realize she'd been holding her breath until she let it out in an explosive gasp. She opened the door to her visitor.

The vet stood only about five feet three, wore bright blue scrubs with a beige hoodie cardigan and had the widest, bluest eyes Emma had ever seen outside of a contact lens store. She swept past Emma and handed her a paper sack in passing.

"Here. Breakfast. Figured you hadn't had time to eat or go out for anything. Where are they?"

"Uh—the pantry. Are you supposed to know about them?"

"Too late now. Sit." She pointed to one of the bar stools at the breakfast counter between the kitchen and living room. "Eat. You get any sleep? Food is an excellent alternative to sleep. Trust me. I know."

Too stunned to disobey, and suddenly ravenously hungry, Emma sat, opened the sack and inhaled. Then she began to devour.

Barbara swept past her, opened the door to the pantry, cooed, "Oooooh," and fell to her knees beside the skunks' nest. "The precious!"

"We have to save them," Emma said around a large bite.

Barbara picked up Peony, who whimpered before she curled into a ball against Barbara's chest. "Honey, you have convinced the toughest, by-the-book, hardnosed ranger in the state of Tennessee to break the rules for you and your babies. It's up to us to protect him from the dire results of his actions. I don't know what kind of hold you've got on him, but unless it's blackmail material, it has to be pure sex appeal."

"I don't…"

"He's my dearest friend. You be good to him, I'll love you like a sister. You hurt him, honey, and you're toast."

SETH SPENT THE morning in his office. For a job that concerned itself with the great outdoors, much of his time was spent staring at a computer screen filling out paperwork. Today he wasn't paying nearly enough attention to it. Emma French's face kept intruding. Didn't matter what program he was officially accessing. He picked up his desk phone a dozen times to call her and see how the babies were doing. Each time he put the phone back in its cradle without dialing. He'd stop by on his way home to see if he could give her a hand moving some of those boxes. He didn't even have to look at the skunks or mention that they were there.

Just before noon Earl Matthews stuck his head in the door of Seth's miniscule office. "Lunch? The café?"

"I had breakfast there this morning. Oh, shoot, doesn't mean I'm not hungry. Let me shut this computer down first. How about we pick up some sandwiches and head on over to the lake to check fishing licenses?"

"You got a deal."

Sitting in the official cruiser beside the dock on the oxbow lake that fed into the Tennessee

River some five miles to the south, they checked to see how many bass boats were out fishing. This late in the morning, there were none in view, although that didn't mean there weren't a few latecomers around the bend, close to the downed trees. Bass, crappie and catfish loved to hide among the branches of trees long submerged.

Seth let Earl run the launch down to the bend while he leaned back against the leather seats, slid his Smokey hat over his eyes and allowed his mind to drift. Emma French probably wouldn't stay long enough for him to get to know her. Obviously she was a city slickeress. Way above his pay grade. He'd generally gone for what his father called pocket Venuses. Like Clare. Five foot three and practically boneless.

Emma's flesh covered strong bones. She'd fight him over those blasted skunks or anything else she didn't agree with. If they ever made love—unlikely—it would be like igniting a thermonuclear device.

"Heads up," Earl said. "Party boat eleven o'clock."

Almost hidden where the high weeds drooped in the water, and under tree leaves that weren't fully open, a large, fancy pontoon party boat carrying a pair of powerful outboard motors was getting ready to hightail it away from them.

There were half a dozen people spooling in fishing lines as fast as they could, and one man hunkered over the two motors attached to the stern. The engines sputtered, then kicked into action.

"Oh, goodie!" Earl said. "Blow the horn, please, Mr. Policeman. I do believe they plan to evade inspection."

"Not if they don't get their anchor up first," Seth said. He shouted into the loud hailer, "Cut your engines now before you swamp!" At the moment that appeared to be an immediate threat. The party boat was built to run perilously close to the water on its pontoons with little freeboard. Normally, in calm waters, that was no problem. In wind and waves, however, the big boat was difficult to handle and swamped easily.

At the moment the two engines were attempting to back the boat against the anchor chain at the bow, but it showed no sign of lifting free of the mud bottom.

The louder the engines growled, the more the boat buried its engines deeper in the lake, lifting the bow perilously high. The people on board had run toward the stern—the opposite of what they should be doing—and now stood ankle-deep in water. The two women in the group were squealing and jumping around trying to keep their feet dry.

"Move forward toward the bow!" Seth yelled.

"And somebody cut those engines! Earl, get me over there."

"Be careful. Don't get trapped between boats, and do not fall into those propellers. They'll cut you to pieces." Earl, calm as always, steered his boat until it gently tapped the left pontoon amidships. Seth said a fast prayer, leaped, slipped, then righted himself safely on the deck.

He was afraid his weight would sink the boat before he could cut the engines. He moved a woman who outweighed him by a good hundred pounds toward the bow. "Get up there! You, too, ma'am," he snapped at her companion, as thin as she was fat.

He reached past one of the men and shut off both engines. Instantly the boat settled back on its pontoons. "The rest of you, go sit down amidships and don't move until I say so."

"You can't tell me what to do on my own boat!" said a grizzled man close to Seth's size, but flabby with age and unsteady on what Seth suspected were drunken legs.

"Yes, sir, I can. Sit down. All of you." Out of the corner of his eye he spotted the smaller of the two women surreptitiously trying to kick what looked like a bottle of Jack Daniel's under the edge of her seat.

"Hey, ma'am, don't try that," Earl called from the launch. She froze.

"Fishing licenses and boat registration," Seth said. Now that the initial disaster was averted, he was starting to seethe. "Earl, can you tie up to us and come on over here?"

"Sure thing."

Seth stepped back. "So, this is your boat, sir?" he asked the grizzled man who'd gone suddenly silent.

"Hell, yeah, it's mine, and you all like to have caused an accident running up on us like that."

"Uh-huh. How many passengers do you have on board this morning?"

"Can't you count? Five. We got five. We was just taking us a little ride…"

"Looked to me like you were doing a little fishing along the way," Seth said.

"Without fishing licenses," Earl said. He shrugged. "That's what *he* said." He pointed at a small man huddled in the seat across from the large woman. "More drinking than fishing, I think."

"Now, y'all lookee here…" The big man puffed himself up and huffed out what he must've felt was an intimidating breath. It didn't work. And it stank of alcohol.

"No, sir, *you* lookee here," Earl said. "There are signs all over this lake. No fishing without a license."

"May I see your current boat registration?" Seth asked. So far he'd managed to sound cool and polite, but underneath, his temper was going from simmer to boil.

The man deflated slightly. "Uh, musta left it back at the marina."

"We'll check it when we get back to the dock."

"Well…could be I left it back at the house."

"That's perfectly all right," Earl said. "We can check the number and expiration date on our computer over there in our boat. By law you're supposed to carry it on board at all times…"

"Lordy, young man," the giant lady said from her seat, "ain't nobody does that. This ain't no big houseboat."

"Shut up, Phoebe," the grizzled man snapped.

"No one seems to be wearing a life jacket, sir," Seth said.

"They in the lockers over there," the big woman said. "Right close, where we can get 'em if we need 'em." She sounded satisfied. "But you don't need life jackets on party boats, do you? Not like they sink or anything. Can't get drownded off one of these things, now, can you?"

"Uh-oh," Earl whispered. "Seth…" He touched Seth's forearm in warning.

Seth thought he sounded calm, but when he saw the sudden fear in the woman's eyes he realized that something in his demeanor had tele-graphed his annoyance. He opened the life jacket locker and tossed a jacket to each of the passengers. "Ma'am, you all nearly capsized ten minutes ago. A party boat doesn't care if it floats on its roof, and it doesn't turn back over on its own. You could've been trapped underneath or caught in the weeds. Please put these on. We are now going to give you a tow back to the marina, at which point we'll write up the offenses you're being arrested for..."

"Arrested?" The gray man inflated again. "You jackasses, write me a damn ticket, and we'll get our own self back to the marina when we feel like it."

Earl reached down and pulled the half-empty fifth of Jack Daniel's out from under the seat and held it up.

"That's not mine!" the man swore.

"It's your boat," Earl said mildly.

Seth never thought of Earl as a big man. Compared with Seth he was just normal. Still, when the boat owner took a swing at him, the man wound up sitting on his rear end. Earl hadn't even disturbed the equilibrium of the boat.

"Your name, sir?" Earl asked just as calmly as before.

"Grady Pulliam, not that it's any of y'all's

business. And I'm gonna sue your asses for harassment. I know the governor."

"So do I," Earl said. "He's my first cousin once removed."

CHAPTER FIVE

AN HOUR LATER, Seth and Earl left the party boat locked in its slip. The keys were with the marina master. He had instructions not to allow anyone to have them, especially Mr. Pulliam, until further notice. The owner would not be partying on his boat for a while. He'd signed off on an expensive ticket and a summons to show cause why he shouldn't lose his boat for drinking on board, plus a long list of other offenses. His wife was crying, and everyone else was shaking with embarrassment.

Earl and Seth could hear the burgeoning squabble behind them as they loaded their own boat on the trailer.

Earl said as they drove out of the parking lot, "Think old Grady will lose his boat?"

"If we were the Coast Guard, maybe, but you and I are small fry. He'll have fines to pay, probably some community service. We didn't actually see any of them taking a drink from that bottle of bourbon, and we don't have the Breathalyzer, so we can't get him on DUI just for having an open container aboard."

"We both know they were drinking. The man's breath stank like a still."

"He's lucky they didn't capsize or pitch pole, dragging against the anchor chain like that. I suspect that one lady would either float like a whale or sink like a stone. No idea which. With the exception of Pulliam, they were nice enough people, but they don't believe the rules apply to them."

"Or why we have rules in the first place," Earl said. "I gotta say, I was right proud of you about those life jackets. I know how you feel about wearing life jackets at all times, and I know how you get when a bunch of idiots stick them away so they can't reach 'em."

"Mrs. Pulliam could tell I was mad. I came close to punching everybody's lights out and tossing them overboard. I don't want to talk about it, okay?"

"Wish you'd stop scaring the stew out of me jumping from boat to boat like that. One of these days you're gonna miss and get yourself hurt."

"Next time, you can do it."

"Nunh-uh. Forget I said anything."

As they drove off, Seth asked, "Is the governor really your cousin?"

"Turns out he is, but I doubt he knows it, much less knows me."

"HAVE YOU DECIDED to come home where you belong?" David French's baritone rolled smoothly down the phone line. No greeting.

"Hello to you, too, Daddy. How lovely to hear from you." Emma let the honey roll off her tongue. He'd pick up on the sarcasm. He seldom missed nuances where she was concerned.

"Have you and Trip made up yet?" he asked.

"Not happening."

"Now, honey. Newly engaged couples invariably hit a few bumps on their way to the altar. Prenuptial nerves. I talked to Andrea about it. She says it's not unusual for a bride to be scared to make the final commitment."

"She say whether she was scared to make a final commitment to *you*, before she married you?"

"Shoot, yeah! But she got over it and not only took me on, but my twelve-year-old motherless daughter, as well. Believe me, you were no picnic." He laughed his professionally warm laugh.

Emma had wondered years ago if he practiced it in front of the mirror while he shaved in the morning.

"Sit down and talk to the man, at least, honey. He's been calling me a dozen times a day. Says you won't answer his calls or his emails."

"He's right. I haven't and I don't intend to.

I've said all I'm going to say. Both of you need to get over it."

"It's all because you got laid off, isn't it? You feel you're letting him down. You shouldn't be embarrassed, Emma. It happens to everyone sooner or later."

"First of all, I didn't get laid off. I got fired. F-I-R-E-D. By Nathan Savage, the boss of bosses. And I did *not* deserve it. Darn right I'm embarrassed. I had to pack up my stuff and drag my pitiful little box out to the car all by myself while the security guard loomed over me. A man I've known for three years. He didn't lift a finger to help me, just glared, as though I planned to steal the office computer. He didn't even want me to take my own Rolodex until I proved it was mine. Letting Trip down was the last thing on my mind. I was concentrating on holding my head high and stalking out while everybody slunk into their offices and didn't even tell me goodbye. It was horrible, Dad." She felt her eyes begin to tear up, gulped and refused to allow the tears to slide down her cheeks.

"I'm sure Trip doesn't blame you, sweetheart. He knows that frankly you got screwed. And if we can manage, it's not going to be long before Nathan Savage knows it, too."

"Dad, Geoff Harrington is the one who signed off on all the contracts, not Nathan and not me.

I advised against them. I told Geoff they were a bad idea, that we'd wind up with egg on our faces. I knew we couldn't possibly meet the deadline to implement a complete new marketing plan. He said he took full responsibility, and my job was to do what he told me. Period.

"I should've gone over his head straight to Nathan, but Nathan was in Switzerland and Geoff was supposedly in charge. By the time Nathan got back, the whole thing was a done deal, and all my memos to Geoff warning against the completion schedule for the new website and ad campaign had somehow disappeared from the original file as well as mine. Geoff convinced Nathan that *I* talked him into signing off on all of it. But, please don't try to intervene. You'll embarrass Nathan so badly, he'll never talk to me again. He hates anyone's catching on when he's wrong."

"How long do you intend to stay out there in the country? You can't possibly find another job working from Martha's old house sixty miles east of Memphis. At least here you'd have the support of your friends and family. You can lick your wounds in comfort. We all miss you. If you don't want to stay in your town house, you can always have your old room back here. Andrea will feed you properly. She told me she'd love to have you back. You could do with some spoiling."

Andrea was an excellent stepmother. She and Emma were fond of each other. Andrea already had her hands full with her committees and her charities and Emma's half brother and half sister. "Thank Andrea, but tell her having a grown child move home is too darned big a cliché."

Emma jumped as something touched her foot. She looked down to see Sycamore patting her toes and mewing like a hungry kitten. "You little devil!" she whispered, scooped him up and held him in the crook of the arm not holding the phone.

"I beg your pardon," David French said.

She giggled. "Not you, Dad. I can't come home, I have responsibilities."

"What kind of responsibilities?"

"Look, don't worry. I'm starting to send out résumés today and signing up with some headhunters. Tell Trip to get on with his life. Thank God we didn't have an official engagement party. Give my love to Andrea and the monsters. I really am all right, Dad. I promise I'll call every day from here on. Love ya. Bye." She hung up the phone, lifted Sycamore up and butted noses with him. "Mr. Hungry, huh? Where are your baby sisters?"

Neither Peony nor Rose had made it across the threshold from pantry to kitchen, but they were gallantly trying to follow their brother. She scooped them up, as well, and deposited them back on their towel. "Okay, you guys obviously need a barricade." She grabbed the big laundry basket, picked up babies and towel, and laid them in the bottom of the basket. Then she carried it into the kitchen, setting it where she could keep an eye on them while she warmed her syringe under the hot water. "Okay, guys. Four hours from now we're going to try mashing a tad of dog food into the milk. We'll see if you can figure out how to handle that. Peony, sweetie, I'll help you, I promise."

CHAPTER SIX

"How's it going with the skunks?" Seth stood on the front porch in clean jeans and a navy polo shirt. His short brown hair was damp, so he must have taken a shower after he came home from work.

"Do you really want to know? Barbara Carew said she'd advised you to ignore them."

"Not easy to do. I worry."

Emma moved aside so he could come in. He stayed on the porch.

"I brought you something that may help." He slid a folded baby's traveling playpen across the step.

"I thought Barbara said you didn't have any children." Her heart had given a major lurch. Children meant wives. She did not want this man—this almost stranger—to have a wife. Go figure.

"I don't. I have it for raising puppies. I don't need it, and I thought you could borrow it to use in place of a crate."

"Can't skunks climb?"

"They mostly don't. Not at their age, at any rate."

"Then please bring it in."

He picked it up one-handed. He held a cardboard box in his other hand. He hauled both box and pen into the pantry, leaned the playpen against the wall and began to unfold it.

"Will it fit in here?" Emma asked.

"It's a country pantry with enough storage area to get through a whole winter, Ms. French. Besides, this is a traveling playpen. Half-size. It'll fit." He didn't even glance at the babies.

"Out of sight, out of mind?" Emma said. "And when did I become Ms. French? I thought we were beyond that after last night."

He wanted to tell her that she hadn't been "out of mind" since he'd walked out of her house the night before. The skunks hadn't been either—well, not much. He set up the playpen, took a fresh towel from a stack on the kitchen counter and made a nest at one end. From the cardboard box he pulled out a folded square. "Brought you a box of puppy pads, too," he said. Unfolding one, he laid it in the other end of the pen. "Might help with cleanup."

"Oh, Seth, thank you! I didn't think…"

"Not my first rodeo, Ms.—Emma. I see you've got a water dish."

She sat on the floor beside him. "I found it on the top shelf of the pantry. I guess my last tenants must have had a dog. I know Aunt Martha had cats."

"The last tenants, the Mulligans, had two Australian cattle dogs. I'm surprised you didn't bring a dog with you as protection out here in the wilderness."

She shook her head and sat on the floor beside him. "I've never had a dog or a cat. My stepmother is allergic to both."

"Well, you sure started out with a bang. Don't know what I'd do without a dog."

"You have a dog? I didn't hear one last night."

"I'm between dogs. Barbara's looking for the right rescue for me. That's why I could lend you the playpen." He ran a hand down Sycamore's back. "You're going to have trouble with this one. Ought to have named him Columbus. He sees new worlds to conquer."

"He already made it to the kitchen this afternoon," she said with a smile.

"The playpen should keep them in for a while. Until you get them weaned and back in the wild."

"How long do I have?" she asked.

"Maybe as little as a couple of weeks or as much as a couple of months. All depends."

"On what?"

"How fast their scent glands develop."

"Oh, Lord!"

"By that time they'll be acclimated to you.

They won't spray you unless you really annoy them. Don't. You'll have to teach them to be afraid of human beings."

"But…"

He heard the longing in that one word and understood it perfectly. He could always recognize someone who cared about animals, any animals. "It's best for them."

One of the hardest choices he had to make was to let nature take its course and to free a wild creature back to the wild. He watched her fingers touch the soft fur between Peony's ears. She had beautiful hands, even if that fancy manicure had pretty much bitten the dust in the past couple of days. He wondered what it would be like to be stroked by those gentle fingers… Uh-uh. Not a safe image. Certainly not when they were sitting on the pantry floor thigh to thigh.

She leaned across him to pet Rose, and her sleek hair brushed his cheek. "How do I teach them to hate me?"

"Not to hate you. Be wary of you." He had no idea which flower her hair smelled like. Flowers weren't his thing. Whatever shampoo she used, it was a darned sight more enticing than *eau de skunk*.

"The playpen won't work for long," Seth told her. He held little Peony in the palm of his hand.

She seemed perfectly content. "They need to get outside."

"But they'll run away!"

"They need a big outdoor cage that's safely enclosed so they can get used to the outdoors. They're going to live in it, after all. They have to learn to forage for food, identify smells... How to be skunks."

"Where on earth do I buy something like that? I've never seen one big enough for what you're talking about."

"You don't buy it. You build it. Should be tall enough so that you can move around inside without stooping, with a roof and a door and someplace they can use as a den. Needs to have a metal strip set below ground so they can't dig under it."

"I have no idea how to do that," Emma wailed. "My daddy tried to teach me carpentry, but I've never been able to drive a nail straight." She looked down at her cracked manicure. Why bother redoing it? One day of hammering, and she wouldn't have any fingernails left anyway.

"If I tried to use a power saw, I'd cut off my hand," she added. "How do I find someone I can hire to build it? Or even design it in the first place?"

He leaned back against the pantry wall and let Peony snuggle against his chest. She made tiny puttering noises that were almost like a cat's purr. "It's not that hard."

"No, no, no, you don't understand. I'm the original klutz. If this wasn't during the school year, I might be able to con my half brother, Patrick, into driving up here to help, but he not only has school during the week, but lacrosse on the weekends. And baseball practice starts in two weeks."

"You have a half brother?"

"And a half sister. Patrick is seventeen, Catherine is fifteen. Daddy remarried after my mother died."

"Then if you have a family in Memphis, why are you up here?"

"I beg your pardon. Why is that your business?" She inched away from him and organized herself to stand up.

He laid his free hand on her arm. "Hey, I didn't mean to upset you. You just don't seem the type to go off to a house like this in the country alone. Rehabbers don't usually admit to being unable to drive a nail." He should've kept his mouth shut. Must be a bad situation at home—wicked stepmother, maybe, although he'd never visualized Cinderella as wearing designer jeans.

"You assumed I came up here to rehab this place?" She shrugged. "I'm going to clean it up, get the yard in order and paint. Cosmetic stuff, but basically, I am up here to *endure* the place while I lick my wounds and get my résumés out. You might as well know. I got fired last week. The last thing I wanted was to run into all my old office buddies while I was pounding the pavement looking for another job."

He had no idea what to say to her. He figured she would hate being subjected to sympathy.

No way would she tell him about Trip. Losing her job and her fiancé in the same week seemed like an ultimate case of bad Karma.

It was probably a case of one thing being responsible for the other. Trip surrounded himself with successful people. Once she was fired and therefore no longer successful, he no doubt went looking for some eye candy to commiserate with him—straight into bed.

Emma did not consider herself a total loser, dammit. It suddenly seemed terribly important that Seth Logan didn't think she was, either.

He set Peony back in the playpen. "How about if I help?"

"They don't get fed for another hour. I thought I'd put a tiny bit of dog food in the milk this time. I was going to check with you first, but since you left the cans, I figured it couldn't do any harm."

"As long as you're starting with a little bit. I

didn't mean I'd help with the feeding, although I will. I meant building the outside cage."

She stammered, "I—I can't ask you to do that. According to Dr. Barbara, you already work all the hours of the day and night until you drop."

"You didn't ask. I offered. I've built several of these cages. I've even built a couple of big flight cages for raptors that were recuperating from head-on collisions with cars."

"I keep telling you. I'll be worse than useless if I try to help with the cage. I don't even know where to buy the raw materials." Or how much they were going to cost. In any case, she hadn't planned to include them in her budget. "I don't own any tools, power or otherwise."

"That's all right. I do. I'll meet you at the Farmers' Co-op in Williamston tomorrow at eight," he said. "By then I'll have worked up some specs. My partner, Earl, will be happy to help, too. Provide pizza and you'll have half the county out here."

"I don't *know* half the county."

"That's okay. Barbara and I do."

Seth had brought a small baby bottle, and Emma stirred a little of the dog food into the milk. While she held the kits, he attempted to get them to suck even a tiny bit from the larger nipple. As usual, Rose and Sycamore caught on fast. Peony, not so much.

"She'll starve if she doesn't eat!" Emma wailed as another tablespoon full of milk dribbled into Seth's lap. He dipped his finger in the remaining mush and rubbed it across her gums.

"Yeah, baby, that's it," he whispered as Peony licked his finger. "She won't starve. Not on my watch."

Emma's landline rang. She ignored it. After half a dozen rings, he looked up. "You ever going to answer that?"

"Hadn't planned to."

"Whoever it is knows when to hang up before it switches to voice mail."

"Uh-huh."

"Might be important. Your family?" He dipped his finger once more and held it to Peony's lips.

"I can guess who it is. Oh, hell." She grabbed the handset from the shelf behind her and answered. She didn't realize it was set on speakerphone until she heard Trip's voice.

"Emma! Thank God! I've been trying to reach you for days. I've been going nuts. Are you all right? I finally convinced your father to give me your landline number, since you won't answer your cell phone."

She glanced at Seth. He was watching her while he seemed to be watching the baby.

"Ow!" He scowled down at Peony. "You imp. You *bit* me."

Emma laughed at his wounded expression.

"What's happening? Who's there? Is it your father? He said he might drive up there if he didn't hear from you. Let me speak to him."

Holding the phone in her right hand, she braced her left against Seth's shoulder, stood and turned away. A second later she turned back and saw that he was grinning at her. She'd touched him so casually. Her hand on his shoulder felt natural; he was no longer a stranger.

She flipped off the speaker and walked across to the fireplace before she answered again. "Trip, nothing is going on that concerns you in any way. No, my father is not here and he doesn't plan to come. He would prefer, however, that you stopped calling him at the office."

"He's damn near my father-in-law! Who else should I call when you disappear and won't take my calls? I had to beg to get him to give me this phone number."

"He is not nor will he ever be your father-in-law. I asked him not to give anyone this number."

"I am not *anyone*. I'm your fiancé."

"No, you aren't. We broke up, remember? I did not run off. I came up here to look for a new job…"

"You don't need a new job. You don't need any job. You need to marry me so I can take care of you. I screwed up…"

"You might say that."

"You must hate me now, but…"

She sat on the arm of the sofa. Seth was hearing every word she said, but hiding in her bedroom was ridiculous. Better get it over and done with once and for all. "I don't hate you, Trip. Although I'll admit I did when I found out about you and Susan. I thought she was my friend."

"It was a one-night stand. You and I had that fight because you didn't want to go to the ball after I bought the tickets. Damn things cost a fortune."

"I told you to find another date."

"I didn't *want* another date. I wanted my fiancée on my arm. You know how tongues would've wagged if I'd shown up with someone else. I would've spent the night explaining why you weren't with me. So I had to go stag."

"Unfortunately, you didn't feel you had to *remain* stag."

"If you'd gone, I wouldn't have run into Susan once I got there. Hell, she came on to *me*. I was mad and I was drunk. That's no excuse, but I swear it'll never happen again."

So it was Emma's fault for not doing what he wanted? "Until the next time you want to schmooze with a room full of VIPs and I am just getting over a hundred and one degrees of fever. Not only did I feel rotten, I was trying to avoid giving everyone there what I had. I didn't blow you off."

"I'm not blaming you."

"Really? Sure sounds like it."

"Anyway, what's the big deal? You break off our engagement a week before we're scheduled to announce it. How's that going to look?"

He'd gone from contrition to recrimination in three sentences. How on earth had she ever considered marrying him? Had she been blind? No, just stupid. You couldn't fix stupid, but she was going to try.

"When we decided to get married, you agreed that infidelity was a deal breaker. I guess that's why you lied to me. It wasn't a one-night stand, Trip. Susan told me she'd been seeing you for the past month."

"That didn't have anything to do with us, you and me!"

How many times had Emma heard *that*?

"Call it a crazy last fling. Now I know for sure you're the woman I intend to spend the rest of my life with. Together we can own the world. I miss you. On Saturday I'll drive up there, take you to lunch." He hesitated, then whispered, "Make up afterward."

When she heard his tone she felt her stomach flip, and not in a good way. She knew what he meant, but making up with Trip no longer sounded appealing.

She slid over the arm of the sofa and swung her legs around to sit. "Trip, I don't hate you. It's worse than that. Hate implies passion. Passion is one step away from love."

"Take that step again, baby, I'm begging you. I'll prove you can trust me."

"Trip, I've realized I don't *like* you. I don't want to have your babies, but I'm sure there are a bunch of women who do. Go marry one of them. Heck, marry Susan. Oh, sorry. I forgot she's already married." She laid the handset gently back into its cradle.

Seth had heard all of that—at least her side of it—but when she turned to look at him he was bent over Peony with his back to her. Trying to act innocent. Discreet. Pretty silly for a guy his size, but she appreciated his attempt.

She'd managed to sound calm—well, calmish—with Trip, although she felt anything but. Her heart was beating like Carlos Santana's rhythm section, sweat slid down her back between her shoulder blades, and when she looked at her fingers, her whole hand was shaking. Her face was probably the color of cherry cough drops.

God, she hated confrontations. She wouldn't recover for a week. Everybody thought she was so tough, when inside she was made of pure marshmallow. By the time Trip got his story straight, the whole breakup would've been his idea. Because she'd failed to live up to his exacting specifications. Because she'd abandoned him when he needed her.

She could hear her father's voice in her head. "I warned you he wasn't good enough for you." Actually, he'd mostly been on Trip's side.

Her father had started denigrating her boyfriends in high school and kept on until she dreaded introducing him to her dates. Her real worry was that *she* wasn't good enough for them. They'd catch on. Better be the *dumper* rather than the *dumpee*. So she usually dumped first.

How come one woman was never enough for one man? How come *she* wasn't enough for Trip?

The answer came roaring back in her head. *Because I couldn't take the chance of letting him know the real me. The one who's scared to fail.*

Trip was supposed to be different. This time she'd planned to marry for all the sensible reasons. On paper she and Trip were perfect for each other. She didn't have a clue whether love even existed, and lots of doubts that it would ever exist for her. She'd convinced herself she was in love with Trip. Obviously, she didn't break his heart. He was probably already setting up a date with her successor.

She went back to the pantry floor beside Seth. "You're a mess."

"More on me than in them," he said. "I'm sticky as a bear in a honey tree. I think you can drop the feedings to every six hours with the food we added to the milk."

"Really? Does that mean I can sleep?"

"*Sleep?* I've heard that word a time or two. Not sure what it means." He stood up and slipped Peony back into her nest.

Emma didn't take his proffered hand to stand up this time. "There's another word I've heard, but not recently. *Food?* You ever hear of that?" She grinned up at him. "I went to the grocery store between feedings this afternoon. I have lots of bacon, plenty of eggs and enough onions for a Western omelet. Plus I bought some artisan bread. And beer. I don't drink it, but I thought you might."

He followed her into what passed for a kitchen. "At this point I'd fight Peony for her dog food. Don't tell me you can cook. Girl like you?"

"What's that supposed to mean? I grew up with hot and cold running servants? Here." She tossed him a big Vidalia onion. "Peel and chop this. You do the crying for a change."

An hour later as he finished his fourth piece of buttered toast, he said, "Okay, so you can cook."

"Very limited menu. And you can eat."

"Big engines require a lot of fuel. So, who's this guy Trip you don't like?"

She took a deep breath. To tell him or not? Oh, why not? It wasn't a secret. Not at home, in any case. "A rich, handsome corporate lawyer on the fast track to being named partner. Just not mine. He's got political aspirations, too. Going to put his name in the race for State senator, maybe eventually governor. Let's drop it, okay? I cook, you clean."

"What? No dessert?"

"You're kidding, right? All you have to do is rinse and load the dishwasher. It may be the world's smallest and oldest, but it works."

As she was scrubbing the kitchen table, she said, "I wish you'd known my aunt Martha. I used to spend my summers up here with her. I loved this place."

"From what I hear, I wish I'd known her, too. Barbara said she was a great gal. After she died, how come you didn't come up here before now?"

"My stepmother and I came up to deal with the estate and the papers and things right after. She left me everything, but there wasn't much actual income to fix the place up, and I didn't have any disposable income myself. Plus I was at a place in my life where I didn't know what I wanted to do with the house. She already rented it out, so that's what I did. I hired an agent who handles it all. When the last tenants—the Mulligans—left six months ago, I missed the little bit of income they brought me, but I figured sooner or later I'd get a new tenant. I was looking for somebody who might want to barter upkeep for rent. Karma, I guess. It hit me when I got fired and unengaged practically the same day that I needed a sanctuary. And thanks to Aunt Martha's kindness, I had one." She glanced around the shabby room. "This, however, needs help."

"Not to mention the skunks."

She leaned back against the table. "I don't want you to think I'm ungrateful, but aren't you going to get in trouble over my skunks?"

"You shouldn't think of them as your skunks, or you'll hate letting them go even more. Yes, I can get into trouble, but if we return them to the wild before somebody reports them, I can ask forgiveness."

"As opposed to permission?"

He rinsed out the sink and hung the dish towel on its hook. And yawned. "Sorry."

"Go home. Go to bed."

She followed him to the front door.

"Don't forget. We meet in the morning at the Farmers' Co-op."

She nodded.

He turned, took one step, swung back and reached for her.

JUST A "meet the new neighbor kiss."

Maybe it started that way, but it got out of hand—fast. She wasn't used to being lifted off her feet. When he wrapped his arms around her, she felt as if she were being hugged by that bear in the honey tree.

He tasted of the fig preserves they'd used on their toast, and when their tongues met and teased, her head seemed to lift free of her body.

He set her down, let her go, wheeled around and almost ran across the street. Thank God there was no traffic, because he hadn't checked either direction, just barreled on inside his house.

She leaned against the wall beside her front door and tried to catch her breath. One kiss, and she could feel her nipples harden.

She hoped he didn't regret it. She didn't. Or did she?

Talk about your rebound! The last thing she wanted in her life right now was another man—any man. Certainly not this big, powerful, difficult man who would not be manipulated. Even if she was any good at manipulation. Which she wasn't.

She'd sworn off the entire sex for the foreseeable future. Maybe forever.

So far, she'd done all right convincing him to help keep her skunk babies safe, but that was only because he had a soft spot for small animals. He could always revert to being Mr. Regulation and take them away from her.

She needed to keep him on her side, but there were limits as to how far she'd go to manage that. On a lifestyle compatibility scale of one to ten—ten being the most compatible—the two of them were about minus a thousand. If her father thought Trip was barely good enough for her, he'd flip out the first time he laid eyes on Seth.

She didn't truly believe Seth was expecting some sort of sexual quid pro quo for helping with the skunks. If he was, he'd made a big mistake.

But what did she know? If some other halfway stranger had swept her into his arms and kissed the stew out of her like Seth had, she'd have sent him flying with a big red handprint on his cheek.

And possibly found herself facing a stalker who wore a uniform and carried a gun.

She sank onto the front step of her porch and leaned against one of the columns that held it up. The guy had majorly overstepped his boundaries.

Even if it was the best kiss she'd ever experienced in her entire life. Not that she'd kissed that many males, but she hadn't been a nun either.

It was just a kiss! she reminded herself.

Emma looked across the street. She could see him pacing back and forth, silhouetted against the front window of his house. She went back into her hall, turned off the lights and shut the front door with its big oval pier glass. He wasn't going to watch *her* pace up and down or keep track of her by the lights that went on throughout the house, from living room to bedroom. She'd undress in the dark.

Tomorrow when she met him at the co-op—assuming he showed up—she would be completely casual, never mention the kiss and dial them back to square one. Acquaintances. Period. She needed him for the skunks. She definitely did *not* need him as a male person who raised her blood pressure.

He had lost his mind.

In two days this woman had put him in the position of breaking rules he was pledged to adhere to. Not just adhere to, but enforce.

And grabbing her up and kissing her like that? She'd be well within her rights to call the police and have him arrested for assault by an authority figure.

Not that she'd left him much authority. She hadn't *asked* him to help her build an outdoor run for the skunks. He'd come up with the idea himself. Now he was committed to a fairly complicated project, one she'd already told him she either couldn't or wouldn't participate in.

She'd intimated that she'd sworn off the entire sex for the foreseeable future. As if he had all the time in the world outside his job to play nursemaid to skunks. Why hadn't she adopted a couple of baby squirrels? Or even a raccoon? He could justify helping her in that case.

Tomorrow morning, he had to meet her as though they'd never shared that blockbuster of a kiss. Casual. Professional. Acquaintances. Neighbors. Nothing more.

He could handle that.

In his dreams.

Then again, what was the use? How long before her fancy, rich lawyer fiancé showed up in a brand-new Mercedes, gave her a big diamond and swept her off to marry him? From her phone conversation with The Jerk—he thought of him in capital letters—the guy was having an affair with a married woman while he was engaged to Emma. Talk about nuts! But with his fortune and social position... No woman would choose Seth Logan over him. If, as Emma said, he was aiming to go into politics at some point, she'd make a smashing senator's wife. Or governor's, for that matter.

Seth had enough experience with domestic disputes to know that in almost every case infidelity was not a deal breaker. All too often, women kept going back to the guy who gave them a broken jaw or a broken heart. His mother had gone back to his alcoholic father again and

again, offered him support and forgiveness and
her belief that he would stay sober. She'd written him off and divorced him only after Sarah
was drowned. She couldn't go on living with
Everett, her husband, knowing it was his fault
Sarah had died.

She barely took her eyes off Seth in the months
following Sarah's drowning. She knew how
deeply he blamed his father. Watching him was
as much for Seth's benefit as her own. She'd continued to look at Seth even when he couldn't bear
to look at himself. She was afraid of what he'd
do if his father showed up drunk and maudlin,
making excuses, casting blame…

She'd been right to worry. At fourteen Seth
was taller, broader and stronger than his father.
Besides, his liver was healthy. He doubted dear
old Dad's was. He'd had to avoid the bastard
so he wouldn't put him in the hospital. Or the
morgue.

The only thing that saved Everett Logan from
his son's wrath was that Seth hated himself more
than he did his father. If he hadn't been able to
hide out in the woods for days at a time, he might
well have followed Sarah into the lake.

He couldn't do that to his mother. So he'd
nursed his anger and avoided his father. He could
thank his father for forcing him to love the outdoors, not that the old man had intended to point

him to his career path. Seth only knew he could *breathe* in the woods.

Poor Earl. He knew about Seth's family and how close to the surface Seth's temper ran when faced with dangerous jackasses like that party boat group. When Seth realized those people on the boat weren't wearing life jackets, it was touch and go whether he could keep his temper or whether he'd tie the idiot captain to his anchor and toss him overboard.

Thank God he'd had Earl there to help him maintain control. He thought he'd managed to stay calm, but that big woman who'd caught his expression had looked scared.

Maybe the alternative was to force the entire party to stare at pictures of bodies pulled from that lake, the *quiet little* lake that could kick up whitecaps in a strong wind and upend half the boats in the water.

As he climbed into bed, he was sure he'd lie awake thinking about Emma with The Jerk. In reality he spent the night dreaming of her instead.

And dreaming of inventive ways to barbecue that Trip guy. Slowly.

CHAPTER SEVEN

"I WASN'T SURE you'd show up." Seth opened the driver's door of Emma's SUV, then stood back. Sweet of him not to loom over her.

"I said I would."

"Ever been to the co-op?" he asked. "It's the farmer's answer to the big-box hardware stores. Little bit of everything from two-by-fours to horse feed."

She shook her head.

"Hey, Seth," a voice from the shadowy depths of the store said. "And who's this pretty lady?" The man who came to meet them wasn't quite as tall as Seth but outweighed him by a factor of two or possibly three. Somewhere under the thick layers of fat could be glimpsed layers of muscle. He wore actual bib overalls that stuck out in front.

"Hey, hon." He engulfed her hand in a rough sunburned paw as gently as though he was holding a butterfly. "Seth giving you the grand tour of our fair city?"

His grin was broad, gleaming, but with something of a mountain lion behind it. A man who could handle himself, Emma thought, and probably Seth, as well.

"Shoot, you're the biggest tourist attraction we got," Seth said. "Emma French, meet the mayor of Williamston, Sonny Prather. Sonny, this is Emma French. She's Miss Martha's niece. She just moved in across the street from me."

"And you figured you'd introduce her to old Sonny. 'Cause you gonna need to buy out the store to get that place all fixed up after the last people. Friendly enough folks, but didn't do much to take care of the place that I could see."

"I'm afraid I can't afford to buy more than a tiny piece of all this," Emma said and waved a hand at the shelves around her.

"Sure you can. We gonna open an account for you like everybody else in the county. That way, you can send your contractor in to buy whatever you need."

"As for the contractor, you're looking at him," Seth said. "This morning, all we need is stuff to build an outdoor run. Emma here is thinking about bringing her dog up from Memphis to stay. He's a city dog."

Emma gaped at Seth. She now knew that he could lie like a rug. Good information for the future. She had to admit, however, that he'd sounded plausible. And not a word about skunks either.

"Lord, yes. Miss Emma, you got to have a kennel for a city dog around here 'less you want him running off after the coyotes or getting hisself snakebit." He turned to Seth. "You know what you want, or you want me to work it out for you? Is it a large dog?" he asked Emma.

"Uh…"

Seth stepped in. "Large enough. Long as we're building, might as well do a decent job of it."

"You got you a new dog yet, Seth?" Sonny asked over his shoulder as he walked off down the store and through a wide doorway at the back. "Know you miss Rambler. He was a good ol' dog."

A fine epitaph, Emma thought. Interesting that Sonny knew the particulars about Seth's dog. But then he probably knew the names of the dogs and horses owned by all his customers. Maybe sheep and goats, too. Certainly bulls. Possibly even cats, although she doubted it. Men tended to ignore felines, but from where she stood, she could see a pair of yellow tabbies curled up in a ray of sunshine beside the front door. No doubt if she mentioned them, Sonny would blush and tell her they were good ratters.

"Barbara's looking out for a rescue for me," Seth said as he followed Sonny. Emma trailed along in their wake, feeling like a third wheel.

The same thing had happened when she first

started working for Nathan Savage. Once a prospective older client sat down at their conference table, turned to her and said, "Get coffee."

Not even a "please." She didn't hit him, but that was because Nathan intervened, explained that Emma was one of their top marketing executives and thus did not act as a waitress. The man never so much as looked at her throughout the meeting. But then he signed a contract for more money than anyone had expected. Guilt, probably. That worked. After she'd engineered the launch of his metal-roofing company with more media coverage than he'd expected for such a specialized top-of-the-line niche product, he became a friend. Who would work with him now that she no longer worked for Nathan?

She glanced over at Seth and Sonny. They weren't cutting her out. They'd simply forgotten she was there. She left them to it.

By the time they'd worked out everything that would be needed for the so-called kennel, she had accumulated a wicker basket full of little cans of cat food, a bag of dry food and several small cat toys.

Sonny said, "Thought it was a big dog."

"We've seen a couple of feral cats around," Seth said. "If they have kittens, Emma may domesticate a few to keep down the mice."

Saved again. She looked at the length of the

invoice Sonny held and groaned. She might have to borrow money from her father, after all, if she didn't get a job soon. When she reached for her credit card, however, Sonny waved her away.

"Don't you know the old saying about farmers, hon? A farmer's solvent one day a year." He grinned up at Seth. "Tell her."

Seth shrugged. "From the afternoon of the day he sells his crop until the next morning when he buys his seed."

"The rest of the time, everybody keeps paying on their accounts," Sonny said. "You gonna move up here, you got to do like everybody else."

"Don't I have to fill out some paperwork? Give you a credit card?"

"Shoot, I know where to find you if I need to. And Seth can track you down, can't you?" He flashed that smile at Seth. "Not that you'll be considered a native, except through Miss Martha. Have to live here a minimum of three generations for that. Now, since Seth has to go to work, and you don't have a pickup, my boys'll be up late this afternoon to deliver your stuff."

"But where?"

"Sonny and I worked it out," Seth told her.

"Got the perfect place up under that big water oak. Plenty of shade, good drainage, close to the house. Sonny, you can put the tools and concrete bags on the front porch."

"Shouldn't they be locked up?" *Tools?* Emma thought. Shades of enormous hammers and four-inch nails! And concrete? What were they building, the Brooklyn Bridge?

"Nobody'll bother 'em," Sonny said. "Now, Seth, when you gonna bring your riding lawn mower and your four-wheeler down for a checkup? You already need to be mowing that little place you got."

Emma waved at them and started out of the store.

"Hey, sweet thing, wait up!" Sonny said. "We're right glad you moved in. Don't you worry. Anything you need, we'll fix you up."

"I'll come by after work," Seth said to her retreating back.

She climbed into her SUV. It was nearly nine o'clock. She'd had one cup of coffee, and she was absolutely starving. Two hours to go before she had to feed the skunks. Must be someplace around here she could get some breakfast. Someplace where she could be a stranger and not the absolute most worthless out-of-her-element female in this universe. She considered she had a fairly good skill set. For the city. Out here she didn't understand the language, much less the customs.

It definitely *was* another universe. Oh, the endearments were the same as in town. She never minded being called "sugar" or "honey" or "sweet thing." There was a wide gap between sexual harassment like the casual hand on her rear end—which she recognized instantly and took care of even faster—and the complimentary appellations from good ol' boys of a certain age.

But it was all too obvious that she didn't belong here. Sonny was right. She'd be a stranger for the next three generations, if it was possible to live that long.

She could make an attempt to slide into the culture, but it would never work. She knew where she belonged, and it wasn't in Williamston. And definitely not across the street from Seth Logan.

"WHOO-EE!" SONNY SAID. He hooked his thumbs into his tarpaulin-size overalls and grinned at Seth. "Yum, yum! She lives right across the street from you?"

"Put your eyes back in your head, Mr. Mayor, before I blacken both of them for you."

"Now, Seth, I didn't mean a thing by it. I'm a happily married man. Besides, Nadine would tear my head off at the shoulders if I so much as looked at another woman. And no way would I give up Nadine's beaten biscuits for a roll in the hay with somebody else. But you—" he pointed at Seth "—are no longer a married man and that—" he pointed to Emma's SUV as it pulled out of the parking lot "—is therefore fair game."

Seth didn't feel like discussing Emma as though she were a side of beef with a man who looked as though he could eat one at a single sitting. "She's in a committed relationship." He very nearly bit his tongue. *Committed relationship?* Not if Emma stuck to her guns after that phone call last night, not to mention her response to that wholly inappropriate kiss he'd planted on her.

Still, she'd been clear that living in Aunt Martha's house was a stopgap measure for a woman who was intended for mansions and French wine. All he knew about French wine was that he couldn't afford it. Mansions? Out of the question.

"I'm late for work," he said. "Thanks, Sonny."

"No thanks needed." Sonny clapped Seth on the shoulder hard enough to make him stumble. "You get that kennel up, and then you pay some attention to that young lady."

Seth decided to stop by the café and pick up a couple of egg sandwiches and a large coffee. When he was close to the turn for the parking lot, however, he saw Emma's SUV already there with no one in it. Darn! If he went inside now, she really would think he was stalking her. He drove by and stopped at the drive-in. The food wasn't half as good as at the café, but the coffee was hot and the sausage biscuits sufficiently greasy. He should've felt good about this morning. Instead, he felt as though he was in way over his head, and not just with the construction.

THE MINUTE EMMA walked into the café, conversation stopped and every eye swiveled to stare at her. Oh, great. Apparently a stranger was sufficiently rare to count as a treat. She put on her coolest expression, noted the sign at the cash register that said, "Y'all seat yourself," looked around and spotted Barbara, the vet, waving at her. She pasted on a smile and walked over.

"Join me, please," Barbara said.

Emma couldn't very well refuse. Besides, not only did she like Barbara, but the vet was a conduit to Seth Logan. Emma needed somebody to clue her in on the man. She couldn't figure him out at all. He obviously had the education and the cultural skills to move up whatever career ladder he chose. Yet here he was, catching poachers and checking fishing licenses—or she supposed that was what he did. He didn't seem to be lazy, not if he planned to help her build the kennel.

"The café's about the only decent restaurant in Williamston," Barbara said.

The waitress laid a menu on the table and, without asking, set down a mug of coffee. "You want cream?" It came out like an accusation.

Emma shook her head. "No, thanks. Just a

couple of poached eggs, bacon and wheat toast, please."

"Huh. We don't do much egg poaching. Hard or soft?"

"Uh, medium?"

"Grits or hash browns?"

"No thank you."

"Velma," Barbara said, "this is Emma French. She's Miss Martha's niece and has moved into her old house."

Emma felt her ears redden. She was certain everyone in the place had heard Barbara's introduction. She might as well be wearing a sign on her back that said "outsider."

"Nice to see somebody fixing up that place," a man in a business suit said from the next table. "Welcome to Williamston." He swung his chair around and held out his hand. "Doug Eldridge."

"How do you do?"

"He's the local doctor," Barbara said.

"Yeah. Barbara heals the animals. I try to heal the humans. She's better at her job than I am at mine. At least to hear her tell it. But if you need me, I'm in the book. And unless you want to drive to Memphis, I'm your best bet."

"More like your only bet," Velma said and walked behind the counter to hang the order for Emma's breakfast on one of the clips by the kitchen.

"How are the *you-know-whos*?" Barbara asked Emma.

"Fine, I guess. Lively, at any rate. Seth says I need an outside cage for them. We came into town to get stuff to build it. He says he's going to help, but I don't see how he has the time. What does he actually do at his job? I don't know a thing about him."

Barbara held out her mug. Velma filled it on her way by the table.

"The first thing you want to know is whether or not he's married. He's divorced, and just as well. No children. Married to his job. Great guy as long as you stay on his good side."

"And if you don't?"

"He'll make you wish you had."

"How come it's better that he's divorced?"

"Clare was a rip-snorting spoiled brat who absolutely hated living in the country, where she had to drive thirty miles for a mani-pedi up to her high standards." Barbara glanced down at Emma's disintegrating fingernails. "She used to drive into Memphis to get her hair cut."

Emma reddened. "I know my hands look awful. I need to at least take the polish off. I just haven't had time what with the *you-know-whos* to find my polish remover. If Seth does build the cage, how do I pay him?"

"Don't you dare! Talk about getting on his bad

side! Fix him a good dinner. That's assuming you can cook. This is the first time since Clare divorced him, moved to Nashville and remarried that he's shown any interest in doing anything other than his job. He's developing a reputation as a real hardnose. His dog, Rambler, died six months ago and he still doesn't have another. I haven't found the perfect one for him yet, but I will. Anyway, he'll probably ask Earl—that's his partner—and maybe a couple of the other guys to help him. So you're really interested in this fostering animals thing?"

"I have no idea. I'm stuck with it now, but I don't know how it works. Obviously I screwed up with my first attempt by picking the *you-know-whos* instead of a baby rabbit."

"You had the right instincts. We don't judge on a cuteness quotient. I've fostered baby turkey buzzards. Cute they are not, except to a mother turkey buzzard. But we need them. We'd be up to our ears in roadkill otherwise. I call 'em God's garbagemen."

Velma set Emma's breakfast plate down just a little harder than necessary. Emma assumed she didn't approve of poached eggs, although these looked perfect.

"You want to find out what fostering animal work is like," Barbara said, "you go home, feed the *you-knows* and drive on down to my clinic.

I've got a menagerie to oversee and no one to work with me, so I need to get back. You know where my clinic is? Just down the road a couple of miles past your house. Can't miss it. There's a big parking lot in front and one behind it, and four horse trailers on the side."

Emma's day was imploding fast. She'd intended to set up her workspace, start sending out résumés and make some telephone calls to friends and former colleagues. Networking always worked better than cold calls. At this point she wasn't looking for a position that paid as well or carried as much prestige as her job with Nathan. Just some way to pay the bills without borrowing money from her dad.

Barbara slid out of the banquette, dropped a couple of dollars on the table for Velma and went off to pay her bill at the front.

Seeing Barbara's clinic and her animals sounded like a bunch more fun than résumés. She'd work on those this afternoon while the babies were napping.

Several people nodded to her as they walked up to the cash register, but no one actually spoke. They obviously knew who she was…heck, they probably knew her shoe size. She didn't dawdle over her breakfast. The babies were waiting for their breakfast, too.

At home, she was astonished by how fast they

were gaining control of their legs. They marched around their playpen like animated stuffed toys and squeaked at her for not meeting their needs earlier. She fed them, cleaned them and their playpen, then went out to call on Barbara with a couple of pats on the head for each one before she left. Peony stood on her hind legs and begged to be picked up, but Emma hardened her heart. "Later, little child. I promise I'll love on you."

She'd been aware of the vet clinic, but she'd never had a reason to stop there.

The clinic building looked as though it had started life as a fancy pole barn and been converted to a business with real walls sometime later. Emma was surprised that the waiting room was empty, without even a receptionist behind the desk. Barbara had said she had no help at the moment, but Emma hadn't realized that no help meant exactly that. Maybe her receptionist was off for some reason or worked only part-time. From down the hall Barbara's voice called, "Emma, come on back, unless you faint at the sight of blood."

Lovely. Just what she needed after a big breakfast. Still, she followed Barbara's voice through an open door halfway down the hall.

Inside, in her signature electric-blue scrubs, Barbara stood over an unconscious tricolored hound with a four-inch gash along its flank. The flank had been shaved, and bits of hair stuck to the globs of blood that had run from the wound onto the table.

"Hey. Put on a pair of gloves—over there in the box—and an apron. You're not going to faint, are you?"

Emma did as she was told.

"When I got back, the owner was waiting in the parking lot," Barbara said. "He helped me get Sidney here onto the table, then he went home to feed his chickens. Big coward when it comes to blood. I guess his wife does the killing when he wants fried chicken." As she talked, she wiped the gash. "Hand me that number ten scalpel," she said and pointed. "That one. Thanks. I have to cut the old skin off the edges so the new skin will grow together when I stitch it."

Fascinated, Emma watched Barbara, who seemed to work almost casually but with skill to remove the edges of the wound.

After cleaning and barbering the wound, Barbara began to suture the cut, using small elegant stitches.

"Can you talk and work?" Emma asked. She couldn't take her eyes off Barbara's hands.

"Sure. I assume you want to talk about Seth."

Emma felt her face flame. "I admit it. I can't figure him out. One minute he's kind and gentle, the next he's snapping at me and convincing me

I'm an incompetent idiot. Granted, around animals he's mostly right."

"He's a complicated man," Barbara said. She continued to suture so that the gaping gash narrowed to a thin line. "He's had a tough row to hoe over the years. He tends to see his job as saving the idiots from *themselves* and the wildlife from *them*."

"How so?"

"Sponge off that dribble of blood. It's getting in my way."

Emma sponged. Surprisingly, the blood didn't bother her.

"He comes from a badly broken home," Barbara said. "His momma's still alive and lives in the only independent-living condos in town. Wherever his father is, you can bet he's drunk. Real pity. I've been told he used to be a fine lawyer. But that was before Sarah died."

"Who was Sarah?" She watched as Barbara tightened and clipped the final stitch on the dog's flank.

"Lucky that chunk of metal didn't slice straight through the tendon," Barbara said. She dropped her used instruments into the metal pan beside the table. "Can't really bandage up this high on a rear leg. Have to try to cover it, but he'll need to wear a collar to keep him from biting it. See that big plastic circle on the top shelf? Hand it to me, please. You're tall enough to reach it without a stepstool. I'm not."

Again, Emma did as she was told.

"Sarah? She was Seth's little sister. She drowned before my husband, John, and I moved here to take up our practice. John specialized in large animals. Since he keeled over with a heart attack five years ago, I do it all, but I'm better with small. I'm fine with horses, but I never trust cows."

"She drowned? That's awful," Emma said.

"Seth always blamed his father. I don't know what happened, and don't you dare ask Seth. He doesn't like to talk about it. My guess would be that his father was supposed to be watching the child—I think she was nine or ten, although don't quote me on that. They were out fishing. Somehow the child fell overboard and drowned. Broke up the family."

"The death of a child often does," Emma said. "So Seth's parents are divorced?"

Barbara nodded. "I don't think Seth has anything to do with his father or even knows where he is. He's close to his mother, though."

"What about the ex-wife?"

"They both graduated from Auburn in the same class and married right after. Big wedding down in Birmingham. Lots of bridesmaids. He was supposed to go to vet school. I have no idea why he decided not to, except that he suddenly had a wife to support. She had some crazy plan to become the lady of the plantation, swanning around and lording it over the local society ladies." Barbara snorted. "She discovered that there *aren't* any society ladies up here, and she wasn't going to be able to have mint julep parties at the country club. I mean, who drinks mint juleps these days?"

"*Is* there a country club?" Emma asked.

"There's a nine-hole golf course about ten miles south of here with a metal storage shed, which passes for a clubhouse. No fancy restaurant. No swimming pool or tennis courts. The women can play on Thursday afternoons. The rest of the time it's men only. That's okay. The women around here are mostly too busy driving combines and feeding cows to drink anything but a slug of straight bourbon after dinner before they fall into bed."

"You're happy, though, aren't you?"

Barbara stripped off her gloves and tossed them in the waste disposal holder in the corner. Emma followed suit.

"I was happier before John died. His doctor called it 'a catastrophic event.' He blew a mitral valve in the middle of cleaning a gelding's teeth. The doctor told me that when such an event happens suddenly to a relatively young man, it is almost always fatal. It nearly killed me, too."

"There was no warning at all?"

"None. He'd checked out perfectly in his annual physical three months earlier. We'd only set up the practice here a couple of years earlier. I felt I had no choice but to carry on. Suddenly I had a family to support alone."

"How on earth do you manage?"

"I'm trying to hire a well-qualified young vet with an eye to buying into a partnership."

"No luck?"

"Not yet. Not many young vets want to come to a tiny practice that does large and small animals both. They want to get their DVM and move into a posh city practice treating French bulldogs. I'm barely getting by. But yes, I'm generally happy. I do not belong in a city. Nobody cares when I show up at the café in dirty jeans or muddy boots. I like that you never know whether that old farmer sitting next to you is poor as Job's turkey or raising prize Santa Gertrudis bulls on his own five thousand acres." Barbara stroked the hound's head and buckled on the collar. "There. That should do it. He can't reach his stitches to bite at them. Give me a hand moving him to a cage, would you? I'll keep him till tomorrow morning and send him home with antibiotics, but he ought to be okay. I'll have to see whether my part-time help is available after school this afternoon. Somebody needs to check on Sidney here when he wakes up. You're lucky. This is generally my surgery morning. That's why there aren't fifty thousand animals in the waiting room."

The big hound required both women to lift him off the table and slide him into a cage to recover. When they stood back, Emma said, "You do nice work, Doc."

"I do, don't I? Never did approve of false modesty. Now, you want me to introduce you to my foundlings? Come on in the back. I keep these guys segregated to avoid any cross-species infection." She opened the back door onto another, smaller parking lot. Beyond it was a metal barn. The two women were met with a cacophony of sound as they walked into the center aisle.

"Let's see. I have four fawns. They're about ready to be released." The fawns stood on their hind feet with their front hooves on the door of a horse stall well bedded with shavings. They still had their spots, but they were fading.

"Two sets of twins," Barbara said. "Their mommas were shot out of season on posted land by poachers. Seth took after the poachers and arrested them. Then he found the babies in the long grass and brought them to me. Not easy, but he and Earl managed it. I've been bottle-feeding them, but they're eating solid food now, so off they go."

"Poor babies. What are their names?"

"Didn't Seth warn you not to name them?" Barbara asked. "Never give them names. After they're released, you don't want them to remember you or any other human being. If you happen to call them by name if you see them in the wild, they may come running. Could be a disaster for them."

Emma looked at the fawns and wondered how anybody could *not* name them.

"Over here we have half a dozen baby squirrels," Barbara said, pointing to a tall wire enclosure with severed tree limbs inside bearing new leaves. "They're learning to find acorns and hide them. This is probably the kind of enclosure Seth thinks you need."

Emma thought it seemed sturdy enough to rate a government mortgage. If this was what Seth intended, she hoped he had a lot of buddies willing to help, because she didn't have a clue. "Where did you get so many squirrels?" she asked.

"We always wind up with a bunch of baby squirrels during squirrel-hunting season. They fall out of the nest looking for their parents, wind up on the ground and unable to fend for themselves. People bring them to us. Out back in the pond, I have a Canada goose with a lame foot from an old fishing line somebody left floating in a tangle. She'll never go back into the wild. She's here for life. She's my early warning system." Her phone rang. "Damn!" She answered, listened, said, "I'll be there in twenty," then hung up and said to Emma. "Choked horse. I have to go. Want to ride along?"

"I really ought to get home and work on my laptop, if I'm ever going to find a job. This, however, has been interesting for someone who's never had a pet."

She drove off in tandem with Barbara, but turned left toward her house while Barbara went right. How on earth could the woman manage with only part-time high school help?

She pulled her SUV into the gravel pad beside her front porch. Home. Weird, she was already thinking of The Hovel as home. She couldn't remember ever calling her town house *home* even in her mind. Despite her stepmother's decorating expertise and her ins at the local decorators' showrooms, the perfect rooms she'd created had always seemed like a stage set for entertaining clients and friends who were, like Trip, movers and shakers. What they used to call "bright, young things" in the 1920s.

Since she had a couple of hours before she was due to feed the babies, she checked on them from the pantry door to make sure they were all right without letting them see her. She knew that the moment they realized she was looking at them, they'd start whining for food. She had to harden her heart, once again, no matter how difficult.

Darn it, they *did* have names, and they had personalities. She couldn't undo that, no matter what Barbara said. She'd have to take them far away before she released them, so they couldn't possibly find their way back to her.

Losing them was going to about kill her, but that was what mothers did. Bring them up, protect them and then, when they were ready, send them out into the world to take their chances.

Maybe she'd better give up the idea of becoming a mother. Andrea had been a more than adequate stepmother after she married Daddy, although she must have dreaded raising the child of a mother who'd died and left Emma when she was only nine. And after the years when Emma alone was her daddy's girl—even if she felt she'd disappointed him all too often.

It made perfect sense that Daddy should take her half brother, Patrick, hunting and fishing as soon as he was old enough. The kid was good at both. Emma wasn't and never would be. How could she explain how much the loss of her quiet times in the jon boat with her father meant to her?

It also made perfect sense that Daddy never

missed one of Catherine's lacrosse matches. He was older now and had more free time to do things like that.

Emma couldn't catch a ball in a lacrosse net if it meant saving the universe.

Patrick loved woodworking with his father. Emma couldn't drive a nail.

Catherine was a cheerleader and one of the popular girls. Emma had practically lived in the library.

Making straight As and winning the Latin contests and the journalism awards didn't qualify the same way as doing well at spectator sports. Crowds didn't applaud or hand out trophies to nonjocks. David French, a brilliant man and a brilliant lawyer, simply expected Emma to do well intellectually. It wouldn't have occurred to him to give her money for getting good grades, as some of her friends' parents did. That was her job.

She was glad that both Patrick and Cathy had turned out to be good kids who loved her and whom she loved. Otherwise she'd probably have poisoned them both out of sibling jealously.

Now she was the young animal sent out into the wild. Her parents had to pay attention to the fledglings who weren't quite ready to leave the nest. It was right and proper. But Lord, it was hard.

She saw now that had a lot to do with her accepting Trip's proposal. He'd offered her the safe, comfortable life she'd been born to. She didn't have to dream big. His dreams would be hers. No chance of failure, of not being good enough, when it was somebody else's dreams.

Except she was sick of being half-alive, of accepting what Trip and her family wanted, even if she didn't.

So, out of the nest we go and into who knows what!

CHAPTER EIGHT

THE TRUCK OF building materials arrived as she was unpacking her laptop on the small dining table after she'd cleaned up her tuna salad lunch. Without being told, they unloaded the wire and wood beside the big water oak and left the tools and bags of concrete on the front porch. She went out and signed for everything. They smiled, but didn't say a word. Just unloaded and drove off.

She forced herself to finish setting up her laptop, printer, modem and all the other stuff she'd brought in her Technology box. Then she sat and stared at the screen without a single idea about how to create her résumé or whom to send it to.

For example, that lovely interview question—"Why did you leave your previous employment?" *Got my ass fired for not covering it well enough.*

"Can we contact your previous employer?"
Not just no, but hell no.

"What are your strengths?'"
I am a great dancer. I speak passable French and can read the first chapter of Virgil's Aeneid in Latin or English. I plan wonderful meetings

and am an expert at setting up h'ors d'oeuvres buffets. I do fabulous flow charts, and I make a mean margarita and a superb dirty martini. I can build a website and create an internet presence. If I'm working for a charity, I know how to raise funds. I can write brochures and prospectuses for clients. In other words, I can help clients work out their goals, figure out what it'll take to accomplish them, write a budget and a marketing plan that include a hefty profit for us, and assemble a creative team to fit the pieces together. Jill of all trades. That's what PR's about.

"What are your weaknesses?"

How do I count the ways! I get impatient. I expect people to do what they agree to do on time, and I can be tactless when they don't. I'm working on that.

"Are you a people person?"

I certainly hope not.

"What do you want out of your career?"

Excitement. New challenges with creative people I like. Control where I have responsibility. And lots of lovely money.

Boy, if they don't make me CEO of a small country with these credentials, they aren't paying attention.

Eventually after she deleted the four lines of *k*'s she'd strung across her screen, Emma gave up. Tomorrow she had to knuckle down and stop the nonsense. She did have skills. She was wicked smart and moderately attractive. Who cared whether she could drive a nail?

Seth did, probably.

She played with the babies on the pantry floor after she'd fed them. They climbed all over her, even got in her hair. Their baby coats were incredibly soft. Their baby claws and teeth, however, were sharp. She could practically see them grow. She sat cross-legged on the pantry floor with all three of them in her lap, thought about how soon she'd lose them and burst into tears.

Seth came in so quietly that she didn't even realize he was in the house until he called out to her. She scrambled to put the babies back in their playpen and wipe her eyes. She'd never mastered the feminine art of crying prettily. Even with no mirror handy, she knew her face and nose and eyes were red and swollen.

The moment she turned to Seth, he stopped dead and said, "Whoa. You look awful. You having an allergy attack?"

"Never tell a woman she looks awful, even when she does," Emma snapped. She ran her fingers across her cheeks and under her eyes. "Actually, I'm feeling depressed and generally worthless. Sort of an I'm-gonna-go-out-in-the-garden-and-eat-worms feeling."

"No time for that. We've got a cage to build."

"I *need* my fingernails."

"You can use a shovel, can't you?"

"Why would I need that?"

"Have you felt those baby claws lately? They'll be able to dig under that new fence we haven't built yet. I said we'd need a metal barrier that goes about six inches below the bottom of the fence. If we're lucky, they'll stop digging down at five. Come on, Little Mother of All the Skunks, time to get your gloves on." He offered her a hand, but she ignored it and scrambled up by herself.

"I don't have any gloves."

"Yeah, you do." Seth slapped a pair of heavy leather gardening gloves into her palm. "I've already marked the footprint of the cage with chalk lines on the grass…"

"How long have you been out in my yard? How come I didn't hear you?"

"I figured you were taking a nap, and I didn't want to disturb you. I don't generally make noise out of doors. Noise scares the deer."

"The better to shoot them?"

He shook his head. "I haven't hunted anything with a heartbeat since I was ten years old, and I didn't like it then. I'm not against hunting per se as long as the rules are obeyed, but it's not for me."

The ground was still damp enough that the

sharp square-ended shovels sliced through the sod and into the ground. By late June, the same job would require a bulldozer to dig six inches down. The dirt would be as hard as concrete. Even now the job was no picnic for Emma. She started digging down the short side, while Seth dug across the long side. He moved like a robotic Ditch Witch. After the first couple of shovelfuls, Emma's arms and shoulders reminded her that she wasn't used to this. She watched Seth and tried to emulate his efficient movements. Watching him was a pleasure. The muscles of his arms and shoulders were so cut that he seemed like a mobile anatomy figure shining with sweat.

He wasn't pretty-handsome like Trip, but he practically trumpeted "male" like a bull elk she'd seen monitoring his harem at Land Between the Lakes. Which had its good and bad points. Right this moment, he was apparently keeping his distance. They were simply two casual acquaintances doing a dirty job. She assumed that, in his mind, their kiss hadn't happened.

In hers it certainly had.

Even when she paid close attention to her job and not the man, her shovel kept landing off the chalk line. Checking behind her, she saw that the path of her trench was more like the wriggly trail of one of those king snakes Seth waxed poetic about. His trench was perfectly straight and at a uniform depth.

Once she nearly drove the shovel into the toe of her boot. She didn't want to lose toes any more than she wanted to lose fingers, but the way she was going, she might.

Shouldn't Seth ask how she was getting along? But no. He didn't even glance at her. Despite the chilly evening, sweat rolled down her forehead, dripped into her eyes and stung. She dropped the shovel and dug in her jeans pocket for a tissue.

Seth peered at her from under his arm. "Something wrong?"

He seemed ungainly all bent over. Kinda cute.

She leaned down to grasp her shovel, caught it on the toe of her Wellington boot, flipped up the handle and narrowly avoided bonking herself on the head. Suddenly the entire operation seemed ridiculous. At the rate she was digging, the babies would be grown and spraying everything in sight before she finished her side of the trench.

She leaned on the handle of her shovel. "I am useless. I can't even dig a straight trench."

"Hey! Careful with that shovel."

"At least Trip never made me dig ditches," she muttered.

He leaned down and picked up something from the ground. "Here," he said. "Bon appétit." The earthworm he held out to her was a good six inches long and extremely annoyed at being kidnapped.

Obviously, Seth was expecting her to scream and run. Forget that! She pulled off her gloves and carefully transferred the worm from his fingers to hers. "My daddy taught me to bait my own hook before I was five," she said and put the worm back on the lawn, where it wriggled away as fast as it could. "Besides, it's not my flavor."

This time he actually looked at her instead of avoiding her eyes, as he had since he'd come into the house earlier. "Come on. You could use a break," he said, then took her shovel and laid it carefully on the ground facedown so she couldn't stomp the handle up again.

Boy, did she need a break, but she wasn't about to admit it. "If *you* need a minute, I have water in the refrigerator. I'll bring us a couple of bottles." She went into the house, got the water and came back looking as relaxed as possible, although she already had blisters on her hands, despite the gloves. No doubt Seth's hands were as tanned as old leather.

But still so gentle, even with an earthworm.

Or a woman? Would she ever find out? Did she want to?

Damn straight.

He sat on the porch steps with his back against the column. She handed him his water, then sat out of touching distance with her back against the column on the other side of the front door. On sober reflection, Seth was undoubtedly regretting last night's kiss. The message seemed to be that he wasn't interested in a repetition.

Fine. No more Mr. Grabby Hands. As if she cared. Wasn't she off men?

She glanced over at Seth, the way he fit into those jeans, the muscles across his shoulders, those lazy gray eyes...

How long did she plan to give up men? Every time she looked at him, the span grew shorter. *Do not*, she reminded herself, *forget that he is a danger to my babies. He could declare they are ready to go back into the woods.* He'd darned well have a fight on his hands if he tried. Yeah, right.

He could pick her up one-handed and toss her into the branches of the water oak.

She'd never had the nerve to make the first move toward a man she was attracted to. Her stepmother said she should always let the man do the chasing. Wait for him to call *you*. How many hours had she sat staring at the phone?

How did men handle rejection? Did they put themselves out there and take the chance that women wouldn't shut them down? They must school themselves to ignore rejection. Either that or women were so interchangeable for a man that it didn't matter which woman he got and which he didn't.

Emma had never been able to be that casual. Every time her father missed a play at school or a soccer game for a fishing trip he'd taken her brother on, she'd gotten better at hiding her hurt. She knew she wasn't being fair. He had three children. He had to keep up with all their extra-curricular activities. But it took Andrea to convince him to cut back on his caseload to spend more time with them. Still, hiding her hurt and not feeling it were two different things. Even Trip's wandering eye hadn't exactly been a rejection. He didn't want to *lose* her. He'd just wanted to add more members to his harem. And that was not happening. Ever.

"What?" Seth asked. "Have I got more earth-worms on my head?"

"Sorry. I'm woolgathering." More like staring at his nice, craggy face. "This isn't getting the trench done." She got up, leaning against the porch column for support. "Come on, tiger. Time's a-wasting." She was going to offer him a hand up, but he was already standing by the time she'd covered the distance between them. He nodded and stepped off the porch to get his shovel.

She'd covered her blisters with plaster strips while she was in the kitchen, but the minute she put on her gloves and picked up the shovel, she realized they wouldn't keep her hands from burning.

She swore she'd have to be dripping blood before she stopped digging.

Eventually she did discover a manageable rhythm after a few more near misses with the shovel. She might not be able to get out of bed in the morning, but she was pulling her weight. Sort of.

She'd been on some peculiar dates, but if this counted as a date, it was weirder than when that guy took her to the wrestling match. She'd almost got them thrown out when she whispered a snide comment and the lady behind them heard her.

That, as she recalled, was the last time he'd ever called her. Just as well, since she would never have gone out with him again.

Trip liked to take her to fancy parties, where they'd get their picture on the society page. She had to admit that kind of publicity had been good for her career, but she really would've enjoyed the occasional picnic.

"Not bad," Seth said.

She jumped. She'd been woolgathering again. It hit her that a picnic on the front porch with Seth held more appeal than strolling to a fancy restaurant in four-inch heels with Trip. Five-inch heels were not possible. She kept having to grab on to tables as she walked by. "What do we do next, oh, great construction engineer?"

"We dig three-foot holes to concrete the corner posts in."

"More digging! You have got to be kidding."

"It's okay. We only have one posthole digger, so I'll do it. You wouldn't by any chance have sandwich makings, would you?" The look he gave her he'd borrowed from a six-week-old puppy. Oh, Lord, he had the softest eyes! Even the bad guy from *Oliver Twist* wouldn't have been able to hold out.

"Better than that. I made spaghetti sauce this afternoon while I should've been updating my résumé. I've got salad makings and garlic bread. I figured we'd be hungry if we did any digging. Do you drink wine? I mean, you don't have to worry about driving home." She pointed across the street.

"I may not *make* it home if I have a couple of glasses of wine."

"Okay. Iced tea."

"I didn't actually say no to the wine. I just wanted you to weigh the possible outcomes." He looked down at her, and their eyes met. *Uh-oh.* They held each other's gaze a little too long. In an instant her skin felt tight and the hair on her arms stood up.

She broke away and fled to the bathroom to

scrub the dirt away. When she was clean, she checked the sleeping skunks, then went into the kitchen. He handed her a goblet of red wine. Not iced tea, then.

This was not happening. Wrong time, wrong place, wrong man.

Any man is the wrong man right now.

HE DIDN'T FOLLOW her immediately. For one thing, at the moment he wasn't all that ambulatory. He needed to relax at least one portion of his body. Emma wasn't anything like the grandmother at the DQ, but he shouldn't react quite so fulsomely *only* at The Look. He'd never had what the French called the coup de foudre—that glance across a crowded room that knocked the world out of kilter. He had a suspicion this was what it felt like.

He watched her in the kitchen as she bent over the oven to put the bread in to warm. Those tight jeans pulled even tighter.

He wasn't about to experience that madness now if it killed him.

It just might.

She might be a city slicker and a poor little rich girl, but she could definitely cook. He liked truffles and caviar as well as the next man when and if he could get them, but he'd rather have spaghetti with Emma than truffles from a fancy chef in New Orleans.

"You can't possibly dig those postholes tonight. It'll be dark in thirty minutes," Emma said as she handed him more garlic bread. "Eat hearty. I don't have any dessert except leftover ice cream from last night."

"I doubt I could stuff in another bite. I now owe you two dinners. We'll have to drive into Somerville for anything fancier than the café."

"I like the café, even if Velma thinks I'm some sort of vampire. So I take it you don't cook?"

"My momma cooks. Clare preferred take-out pizza to cooking. Take-out anything, actually. I usually came home too late and too tired to care."

"Clare?"

"Ex-wife. I figured Barbara told you."

"I didn't remember her name. And you didn't have any children, right?"

"Putting it off to be able to buy a house in town. Clare hated living out here."

"But you own all that land. Don't you have a barn?"

"It's falling down. Earl and I work on it some when we have the time. I no longer even bushhog the pasture. You have a barn, too. It's in pretty rotten shape."

"I do not have a barn."

"Sure you do. And a pond," Seth said.

"Listen, I spent five summers up here when I was a child. I'd know if Aunt Martha had a barn and a pond."

"Granted, it's a small barn in poor shape. I heard Martha's daddy used to run a few beef cattle back there when she was growing up. The walls are concrete block and still standing, but the roof's fallen in. She wouldn't have wanted a kid going back there."

"I *know* there's no pond. I begged Aunt Martha for one of those aboveground pools. She always said she couldn't afford one for the couple of months I spent up here in the summer. She was right, of course, but kids don't think that way."

Seth grinned at her. "How do you suppose those cows got water? Sure as heck no water lines back there."

"Buckets, I suppose."

This time he actually laughed. She wanted to hit him. "You have any idea how much even one cow drinks per day?" he asked.

"Then they used rain barrels."

"Very good," he said as though he were rewarding a truly backward student who'd made an intellectual breakthrough. "And when the water froze in the winter or we went without rain for six weeks every summer? Sorry, there is a pond. Man-made and fairly shallow, but it's spring fed and never goes dry. If she didn't want you messing around in that old barn, think how she would've felt if she thought you were wandering around alone where you could drown. She was right to ride herd on you." He stared out the front window as though he'd forgotten she was there. "I wish all guardians were that careful."

Emma said, "She told me she didn't own that piece of land, and I had to stay away from it because the farmer was mean and might shoot me. I was forbidden to go through the barbed wire at the edge of the backyard."

"So you didn't. According to my mother, that's a secondary characteristic of little boys versus girls. I'd have been through that fence the first night I could sneak out my window."

"I thought you were the big obey-the-rules guy."

When he didn't answer, she turned to stare at him. His face looked frozen, his eyes empty. Finally, he shook himself and said, "That came later. I was a hellion growing up. I had to learn."

"Come on, let's go check out my barn! I want to see it."

He grabbed her hand and pulled her back down. "It's behind a thicket of locust trees with three-inch thorns that can puncture a femoral artery. It's covered with wisteria and poison ivy. The pond is overgrown with so much duckweed you could fall in before you knew there was water."

"It's mine and I need to see it." She knew she sounded petulant, but she *did* need to see it. Why hadn't anyone ever told her about it? After she grew up, why hadn't Aunt Martha?

He breathed deeply and ran his hand down his face. "Yeah, okay. Tomorrow afternoon, if I can get off a little early. You do *not* go alone. This time of year the water moccasins and copperheads are too slow to avoid you."

"Why couldn't we fix it up to use for rehabilitating animals?"

"Too far away and completely overgrown. You'd have to traipse out there in the middle of the night to feed. You'd fall in the pond."

"No, I wouldn't. Besides, my babies are not staying outside at night."

He didn't bother responding. When the cage was done, the skunks *would* go outside the house. They had to learn to live in the wild. They needed to be released as soon as they were relatively safe on their own. Once the cage was finished, he and Emma could have what promised to be an unpleasant confrontation about where the skunks spent their nights. No sense borrowing trouble.

"Last but not least," he said and suspected this would be the capper, "not only are there snakes in the barn and the pond, but some great, big snapping turtles, too. They pretty much stay around the pond, where there are plenty of frogs to eat, but occasionally one of them will wander up in the yard looking for birds' eggs that've fallen out of the nest. I'll enlist Earl on Saturday after we put up the kennel, to try to net the big ones and transplant them to the river bottoms ten miles away. It'll take two of us. Some of them weigh over a hundred pounds."

"I'll never walk into the yard again!"

He laid his hand on her arm and glared at her. "You are living in the country. Not the city. Not the suburbs. This fall you'll have deer on the lawn, and I've spotted both fox and beaver. Oh, and coyote. Then there's the occasional bobcat. Saw a puma once, but I suspect he was just trekking east. Haven't seen him for a couple of years."

She jerked her arm away. "My God! What else? Grizzly bears?"

He grinned and shook his head. "No grizzlies. Spotted a black bear in the bottoms a couple of years ago. The only one I've ever seen around here. They're generally east and north of the Kentucky border, and they're rare even there. Our bear was simply lost. We followed it north out of our territory, where it became another ranger's problem. It was a young male bear. No cubs to worry about."

"Would you have? Worried?"

"If we'd had to. If they'd been abandoned or orphaned. Barbara would've taken them on until we could get them to the zoo in Memphis."

"So bears are fine to foster, but skunks aren't? That's nuts."

"It's the rules, and for good reason. That's why we bait the bottoms with rabies protection. So far we've never had a single case of rabies from any animal around here, not even bats. The few cases in Tennessee are in the hills east of here and in North Carolina. No incidences anywhere in west Tennessee for many years. The regulation about bats and skunks may be outdated, but it's better to err on the side of safety. We warn the public to stay the hell away from all wild animals. If any of the critters become a nuisance, we'll trap them, vaccinate them, and if they are clean, we'll move them."

"What else am I likely to run into around here?" she asked.

"The ubiquitous raccoons. Once a year we try to move them back to the river, but they come back when they start to wean their young in the spring."

"Baby raccoons are so cute."

"But a full-grown raccoon can tear you up. The males can weigh over fifty pounds. Actually, Memphis has more of a problem than we do. People leave dog food outside, and raccoons love dog food. Then we see the occasional possum. They really do roll up in a ball when they're scared. You don't want them around horses. They carry EPM, which can kill a horse. There are armadillos, of course. They can carry leprosy."

"Leprosy? Good grief! How about bubonic plague?"

"Not yet. No hantavirus either."

"What's that?"

"Mostly in Arizona and New Mexico. From mice." He grinned at her again. "Don't worry. The only armadillos you're likely to see are dead on the road. We get weasels, beavers and marmots around the lakes. They eat the insulation off wires on people's boats. Woodchucks. Mice and rats. And the hawks and owls that eat them. Turkey buzzards, too. The occasional eagle strays down from Reelfoot Lake. So far, no alligators this far north, but with global warming, who knows when they'll show up? I'm sure I'm forgetting some critter or other. Like your skunks."

"And massive turtles to chew your foot off and eat your fingers. Please stop! I don't want to know. All we're missing is your friendly neighborhood Tyrannosaurus Rex." She pushed her chair back, picked up the plates and set them in the kitchen sink. "I may never leave the house again. No wonder I have skunks! What on earth is lurking under my bed? One of your king snakes?"

"You shouldn't get so much as a dirt dobber inside. Miss Martha had this house buttoned up so critters can't crawl in."

"Like skunks?"

"The Mulligans must not have latched the back door properly, so it didn't close all the way when they left. The rainstorm could've blown it open enough for the momma skunk to squeeze in with her kits. She needed some safe place for them while she went off foraging."

"And never came back."

"She would have if she could have, I promise you," Seth said.

"Could a snake have slithered in after the skunks?"

"Your pantry door was shut, so nothing got into the main part of the house. And if there'd been a snake in the pantry, those skunks would not have been sleeping peacefully. Little as they are, their instincts would've kicked in. They'd have tried to kill it. Your house is safe. No snakes, no varmints. No basement for anything to hide in, and no way for critters to sneak into the attic. The vents are all stuffed with steel wool."

"What about outside motion sensor lights? Don't I need them?"

"You need new bulbs for the ones you already

have. I'll pick some up tomorrow. Earl and I can put them in for you. He said that, barring the unforeseen, if we get the posts in and set, he'll bring his wife over on Saturday morning for a couple of hours to help attach the wire and watch us net turtles. Probably some of the others guys will come by to help, too."

"I can't ask them to do that!"

"Earl wants to meet you. So does his wife. She was raised in town, so she knows the local gossip. They may even bring the kids if that's okay."

"Of course. I'll get some hot dogs and hamburgers for lunch. If they're going to help, they deserve to be fed."

"Not necessary, but a great idea." Seth got to his feet. "Now that I've frightened you half to death, I'd better get on home," he said.

She followed him to the front door, expecting him to reach for another kiss. This time she forestalled him by shoving him away—just barely. "I dumped a perfectly good fiancé less than a week ago," Emma said. "Well, Trip wasn't so good, but I thought he was, until the last minute."

"I am not this Trip person."

"No, you're not. You're much more dangerous than Trip ever was. You look right at me and you listen to me and you scare the living daylights out of me."

"Scare?"

"And I'm not going to fall into bed with you or anyone else a week after I became unaffianced. Can you say *rebound*, boys and girls?"

"I don't think *unaffianced* is a word."

She considered smacking him on the shoulder, but decided that would be counterproductive. "If it's not a word, it should be, even if I just made it up."

"Am I asking you to fall into bed?"

"You're not?"

"I won't deny I'd be delighted if you did. Any male who's attained puberty would be. But I'm not some Viking warlord raiding the neighboring villages to capture Valkyries to carry off to Valhalla."

She tried to stay serious, but she wound up snickering. "You've got your metaphors mixed up, not to mention your Norse mythology."

"The heck with my metaphors and my mythology, too." He reached for her shoulders, pulled her against him.

She was expecting another of those blowout kisses. Instead, he stopped short of her lips, then brushed them gently, teased them with the tip of his tongue. She opened to him, met his tongue with hers and sank against his chest while little spurts of fire ran up her spine. When at last he broke the kiss, her head fell back and, eyes still closed, she whispered, "Oh, my."

"Yeah," he whispered back.

"Go home. Please. Now."

"If I have to." This time the kiss was indeed one of the blowout ones that made her knees go weak. She eventually—but not too quickly— moved back. "Git!" she said. "This is not fair."

"By whose rules?"

"Mine, damn it!" She fled inside and shut the door firmly against him.

WHEN EMMA GOT her breathing under control, she considered that, for all intents and purposes, she was having a party on Saturday. That meant another trip to the grocery store. Who knew how many others would show up to help and stay to be fed? Emma sighed. She'd never done much impromptu entertaining in the city.

She'd have to make a stab at cleaning up the house for company. Fresh towels in the bathroom. Cold beer. Sodas. She had a yard that needed cutting and no lawn mower available. She wanted a used one she could afford. Another unforeseen expense. Whoever came would have to put up with uncut grass. She couldn't even borrow Seth's. She didn't know how to drive a riding lawn mower, and the mayor had said Seth's wasn't working properly. She wasn't familiar with any landscaping services out here, never mind the cost.

On top of that little problem, she apparently had an entire zoo wandering around her property. A phantom barn choked like Sleeping Beauty's castle in wisteria and thorny locust trees. A pond filled with poisonous snakes and vicious snapping turtles. Seth inviting people first and asking later. Seth planning and building the cage. Seth getting the lightbulbs and putting them up. Okay, he was trying to be helpful, because she was obviously a greenhorn, even if she *had* spent summers here as a child.

She wasn't a child now. She'd kicked a man to the curb for trying to run her life and groom her to play his own little Galatea to his Pygmalion.

There was a definite divide between being helpful and taking control of her life. No matter how sexy and competent and handsome and knowledgeable Seth was, and as much as she needed his help, if he tried to run her life for her... She'd see about that.

Tonight he'd kissed her again, but a totally different kind of kiss. She should've been clearer that she was *not* looking for a replacement for Trip. If she responded as she had tonight, it was no wonder if he thought she was beddable. Which she wasn't. Not at all.

Pheromones were the darnedest things. She should be so devastated by her breakup with Trip that she wouldn't notice Brad Pitt if he walked into her kitchen. As a matter of fact, she'd never had such an immediate reaction to a male. She'd thought she was invested in Trip—after all, she'd agreed to marry him—but this ka-blam reaction she had to Seth was outside the scope of anything she'd ever felt before.

But that was simply rebound. All that adrenaline had to go somewhere, and he'd appeared at the optimum moment.

She fed the kits, who barely woke up long enough to take their gruel before they went back to sleep.

It wasn't too late to call her father. She had promised.

Neither of her siblings ever answered the landline at home. They were too busy texting and talking on their cells. If a tornado destroyed their cell towers, teenagers across the nation would have a meltdown.

Andrea, not Daddy, answered the landline. "Ah, so this is Green Acres reporting in?" she asked.

"I'll have you know I do not have a thousand-pound pig in my living room like on the TV show."

"Good thing, too. The idea of cleaning up pig poo on the carpets does not bear thinking about. How are you really? Any job offers yet?"

Emma felt a surge of guilt roll over her. She

couldn't get a job of any sort if she spent her time playing nursemaid to small animals. Better not mention the skunks. Andrea would definitely not understand the need for secrecy. She'd have to talk about them at her golf foursome. They'd make such a good story. "Nope. Trying to get the house in order and the boxes unpacked. I thought I just brought the bare essentials."

"Met your neighbors yet?"

Another wave of guilt. "The only close neighbor I have is a game warden who lives across the street." Emma had no intention of telling Andrea anything else about him. "And I've met the local veterinarian and a couple of people in town, including the mayor."

"Great. Is the mayor married?"

"He's bald and weighs close to four hundred pounds. I think he has a wife and a passel of children."

"Then are there any handsome, rich, unmarried farmers around?" Andrea's voice dropped to that throaty whiskey baritone she always used when playing around in Emma's love life. "Oh, Lord, Em, honey. That was inappropriate. I'm sorry."

"Don't be. I'm realizing I had a narrow escape from Trip."

"Trip has called your father a dozen times a day. Tonight, he got me instead. I thought he was going to burst into tears. What did you do to him?"

She doubted Andrea would have broken up with David French because of a casual infidelity. But then Andrea put up with a lot from him at one point in their marriage. He started working what sometimes seemed like 24/7, and playing golf the few hours he had left over. With three children at difficult stages, Andrea told Emma later that she felt as though David had opted out of the family, and left her to deal with them single-handedly. He stopped coming to their games or Emma's horse shows. At Andrea's insistence, they went to marriage counseling. It worked. Emma felt certain that was because even when the situation was at its worst, they never doubted their love for each other.

"Trip and I didn't want the same things anymore," Emma said.

"Better to find out now. Even when we were going through that rough patch with you three hellions, David wasn't unfaithful. Not sexually, anyway. One of the things I've always loved about him is that he can see a problem and change to fix it. Most men either can't or won't.

"That's when I went back to working part-time with my decorating. I love you all, but I needed to get away from you to do my own thing, too. Better to have no man than the wrong one. That's what I tell Catherine, but at this point she falls for a different boy every day or so."

Actually, that surprised Emma. She'd always figured that Andrea would take the best available man as opposed to none.

"Your father is off playing poker at the club," Andrea said. "His usual once-a-week game."

"Do you mind?"

"Lord, no! The dynamics have changed now that you children are more grown up. I don't feel abandoned when everyone's gone. In fact, I'm grateful for the peace and quiet. Call him on his cell, why don't you?"

"And interrupt a royal flush? I promised to check in, so you can count this. Tell him I really am fine. Tell the brats I miss them. You, too."

"I love you, kiddo," Andrea said. "Get yourself together and come home where you belong. Mrs. Miller from next door to you is checking on your town house. I hope you're back before somebody offers to rent it."

Emma hung up and leaned against the couch. She hated the idea of renting her town house, even on a short term lease, but it was the sensible thing to do. The mortgage was expensive. She regarded moving back to her parents' house as failure, even if it was only for a short term. At least she had options. So many people didn't.

She was also lucky to have landed a step-mother she'd come to love. That had taken a while on both their parts. Andrea was considerably younger than Emma's dad and had not signed on to marry a widower with a mother-less child. Still, she was game. After the other two were born, the nanny costs skyrocketed, but like so many second wives much younger than their husbands, she'd been expected to pick up and travel with him at a moment's notice. Not quite a trophy wife, because Emma's mother had died and not divorced, but a trophy nonetheless. And she was good at her role. She had been a top interior designer when she met David French, and only started working part-time after the children stopped needing her so much. Emma could thank Andrea for teaching her how to raise funds for everything from the symphony to the ASPCA. She could charm big bucks from Scrooge.

Now, there was a thought. How did the local rescuers interact with the other animal rescue organizations? She'd have to ask Barbara. She hoped she'd be back in Memphis soon with an interesting job like the one she'd had, but until she was, she might as well do some work with the animal people. She'd talk to Barbara about it tomorrow.

The alternative was to sit on her broadening rump and feel sorry for herself. Even Trip might start to look good. Nah.

As for his calls to her father... She felt certain Trip wanted to win her back so he could dump her. His sense of his own worth had taken a hit, and he obviously didn't like it. How had she not known what he was? How could she have agreed to marry him? The next guy she liked, she'd plumb the depths of his history and his character before she took any irrevocable step.

Such as what?

How could she be so totally over Trip so fast? Was she that shallow? Apparently so. Because she was a whole lot happier than she should have been with no job and no fiancé and no prospects.

Her thoughts flashed to Seth. Bon appétit! She went to bed laughing.

She remembered that the vet's clinic opened for business at eight thirty, but when she called, the line was already busy. Maybe she should forget about talking to Barbara. As she waited for the babies to finish their gruel, she went down the list of chores she had to do before Saturday, when she had company coming. She could put the pedal to the metal tomorrow and concentrate on résumés and phone calls today.

The third time she called Barbara, she got through.

"Barbara," Emma asked. "Are you on your way out or can you talk?"

"Both. I've got a tup with an abscess on his jaw. I'll pick you up in ten minutes. You can ride along. Shouldn't take long, and I could use the extra hands."

Why not? Another morning of boring résumé writing down the tubes, but hey, what was money? She hadn't put on a pair of panty hose or a skirt since she'd moved into The Hovel. That felt like winning a nasty battle.

The first thing she said when she climbed into Barbara's monster truck was, "What kind of animal is a tup?"

"It's what the Scots call a breeding ram. And the required action is called 'tupping.' So if some guy with a Scottish burr asks you if you'd like to tup…"

"Say no."

"Not necessarily," Barbara said with a grin. "Depends on the guy."

"What about you? Have you ever considered remarrying?"

"At my age? With grown—well, semigrown— kids who keep me broke and on the verge of a heart attack? I have no intention of getting naked with a strange man. Even if I knew one strange enough to be interested."

"You look great."

"The corollary to that is 'for my age.' I don't think after the years without my husband I could adjust to having a male living with me again. They want their laundry done and folded or—God forbid, ironed—and meals cooked for them and a reasonable schedule they can count on. Not happening with my job. If I was supposed to be doing corporate wifely things at some fancy function, and a cow got stuck in the middle of delivering a calf, I'd pick the cow every time."

"You'd never marry a man who didn't support your decision."

"So far as I've found, there ain't no such animal. Not after John. The turn-in we want is a couple of hundred yards along on your side of the road. It's only a break in the privet hedge, so look sharp."

Barbara made the turn and found their way blocked by a five-bar steel farm gate. Without being asked, Emma jumped out, held the gate open, shut and fastened it after Barbara drove through, then jumped back in the car.

They followed a narrow dirt and gravel driveway that had probably not been graded or had gravel added to its surface in years. Barbara's truck didn't have the finest shock absorbers either. Once, Emma bounced up and hit her head on the edge of the closed sunroof and saw stars. Eventually, however, they pulled up in front of a medium-size red barn that had not seen a lick of paint since the gravel driveway was new and smooth.

The man who loomed up out of the darkness in the barn looked a lot like the mayor, except that his weight was stretched up to at least six and a half feet instead of being squashed down like the mayor's. He wore muddy boots, muddy jeans, a muddy shirt and a sweat-darkened John Deere baseball cap. "Hey, Dr. Barbara," he said, holding out a giant paw with patches of dark hair on the knuckles. "This here pretty lady must be Miss Martha's niece." He enveloped her hand after he shook Barbara's.

Emma nodded. Of course he would have heard about her. "Are you by any chance kin to the mayor?" she asked as she rubbed feeling back into her fingers.

"First cousin on my momma's side. How'd you guess?"

"Just a hunch."

"Growin' up, folks thought we was twins. Then he started growin' sideways while I kept on straight up."

"Where's your ram, Holloway?" Barbara asked as she pulled her travel case from the backseat. "I hope you've got him confined."

"Well, now, as to that…"

"I refuse to chase your ram all over the pasture."

"Not as bad as that. We got him in a stall. Just that it's the foaling stall."

"Holloway, it's half the size of this barn!"

He held up his hands in a placating gesture. "Gimme a little minute. We'll get a couple ropes and hog-tie him."

"Until I can get some tranquilizer in him," Barbara said.

"He's a real sweet ram generally, but his jaw hurts, so's he can't eat. He does like to eat almost as much as he likes his ladies."

From outside came three young men, also giants. "Sons?" Emma whispered.

Barbara nodded. "Boys, y'all go help your daddy."

They didn't meet the eyes of either woman, but marched off toward the far end of the barn and through a stall gate.

"They're kinda shy," whispered Holloway.

"Here we go," Barbara said.

The boys were huge compared with the ram. He, however, had large horns, four sharp hooves and apparently the temperament of the Tasmanian Devil in the Saturday cartoons.

"Should we help?" Emma asked Barbara.

"Are you completely insane? Just watch." She brought out a syringe, filled it with some sort of liquid, then waited by the gate.

Emma had watched children's goat rodeo

classes at the fair. This was the same sort of thing, except it was one goat versus four large men. At one point they cornered the ram against the fence, only to have him rise up on his hind feet and drive his horns into the belt buckle of the largest of Holloway's sons, who flew back six feet and landed on his rear end.

He clambered to his feet, brushed off the seat of his jeans and said, "That's it." He rushed the ram, grabbed one front and one rear leg, flipped the ram flat on his side, then sat on him.

Barbara hurried into the stall and emptied her syringe into the ram's rump.

"You can get up as soon as he's unconscious," she said.

Five minutes later, the ram snored peacefully. The lump on the side of his jaw was the size of a softball.

Emma brought Barbara's case to her.

"Stand back," Barbara said. "I'm going to drain this thing. It'll be nasty."

It was. Smelly, too. After Barbara had lanced and emptied the wen, she cleaned it and felt around inside. "Hello," she said. "Here's his problem." She took her forceps and carefully withdrew a five-inch-long twig from the wound. "He must've run into the hedge when he was chasing down his harem."

She finished cleaning, dosed with antibiotics and gave instructions for Holloway to keep up the treatment. "Needs to stay open so it can heal from the inside. You'll have to irrigate twice daily. He ought to be good as new in a couple of days."

When the two women drove back down the driveway, the four large men watched them silently.

"Well, that was fun," Barbara said.

"I didn't do anything to help," Emma said.

"You stayed out of the way and handed me stuff. That's plenty. I don't mind blood, but I do hate pus. Bleh."

"Poor little ram," Emma said.

"If you can put up with that without turning a hair, you can probably handle anything. Come on, I'll make you a double latte when I get back to the clinic. There'll be folks waiting for me to open up and mad as snakes because I'm late. I really have to get somebody in full-time to answer the phone and schedule appointments."

Half a dozen trucks, two horse trailers and three SUVs waited in the parking lot of the clinic. Not a single sedan. As Barbara parked, doors opened and prospective clients piled out and followed her to the door.

"Sorry, y'all," Barbara said. "Let me get the coffee on and clean myself up, and we'll figure out what sort of order to see you in."

Without being asked, Emma slid into the vacant seat behind the receptionist's desk, opened the appointment book to a new page, entered the date and began to check in the clients who were waiting. For twenty minutes she fielded clients' questions, wrote notes and generally did the job as she guessed it should be done. She'd worked the reception desk during the summers she'd been an unpaid intern at a couple of temp agencies, so this wasn't completely unfamiliar. But she discovered that the computer was password protected and she didn't have a chance to check with Barbara. She didn't know how to open it, much less bring up the data. She did the best she could by taking hand-written notes. The clients seemed to have evolved their own way of working out the order in which they were seen. Since there didn't seem to be any genuine emergencies, that turned out quite well.

An hour later, the chaos had resolved itself to semiorder, but semiorder punctuated by meows, barks, the screech of one red macaw and the squeal of a small potbellied pig. Emma met her neighbors, overheard more gossip than she had in a dozen years in Memphis, and actually enjoyed herself. As she saw the last client with her beagle puppy out, Barbara left the exam room. "Put the closed sign up," she said. "I'm starved."

"Good grief," Emma said. "So are my babies! I have to get home."

"Can't thank you enough for helping out. You really jumped in there."

"I couldn't even turn on the computer. You'll have a lot of notes to transcribe."

Barbara collapsed into the nearest client seat. "How desperate are you for a job?"

"Desperate for the right job."

"Meaning not one that pays just over minimum wage and works your tail off?"

"I may be at some point. But if I keep not sending out résumés or networking, that may be sooner rather than later."

"So, stave off the wolf at the door a little while longer. If you could do what you did this morning, I would bow down and kiss your feet."

"I thought you had a high school girl."

"She does a couple of hours after school three days a week and a couple of hours Saturday morning. She cleans the cages and scrubs the floors, and if she has a few extra minutes, she does some computer work. But mornings are crunch time. Say, eight thirty to noon, or eight thirty to two? Not even every day." Barbara was starting to look pitiful.

Emma laughed. "I'd rather ride with you. Tell you what... I'll work for you eight thirty to noon three days a week if you'll teach me about fostering animals."

"Done. Which days?"

"Which are the heaviest?"

"Mondays, Thursdays and Fridays. Saturday is covered."

"Let's give it a shot," Emma said. "If it doesn't work out, no pain, no foul." She flipped the sign on the door to Closed. "Now, I have babies and me to feed."

"I could maybe scrounge up a can of soup or something…"

"Nope," Emma said. "Let's start as we mean to go on. Anyway, so far it's been fun. See you Monday."

CHAPTER NINE

"I NEVER SHOULD'VE told Emma about the barn and the pond," Seth said to Earl. He finished his chef salad and corn bread. Velma took his drink glass to put in a to-go cup so he could take it with him on his afternoon rounds. He hadn't asked. She always did it and fixed it up properly with lemon and sweetener. "Emma wants to hotfoot it down there and see if the barn can be saved."

Earl snorted. "Hope you got your snakebite kit up-to-date."

"What I told her. Come on, we got a poacher to track."

Thirty minutes later, Seth turned left onto the gravel road into a dense fir tree plantation. Some optimistic farmer twenty years earlier had planted the trees in serried rows in hopes of cutting them down to sell as Christmas trees. Unfortunately, Southern forests weren't good places to grow the fancy Norway spruces that people seemed to prefer these days. Those were brought down by the truckload from Minnesota and Wisconsin the week before Thanksgiving. Trees that weren't sold by December 15 were given away. Any scruffy leftovers were turned into mulch after New Year's Day, and that was given away in the spring.

Seth had no idea who currently owned this tree farm, but whoever held the title ignored it except for large "No Trespassing, No Hunting, Private Property" signs posted at irregular intervals.

The deer didn't ignore the property, however. Therefore, neither did the hunters. Or the motorcycle and ATV riders. Every ATV ride off the dirt roads, even on deer paths, set up ruts that eroded with every rain until the roads themselves were impassible. At least Southern wardens didn't have to worry about snowmobiles. Except for one good snowstorm a year, more or less, snowmobiles weren't usable.

The laws of Tennessee said that a property owner could cull the deer on his own property if they were destroying his crops. He didn't have to hold to restrictions as to permits, seasons for rifles or for bows and black powder antique weapons, or even does versus bucks.

Seth hated that law. Most farmers were protective of their wildlife and didn't abuse the law. Some big corporations, however, saw their large tree farms and soybean fields as an excuse to bring in rich clients to hunt in or out of season.

Seth considered that pure poaching. So did all the other game wardens, although there wasn't much they could do about it. Farmers did suffer predation from deer, especially after particularly cold winters—and more to the point, horribly hot summers. Human predation, however, meant orphaned fawns, and orphan fawns largely wound up being cared for by Barbara and her animal rescue group. They spent time and money, often their own, rescuing. They held fundraisers, but according to Barbara, they always worked on a narrow margin at the edge of penury.

He could remember seeing *The Yearling* as a kid. When the father shot the deer, Seth walked out of the theater. He'd never willingly gone to another movie about animals. He'd never seen *Turner and Hooch*, or *Benji*, and definitely not *Bambi*. He took a lot of teasing from his buddies at Auburn and even now. Earl understood, but plenty of others thought he was a wimp and told him so. He really didn't care.

At this point, he was checking the trails through the Christmas tree farm in search of an ATV that had been reported as hoorahing full blast day and night, possibly jacklighting deer and firing what sounded like howitzers much too close to houses.

There was always shooting in the country. Most everybody ignored it. Everybody owned at least one gun and probably several. In dove season, however, he'd been forced to comb bird shot out of his hair on more than one occasion, when some fool hunter had gotten off his beer-stocked cooler and let fly. Hunting drunk was right up there with—or above—driving drunk. He and Earl came down on excessive blood alcohol levels like a ton of bricks. He'd badgered the powers that be unmercifully until they'd purchased a Breathalyzer. Half the time, however, it was in the other car.

But this wasn't dove season. Or deer season either. Because there'd been no rain for several days—not since the night Emma moved in—any ATV tread marks had practically disappeared. Enough remained so the two men knew they were following a big ATV with balloon tires.

"You gonna be ready for me to come over Saturday morning?" Earl asked. "Finish up that cage for you? Sounds like it's gonna be big enough to use as a flight cage. Barbara's is pretty puny when you're trying to exercise a broken wing on a big hoot owl."

"Not that big, unless it's a very small bird," Seth said. "Damn!" he shouted as the SUV bottomed out in a hole as wide as his wheelbase.

"What's with you and Miss City Slicker?"

"I'm being neighborly. Period."

"Uh-huh."

"If she hadn't moved into Miss Martha's place, I never would've met her," Seth said. "Our orbits do not mesh. My guess is she'll get a new job in the city and be out of here in a couple of weeks. Back with her fiancé and setting the date. You know that dating site where they try to match country boys with country girls?"

Earl nodded.

"Well, I am and she isn't. Barbara told me she was a debutante."

"And that means?"

"Where all the rich daughters get displayed for all the rich eligible bachelors to get 'em married off to go live in somebody else's McMansion instead of Daddy's."

"You sound a tad bitter."

"After Clare, you can see why I'm not real high on city girls."

"Not every city girl is like Clare," Earl said. "Anyway, seems like all the classifieds I read are about selling a hobby farm to city execs who want to move out of the rat race that they largely created."

"Farming, as we both know from experience, is not a hobby. That was Clare's problem. She thought she could swan in to Memphis every whipstitch to get her nails done and have lunch at chic little restaurants with her rich girlfriends. And I'm not."

"A girlfriend? You got that right."

"No, idiot. *Rich.* Hello. See that little bit of red over there in the brush?" Seth pulled to the side of the road. Both men got out and slid through the trees.

The rear end of a large ATV stuck out from under a dark green tarp obviously meant to conceal it. The way it was parked, it posed a threat to any vehicle that came up on it.

Earl checked the plate. "A year out of date. That would seem to constitute a violation." He got out his phone and dialed in a series of numbers. "The last license comes back to a Tyrell McKee." He waited. "My, my, Mr. McKee is not one of our more saintly citizens."

Seth pulled the tarp forward to uncover the hood. The engine was cold.

"The gentleman who's the registered owner of this sweet little baby girl already has three tickets for joyriding and a bench warrant for a DUI and poaching an out-of-season doe," Earl said.

"You got an address?"

"And an arrest warrant all ready to be made out and signed. Would you like to take us on a little joyride, too?" Earl asked. "House is only a mile down the road."

"He hears us coming, he'll book it sure as this world," Seth said.

"We can park the cruiser across the road

where he can't get past. Can't fit an SUV between the pines."

"But he can T-bone us, shove us out of the
way and total the cruiser. How about we park
his ATV crossways up ahead of us, take the keys
and remove the plugs. Either he stops or he hits
his own vehicle."

Ten minutes later, the two men walked down
the track along the edge of the trees where their
green uniforms blended in so perfectly that only
their movement gave them away. Whoever was
in the house would have to be looking hard to
see them.

The low farmhouse desperately needed paint-
ing. The porch stairs sagged on one end, and the
window in the storm door was covered with a
square of cardboard. But at the doorway sat a
shining, silver crew-cab diesel pickup that was
in showroom condition. The two men could see a
gun rack through the rear window holding what
looked like a shotgun and two rifles.

Both men loosened their sidearms and stepped
behind the truck to keep it between them and the
front door of the house. With luck, the only guns
available to the owner were safely on that gun
rack, or if not, McKee wouldn't want to put bullet holes through the cab of his truck on the off
chance of hitting a game warden or two.

"Mr. McKee?" Earl called. "Tyrell McKee?

Game wardens here. Would you come out and talk to us a minute?"

Nothing. Seth made the same request. His baritone was deeper and louder than Earl's tenor, but both men sounded calm and reasonable. Neither wanted a gunfight. Lord only knew who might be in that cabin. The two of them wouldn't fire the first shot—or any shot if they could help it.

"He's not here," came a female voice from inside. "He's at work."

"Ma'am, his truck's here," Earl said.

"You think he drives his good truck to work? Let it get repoed?"

"Where would we find him?" Seth asked. "Ma'am, could you open the door so we can talk to you?"

Nothing happened for more than a minute, then the front door opened. *At least the family isn't starving,* Seth thought when the lady barely fit through the door sideways. Inside Seth glimpsed a restaurant-size freezer and saw a propane tank around the corner of the house. He didn't have a search warrant to allow him to check the freezer, since it was inside the house, but he had no doubt it was filled with venison, squirrel, possum, raccoon and probably bass and crappie, as well.

"Where's Tyrell working?" Earl asked.

"He's working construction downtown. Don't know where exactly."

"When will he be home?"

"This evening sometime. He generally stops off for a couple beers after work."

Or more, Seth thought. He'd be unlikely to go nuts joyriding with his ATV and shotgun in the middle of the night if he had only a couple of beers under his belt. More likely a six-pack and a few shooters.

"Ma'am, we do need to talk to him. We've had reports his ATV's been driving through people's fields and front yards full throttle at all hours of the night, and he's been shooting off guns and scaring people to death."

"It ain't Tyrell."

"It's his registration, ma'am."

"Quite a bit out of date," Earl added. "Need to see a current registration and proof of insurance. He has to move his ATV up here, park it in his yard and not hide it in the brush at the side of the road where somebody could run into it. And he needs to come into our office and take care of his fines. Bring his paperwork up-to-date and clear this matter up before he drives it anymore. It's only because we didn't actually see him driving it that he's not getting fined right now." Best not to mention the DUI. The chances that he'd come in on his own were slim anyway, but if he had an inkling that he could be arrested for the bench warrant, he'd be halfway to New Orleans before they saw him.

"Huh. Yeah, I'll tell him. He's mighty busy, though."

"Ma'am," Earl said and handed the woman a folded piece of paper. "This isn't a subpoena—yet—just a friendly reminder. If we have to come back here again, though, ma'am, things might get real unpleasant. I don't expect either one of you would like sitting in jail waiting to be arraigned. Sometimes that takes weeks."

It didn't, but it could, so they weren't actually lying.

"Jail? Now, you lookee here! I got kids in school."

"Child protective services would take care of them, unless you got kin to look after them."

"Kin?" she screeched. "My good-for-nothing brother-in-law is why Tyrell's in this mess. Fool likes to drink and joyride, and sometimes Tyrell goes along with him." She snatched the letter from Earl's hand. "I'll go move the ATV right now, and I'll get Tyrell to come by your office tomorrow morning. I ain't never been to jail, and I don't plan to go now. And no child protective *anybody* is going to look after my kids. Plus every bit of the meat in that freezer is legal with stamps and everything. Whatever y'all may think, Tyrell and me's not trash. Tyrell's got him a bad back, can't work all the time. Sometimes if Tyrell don't hunt, we don't eat. Y'all said your piece. Now git."

"Would you like us to accompany you to the ATV?" Seth asked.

"Oh, for… Just git."

They got.

They replaced the plugs and keys before Mrs. McKee reached them. She climbed aboard, backed around and gunned the ATV up the road toward her house. Even the engine sounded irate.

"Think he'll come in?" Earl asked. "She's bound and determined to protect him."

"If she has her way, he will," Seth said. "She doesn't want him in jail. If that freezer is full of legal meat like she says, why did he poach a doe? I suspect he's processing illegal meat and selling it. But we can't check without a search warrant."

"No judge will give us one unless we have more evidence."

"Pity. If we could prove that, then he *would* be going to jail. We'll need to keep an eye on him. Lord, Earl, life would be so much simpler if people just did right and obeyed the rules."

"It's natural to protect the people you love," Earl said. "Even from themselves."

Seth's mind gave him a swift kick. *The way I have with Emma and her skunks.* But that wasn't love. He hardly knew the woman. He felt protective of her because she was so obviously out of her depth here in the country with no family, no friends, no job, no fiancé and, for all he knew, no money. Maybe Barbara could find that out. Seth didn't have any idea how to go about it.

"How you coming with your kennel?" Earl asked. The two men had a tacit agreement that was what Emma's enclosure would be called. For a dog, say. Anything but a skunk.

"I think we'll be ready to tack the wire on and hang the door Saturday," Seth replied. "You and Janeen bringing the kids over? We'll come up with something for lunch. Hot dogs, probably."

"The kids' favorite. They'd live on hot dogs if Janeen would let them."

"I'll keep the skunks out of sight in the pantry. The kids don't even need to know they're around. If they catch a glimpse, they'll go ape. Those little devils are seriously cute and completely tame at this point. Their idea of heaven is curling up in Emma's lap."

"How about yours?"

"My lap?"

"Your idea of heaven, ol' buddy. From what I've heard, curling up in her lap sounds like an appealing proposition."

Seth felt himself blushing. His ears burned. Men didn't blush. "We're friends, period. She's a thorn in my flesh right now. I want to get those babies in the woods and Emma back in the city, so I can go back to doing my job without worrying about her."

"You're telling me you haven't hit on her?"

"None of your business, ol' *buddy*."

"Woo-hoo, hit a sore spot, didn't I? Tell you what, how 'bout we fall by your house for a beer on the way back to the office. If she's at home, I can meet her and give you my honest opinion as a serious connoisseur of ladies if she's worth all the problems she's causing you."

Seth grumbled, but complied. He didn't know if he wanted to see her SUV in the driveway or not. When he drove around the curve in the gravel road and saw the SUV outside her front door, he felt a jolt of anticipation that he didn't like.

He told himself he didn't give a darn if Earl approved of her or not.

But in reality he wanted Earl to be as knocked out by her as he was. Like winning a blue ribbon at the fair with your Duroc sow. Not that she looked like a sow. But she was no cuddly bunny either. More like a swan—beautiful, graceful and capable of removing your head from your shoulders if you provoked her. They climbed out of Seth's truck, expecting her to come to the front door when she heard them.

Seth rapped on the door, checked around the side of the house, but saw no sign of her.

"She's got to be here somewhere," Seth said. "Maybe she went across to my house to ask me for something."

He stood on her front steps and surveyed the big front yard. He did not have a good feeling about this.

"You hear that?" Earl whispered.

"No, what?"

"Listen. Sounds like somebody…" Earl held up his hand for silence.

"Emma!" Seth shouted. Earl had ears like a fox. He could hear things no other ranger could. If he heard a sound, it was there to be heard.

"Help, somebody!"

CHAPTER TEN

SHE KNEW BETTER. She'd promised Seth she'd wait for him to show her the way to the pond and the barn, but it *was* her pond and her barn. She didn't need his permission or his assistance to check out her own property. He'd sworn he'd be home soon enough this afternoon to take her back there. Still, he'd said it was less than half a mile from her back door. Even a dilapidated barn was a sizable structure and should be simple to spot through the trees and brush. She couldn't get lost in half a mile. She was unlikely to fall in the pond either. You could see water before you walked into it.

She was sick of his "countryier than thou" stance. She'd sneak out on her own, be back before he got home and prove she could handle herself.

People who promised to do a job, then when push came to shove, didn't deliver, annoyed her. The heck with Seth. She'd show him.

Okay, she was scared. That was nothing new. She couldn't remember a time since her mother died that she hadn't felt a modicum of fear. It was a point of honor to keep going, whether it was riding horses or learning to drive a car, or auditioning for the school play, or walking into a big party where she didn't know a soul. None of that mattered so long as nobody could tell she was scared. Her father had taught her that. If she failed, she disappointed him, and he didn't deserve a disappointing daughter.

As far as he was concerned, his daughter could take on anything. She'd tried to convince Seth of that, too, and she wasn't about to back off now.

She did not, however, intend to be stupid. She collected her cell phone and made sure it was charged. She checked the batteries in her big flashlight, sprayed herself with sunscreen and bug repellent tough enough for the Amazon delta, pulled on a long-sleeved shirt and jeans, then her theoretically snake-proof knee-high boots. She stuck her Swiss army knife in the front pocket of her jeans, along with a wad of tissue. Then she picked up the heavy gloves Seth had given her to work on the cage, ran over her checklist in her mind and turned on the porch light in case she did need a light to guide her home. Finally, she headed out the back door.

A very small voice in her mind dared to whisper, "Why are you doing this?"

Because I'm mad and scared and I have no intention of letting either one control me.

The Mulligans, or whoever had attempted to keep the yard up, had stopped mowing at the edge of the azalea beds near the back of the property. The azaleas were old, as tall as Seth and as thick as a grizzly bear.

Past the barbed-wire fence, as far past the tree line as she could see, the abandoned pasture was choked by brush and scrub trees and nettles and all sorts of greenery she didn't recognize.

Before she attempted to climb through the three-strand barbed-wire fence behind the azaleas, she tried to spot either the pond or the collapsing barn, but could see neither through the brush and trees.

Seth had told her the barn was to the northwest, so she headed in that direction.

She should've brought Aunt Martha's foxheaded Malacca cane. And maybe her binoculars.

Okay, two things that should have been on her list but weren't. At this point she was not walking back to the house for either one.

She'd considered bringing a bottle of water, then told herself she wouldn't be gone long enough to get thirsty. Probably because she was uptight, she already felt like spitting cotton with thirst. She'd simply have to put up with that.

She did twist off a straight branch from one of

the trees and strip it of leaves and twigs. It would be an adequate walking stick. She had no idea what kind of wood it was. Not locust, because it bore no lethal four-inch thorns. She could recognize oak or pine trees—one because of the acorns, the other because of the cones.

Now she could sweep her stick ahead of her to brush aside some of the taller meadow daisies and Johnson grass. And scare off the snakes. She was beginning to agree with Seth's ex-wife. At this point, a snake was a snake.

The ground beneath her feet wasn't hard, but it was dry enough that her boots didn't sink in but left shallow prints. Actually, it was pretty back here, if too overgrown. It would take a giant bush hog to even begin to clear it. Bringing in expensive equipment to reclaim land she didn't need was way down on her to-do list.

If she only knew where she was going. She caught the glint of water a dozen yards to the left at the same moment she buried her boot ankle-deep in ground that a minute ago had seemed hard.

Drat! She managed to pull her boot out, although the mud tried to suck it off her foot. She backed up and turned in a 360-degree circle to get her bearings. She could no longer see either the barbed-wire fence she'd climbed through, or The Hovel. No big deal. She knew where they both were, of course she did.

She pushed aside the lower branches of what she thought was a sycamore tree and spotted an obviously man-made structure some distance ahead. The old barn was the only structure back here, so that must be it. The building was draped with vines and creepers. A good many looked like poison ivy. She sidestepped, careful to trust her weight only to ground that didn't give. Before each step she pushed her stave into the ground ahead of her. So far, the ground was solid. She had seen no snakes. Yet. She got about twenty feet from the structure, then hesitated.

The walls of the old barn were, as Seth had said, built of concrete block. They looked in remarkably good shape. A few at the corners had crumbled, but the walls were structurally sound, although she could see daylight through the roof.

She pointed her flashlight into the barn, heard a rustle up in the rafters and froze. Raccoons, maybe, or rats. Possibly doves. Surely nothing big enough or bad enough to be dangerous.

Did snakes rustle?

She hesitated to move closer in case the remaining rafters in the sagging roof collapsed…

She should've left a note for Seth on her windshield to tell him where she was. What if he showed up before she made it back to The Hovel? Her SUV was there. Surely he'd figure it out. By then she'd be back inside the house with her babies, anyway.

He'd never need to know she'd made this crazy trek that seemed more and more like a bad idea. Nonsense. Nothing bad had happened—the muddy boot didn't count. Not like it was quicksand.

Off to her left side, the pond looked placid and calm in the setting sun. All around its edges were giant lily pads, not yet in bloom. In another month the whole lake would be covered in blooms and redolent of perfume.

As she watched, a turtle with a shell big enough to cover the hood of her SUV surfaced in the center of the pond, floated for a moment, then disappeared under the water again like Moby Dick luring Ahab. *Guess which one I am?*

She choked back a scream. How many more giants lurked just under the water?

Or out of it? On the banks, among the lilies, under the brush?

I need to get the hell out of here. This place, these creatures, do not want me here. I don't want me here either, and definitely not alone. Why didn't I wait for Seth?

She took a deep breath to calm down. As she turned to retrace what steps she could see in the mud, two does and a fawn exploded from under the shadowy barn eaves and bounded straight at her.

She screamed.

The deer—no doubt more terrified than she was—spotted her, turned their white tails in midair and splashed across the end of the pond to disappear into the trees.

For the first time in her life, she understood true panic. The great god Pan held her in his atavistic grip and she wanted *out*!

She ran back the way she'd come—or at least she thought it was the way she'd come. She stumbled out of the trees and up to the muddy edge of the choked pond. When she turned away, she could see the faintest trail, where she'd come through what seemed like hours ago but must be only minutes. Nothing looked familiar except her own barely discernible footprints.

Then she glimpsed the roof of The Hovel straight ahead, past the barbed-wire fence separating the pasture from the azaleas. Once through the fence and the shrubs to the back door she'd be home. She pulled her gloves back on to get through the barbed wire.

She had her eye on the prize.

Not, however, on her feet. The toe of her boot caught under a thick root.

And catapulted her face-forward directly toward the barbed wire.

Somehow she managed to twist so the back of her skull struck the wire and crashed through the top two strands. Her foot stayed trapped and twisted under the root.

She'd always hated that feeling—when you know you're going to be hurt, but not how badly, and there's not a darned thing you can do to change the outcome. Like falling off a horse or being knocked down at lacrosse. She definitely felt it now.

The thud took only nanoseconds. Getting breath back into her lungs took more than half a minute and seemed like an hour. A minute after that, she began to assess the damage.

She lifted her head and found she couldn't move it more than a couple of inches before the barbed wire threatened to scalp her. She wished she had a crew cut. Better yet, a Mohawk. She pulled off her gloves and felt her scalp.

Her head had landed right between two fence posts and ripped loose two strands of wire when she fell. A foot to either side, and she would've cracked her head on a fence post and knocked herself silly. Or worse.

She touched her scalp carefully. Her fingers came away bloody from the embedded wire. She wasn't badly hurt. Scalp wounds always bled a lot. She was, however, stuck. She couldn't see the back of her head, and every time she tried to loosen her hair from the barbs, she ended up pricking her fingers.

She'd been so concerned with her scalp that she hadn't paid much attention to the rest of her. Now the foot caught under the root began to throb for attention. She couldn't sit up because of her trapped hair, so her hands couldn't reach her ankle to free herself. She scraped dirt away from under her trapped boot with her other foot to get a little maneuvering room. Any movement hurt her ankle. Sprained? Broken? Surely not broken. It still worked. Well, sort of.

She realized she'd been grumbling words that her mother would have smacked her for. She closed her eyes, took a deep breath, planted her good toe on the instep of her trapped foot and shoved down hard.

She snarled every cussword she knew in several languages—one of the benefits of the private education she hadn't paid much attention to before. She rested a moment. Her twisted foot now had wiggle room. She took another deep breath, put her good foot on her instep again and shoved down hard. She gasped with the pain, but yanked on her trapped foot and pulled it out.

She was free! Barbed wire or not, she laid her head gently on what she was beginning to think of as her bed of nails and gulped for air until she could breathe.

The ankle throbbed. Bound to be swelling, but she gritted her teeth and wiggled it anyway.

She refused to allow her ankle to be broken. She could hobble inside the house and soak it in ice water while she assessed the damage to her scalp. If she could get her hair untangled...

Should she call Barbara? She'd still be having office hours or out on a call. She didn't know another soul closer than two hours away.

Should she call Seth on her cell phone?

No, not just yet. She wanted to make her way back to the house alone, preferably before Seth found her. "I got me into it, I intend to get me out of it," she said aloud. Even talking to herself made her feel a tad less alone. "At that point everyone's welcome to laugh at the idiot. Oh, God, what if I have to stay here all night?" When the snakes and the turtles came out to play, not to mention the beavers and the skunks and the armadillos and...

She yanked on her hair. Big mistake. Just as well she couldn't see what she was about to do. Her hairdresser was going to kill her.

She managed to slide her knife out of her pocket—not easy lying flat on her back wearing tight jeans. She bent her knees and shoved herself up as far as she could. That pulled the hair entwined in the wire taut.

She opened the tiny sewing scissors attached to the knife. Better those than the knife itself. She spent the next ten minutes clipping her trapped hair free as carefully as possible, a few hairs at a time. She had to work strictly by feel.

Finally, after what seemed like years and years, she was free. The scissors were bloody from contact with her scalp. Small price to pay.

Her arms, shoulders and abs hurt from the strain. Using the nearest fence post and only her right foot, she scooched herself up to a standing position.

She was still on the wrong side of the fence.

She put her knife away, ready for her next disaster, and tossed her walking stick across the fence and past the azaleas onto the lawn. She tugged on her gloves again, separated the strands of wire, then slid her good foot through and forced it to take her weight. She bent as close to double as she could manage, climbing through the wire with only a few rips on the back of her shirt, then pulled her bad foot through.

And fell onto the azaleas. She'd never be able to stand on her bad foot without that walking stick as a crutch. It had landed a good eight feet away. She'd have to crawl on hands and knees to reach it.

She'd hardly ever felt this tired in her life, or this dispirited. And so thirsty. She longed for that bottle of water she'd left on the kitchen counter. She couldn't do this. She was done,

done with this place, the animals, Barbara, Seth—mostly Seth.

He'd laugh at her, then he'd yell at her. She felt diminished.

And stupid.

And hurt. She yelled out her frustration.

"Emma?" Seth's voice. She heard two sets of footsteps thudding toward her out of the twilight. He wasn't alone! Bad enough for Seth to see her like this, but a stranger?

The final indignity.

"Emma, where are you?"

He loomed up out of the twilight. Linebacker, superhero, Prince Charming. But she sure wasn't any fairy princess, and he was more like the dragon than the prince.

"Go away. I'm fine."

He stopped in front of her. "Then why are you spread-eagled on the azaleas? Doesn't seem comfortable. What's with your hair?"

"My new look. Witch of Endor."

"Damn, you're bleeding!"

He reached for her, caught her under the arms and lifted her up and across the plants.

"Ow!"

He set her down, but she crashed to the ground again.

He dropped beside her. "You're hurt."

"I twisted my ankle. At least I think that's all

it is." She looked up at the man standing behind Seth, and offered him her muddy hand the way she'd been taught at tea parties when she was ten. "How do you do? I'm Emma French, and you are?"

The man took her hand. Emma watched for any sign of a snicker, but he managed to act perfectly serious. Emma suspected it cost him major control points.

"I'm Earl Matthews, ma'am. I work with Seth."

"Oh, yes, he's told me nice things about you."

Seth made a growling sound, stood and started to sweep her into his arms.

"Don't do that! I'm too heavy!"

"You are not."

"I know how heavy I am. Help me up. Earl, please get me that stick. Seth, please just help me into the house." Ha. Back in control. Now that it was over and he was here, she felt herself tearing up and thought, *No way. I will not cry.* She leaned against him, however, as he supported her into the house and to the sofa.

He knelt in front of her. "Give me your foot."

"I can do it."

"Shut up and give me your foot. This is the kind of thing I do for a living. Folks are always getting bunged up in the woods."

Earl had disappeared, but the refrigerator was making ice cube noises. Good.

She figured Seth might try to cut her boot off and prepared to fight him. They were expensive boots. But he eased it off so gently that she only caught her breath and whimpered once. He did cut her sock off with one of the blades of his big woodsman's knife. After five agonizing minutes in which he manipulated her foot and ankle, he pronounced, "Sprain. Not a bad one."

"I do not want to go to the doctor."

"Fine."

"We'll ice it and wrap it," Earl said. He held a basin filled with ice cubes and one of the clean towels from the counter. "You should be able to walk on it tomorrow."

Seth didn't lift his head to look at her as he said, "Tell me."

She fell back against the sofa, felt a surge of fury. "I did something stupid. Big surprise."

"Earl, mind bringing my first aid kit from the truck?" He turned back to Emma. "We need to rinse the blood out of your hair and assess the damage. Did you hit your head? Were you unconscious even for a second?"

"No. The barbed wire saved me, much as I hate to admit it."

So far he was taking this seriously. But of course he was. He was used to this. Dumb human tricks. Dumb city-girl tricks. If she'd really been hurt, he could get in trouble if someone found out about the skunks and building the cage. She'd done nothing since she got here except screw up his life. He'd done everything for her, and she repaid him by getting hurt in the woods.

What was she thinking? *Selfish and spoiled. Need to get back to where I know who I am and what I'm supposed to be doing.*

CHAPTER ELEVEN

EMMA KNEW HOW to set up for parties. Her mother had begun her lessons when she was hardly old enough to learn which side of the place setting the knife went on and how to fold the towels. She'd polished silver for Christmas dinner when she could barely climb onto the kitchen stool. She was skilled at organizing, so she usually wound up doing it.

She was going to make her first country party as perfect as she could.

She started by hunting through Aunt Martha's attic to see what kind of linens remained without holes or mildew. The Mulligans had been good tenants, thanks to Aunt Martha's lawyer, and had apparently never touched the boxes in the attic. Emma knew which ones they were. She'd helped pack and label them after Aunt Martha died. She'd also spent hours ironing linen napkins and tablecloths before they were put away. Aunt Martha did not approve of anything but plain white linen on her table.

She dragged two heavy plastic boxes down the

attic stairs and opened them on the living room floor after having sprayed around and over them for brown recluse spiders. Although Aunt Martha had been dead for almost five years, the bags the table linens were stored in had kept them clean, not moth-eaten, and without a speck of mold or mildew.

The two folding tables on her back porch would do for serving, so spent several hours scrubbing them so her guests wouldn't die of cholera if they used them.

She found enough matching linen napkins to feed Aunt Martha's entire church circle. Unfortunately, all the bags were of the kind that you stuffed, closed, then vacuumed until you sucked all the air out, leaving a tight rectangle about a quarter the depth of whatever you started with. They worked really well to conserve space, except that every crease and wrinkle was smushed into them as the air was smushed out.

Emma would have to iron creased napkins and tablecloths while spraying them with starch and air freshener to remove even the slightest odor. She didn't have any dowels long enough to roll the cloths on, so she'd have to lay them on the bed in the guest room to keep them from getting wrinkled again.

She'd learned at least half a dozen ways to fold dinner napkins from the waiters she knew. For a picnic, swans seemed appropriate. Easy and kind of country. Not quite ducks, but close.

Next she went back to the attic to hunt for serving dishes. Emma came across another heavy box that contained Aunt Martha's second-best silver-plated flatware. Emma had the antique sterling at her apartment.

She didn't need the silver candlesticks—not for a picnic—but she did need some of the enameled bowls and a couple of platters. Nothing fancy, although one of the bowls was Waterford crystal.

She could use the *famille rose* divided plate for mayonnaise and mustard—two kinds of mustard, since the kids would probably want ballpark and the adults might prefer Dijon. Two kinds of pickles and pickle relish, of course. And sliced onions and tomatoes and lettuce. Add sliced lemon and fresh mint that grew in abundance outside her back door for the iced tea.

All the dishes would need to be scrubbed by hand, but the alternative was plastic bowls. Aunt Martha would whirl in her grave if Emma served a meal in plastic bowls. Earl's wife, Janeen, would probably bring the potato salad in plastic, but that was fine.

She'd have to spring for plastic goblets for the iced tea and soft drinks, and plastic wineglasses. With kids around, it would be crazy to serve drinks in crystal. The yard would wind up full of shards. Not safe.

For the same reason, she decided to invest in really fancy paper plates. It was tacky, but better a little tacky than broken glass and cut fingers. Since she couldn't fit everyone around her dining room table, she'd have to provide quilts for people to sit on under the trees.

Finally, she found a lovely shallow majolica vase that would be perfect for flowers in the center of the serving table. Very country.

She'd pick up a bouquet of spring flowers at the supermarket when she went to get the food Friday.

She sat on the floor in the living room and went over her finds. Getting everything ready before the first guest—well, worker—showed up would be challenging, especially when she had to clean and straighten the house, as well. Good thing she'd agreed to start working for Barbara on Monday and not before.

Although the party was supposed to be outside, people would wander in and out of the house. *She* might call it The Hovel, but she didn't want anyone else to feel free to do so.

She set up the ironing board in the kitchen where she could watch daytime television and iron. After ten minutes of that, she put some Mozart on her CD. Aunt Martha had taught her that Mozart was absolutely the best accompaniment to any sort of household chore. Chalk up another one for Aunt Martha. "I wish you were here," she said with a sniff. "But thanks to you, I can do this at a walk."

She'd always enjoyed getting ready for parties, big or small.

Nathan had given her an internship and then hired her fresh out of college not only for her marketing degree, but because he trusted her to handle any function that required food and drink, from a sit-down breakfast for prospective clients in the boardroom to cocktail parties for three hundred people at The Peabody. He said she could feed 'em as well as schmooze 'em into signing large checks to the agency. Lately she'd helped create whole marketing presentations, ad campaigns, websites, once even a proprietary comic book, but she'd never been allowed to let go of the entertainment end of her job.

She managed to fit in serving on committees for the symphony ball and the ballet ball and the opera garden party every June. She called banquet captains at the big hotels and country clubs by their first names and had the reputation of being able to pull triumphs out of impending disasters. She spoke fluent "caterer" and "florist" and occasionally "limousine."

She could do everything to make a party

a success—except cook for it. Other people, mostly caterers, handled that. She made certain the hors d'oeuvres that were supposed to be hot were hot, and those supposed to be cold were properly chilled. Hot coffee was piping, chilled white wine was cold enough, but never too cold. She expected perfection and usually she got it.

Seth thought she could cook. In fact, she could manage chili, spaghetti Bolognese, salad and a couple of other simple dishes. Period.

She liked dressing up. She enjoyed meeting strangers. She liked snatching success from the jaws of disaster. She loved being a fixer. It was only a small part or her job, but it was fun to spend other people's money on things she would never be able to afford.

She had met Trip at a particularly fancy cocktail buffet over glasses of imported champagne and blinis made with fresh beluga caviar. She'd impressed him by going into the kitchen and calming a hysterical chef who decided his beef tenderloins were overcooked and tried to throw them in the garbage. They weren't, thank heaven. She hadn't the foggiest notion how to rescue them if they were.

Trip asked her out for drinks the following night. And from there… She realized now that he wasn't looking for a wife—a helpmate—as much as he was looking for a hostess who gave him privileges.

After they'd been dating for a while, Trip had suggested she take a course at the local French cooking school before they married. It was important to entertain important clients at *home*. She replied that she had a dozen caterers on speed dial. Who had time to go to cooking school? Anybody ought to be able to read a cookbook, right? Except that for her, the average cookbook seemed to be written in ancient Sumerian.

For this first small country weekend thing, Seth had promised to do the grilling. The ancient charcoal grill on the far corner of her front porch wasn't anything fancy, but according to Seth, it would work just fine. He'd brought over a big bag of briquettes, starter fluid and cooking spray the day before, then spent an hour scouring the grill.

Earl's wife, Janeen, had offered to bring homemade potato salad. Emma ordered the big chocolate cake and bought already "pattied" hamburger patties, hot dogs long enough for their buns, drinks and everything else she'd need.

She figured even *she* was capable of slicing onions and tomatoes and washing lettuce without opening a vein.

The skunks would be carefully locked in their

pantry with food and water. No one who didn't already know would find out she had them.

When she collapsed with an iced tea on her porch steps Friday afternoon as she waited for Seth, bringing the cake, she couldn't click off the big checklist in her mind. It still held too many unchecked squares.

I have run banquets for five hundred people, complete with flaming baked Alaskas. Why on earth am I as terrified as if I were serving the queen of England and all the court? She swallowed a cube of ice, choked and coughed as hard as though she'd inhaled phosgene gas.

Because they're Seth's friends and colleagues, dummy, she thought as she wiped the tears from her eyes and coughed a final time. *I want him to see me as competent. So far I haven't managed competence in any way, shape or form.*

She chose to ignore the great barbed-wire debacle and hoped Seth would do the same. She no longer limped on her twisted ankle, and she'd washed the dried blood out of her hair. Plenty of hair spray kept the little spiky bits lying flat. Occasionally they popped up so she looked like Buckwheat in the old *Our Gang* comedies, but she couldn't help that.

She was worn out from ironing and scrubbing, but she hadn't cut the grass or pruned the azaleas. Too late now.

At the rate she was sending out résumés looking for another job, she'd be working for Barbara as a part-time clerk when she filed for Social Security.

Would that be so bad? It was more fun than being charming to corporate executives who thought she appreciated being hit on by drunken, middle-aged men who considered her a perk of whatever deal Nathan pursued with them.

If Nathan offered her job back, would she take it? If she didn't, she should be locked up in the local home for the seriously deranged. But it no longer sounded as much fun as it once had.

And scrubbing rust off tables was?

She saw Seth's SUV roll into her driveway, and her heart did that thing it did whenever she saw him. It was extremely annoying that she felt her ears turn red and the pulse in her throat begin to thrum so loudly that she worried he could hear it from the road. That sort of reaction was supposed to happen when you had a crush on the paperboy when you were thirteen!

SHE WAS SITTING on the top step of her porch drinking a big glass of iced tea. He hoped she was waiting for *him*. Her chopped hair shone in the afternoon sun like a bucket of doubloons from a Spanish treasure shipwreck. How had he thought when he first met her that she wasn't beautiful? Granted, she'd looked like a drowned, angry bobcat, but he should've been able to see through that. His hormones certainly had.

It would seem that he preferred streaky-haired blondes with eyes as gray as thunderclouds to brunettes with hazel eyes like Clare.

Emma's eyes met his head-on. No sideways, flirty glances. He got those a lot. Must be the uniform.

As he walked across the road to bring her the cake, he wished she'd jump up from the porch stairs and fling herself into his arms. If she did, he wouldn't let her go.

Except it would smash the cake.

Cake or no cake, that wasn't going to happen. She might not admit it even to herself, but she was wounded. He saw the wounds in her psyche from the way she moved toward him one minute and backed away the next.

Okay, he recognized her wounds because he was wounded, too. Nobody plans to get divorced, and nobody comes out of a divorce unscathed.

Either losing her job or dumping her fiancé would've been enough to crush most women, but combining the two gave Emma a big load of history to fight through.

Seth could be as big a jerk as the next man when it came to beautiful, sexy women, but he didn't want to carry the guilt that taking advantage of her vulnerability would entail. He refused to be the *rebound* guy. When and if they came together, he wanted her to come to him with a whole heart.

On the other hand, he was sick of being the *good* guy. He wondered how long he could avoid grabbing her and tossing her on the nearest bed.

Something in the way she looked at him, when she didn't think he could see her, made him believe she'd stay on that bed…

He couldn't take the chance she'd stay there for the wrong reason. To prove she was over Trip.

"Cake delivery," he said, and almost stumbled when she flashed that smile at him. "Velma swears if you put it in the refrigerator overnight, it'll be perfect for the picnic."

She put her glass down and walked over to him, but not to throw herself in his arms. She seemed more concerned with the cake.

"Thank you so much for picking it up on your way home," she said. "It's beautiful. I had no idea the folks at the café could do a cake like that."

"We're not all hicks."

"I didn't mean that. But it's no fancy French bakery either. I wish I could cut into it right now."

"Back off," Seth said, and swung the cake beyond her reach. "Put it in the fridge. Now, come on. I'll take you to dinner and buy you chocolate cake for dessert."

"I'm not dressed."

"You're clean, aren't you? You smell like soap and your hair's still damp. In country terms, you're dressed for a formal dinner."

She took a deep breath, considered for a second that seemed much too long to him, then said, "Okay. Let me check on the babies and get my purse."

CHAPTER TWELVE

HE WISHED HE could offer Emma the sort of fancy dinner she was used to. Instead, they ended up with country fried steak, salad and fresh vegetables at the café. She turned down the chocolate cake on the menu. "It'll go straight to my arteries or my thighs," she told Velma.

"Sorry it's not fancy or French," Seth said. "Pickins are limited."

"Can't get tomatoes that actually taste like tomatoes this early in the city. And I love okra. Don't apologize. Anyway, I forgot to have lunch, so I could eat the rest of the cow this came from. And an entire chocolate cake is waiting for tomorrow. When will people get there?"

"Not too early. Nine or so."

He saw her go instantly on alert. "That early? I'll have to have coffee and orange juice and fresh doughnuts at a minimum…"

He reached across the table and laid his hand on hers. He could feel her trembling. "Whoa! Not one mouthful. You give them doughnuts and coffee, we'll never get any work out of them."

"But I can't just…"

He shook his head. "Yes, you can. We'll be through in time for lunch. This isn't tea at the White House. It's a work party and a picnic. Those boys of Earl's are good kids, but they go into overdrive. You'll probably need to help Janeen keep an eye on them. Make sure they stay out of the back pasture. They're perfectly capable of falling into the lake or bringing what remains of the old barn roof down on their heads."

"How old are they?"

"Earl Jr. is eleven. Carl is eight. They're tough and self-sufficient, but they're still boys."

Seth had parked his SUV a block away from the restaurant. The night was perfect for a stroll down Main Street. Seth longed to take her hand, but figured she'd look at him as if he'd lost his mind. They'd both gone silent, and yet it was the companionable silence of two people who were beginning to know each other and liked what they found.

They were nearly at the car when a voice said, "Seth? Is that you?"

Seth froze. Instinctively he reached for Emma's arm and held her back, as though they were walking into danger. In a sense, they were. A second later, he said, "Come on." He clicked the lock, opened the door for her, then put a hand on the small of her back to move her into the car.

He felt her stiffen.

"What?" she said and turned back.

He knew the man who stood ten feet from them by the only streetlight on their side of the street. "Get in," Seth snarled.

She stared up at him. It had definitely been a snarl. She could picture him using that tone on DUIs or poachers as he shoved them into his squad car. He reached up as though to place a hand on her head the way cops did when they put a suspect into a squad car.

"Seth? Wait a minute." The man walked toward them fast, apparently afraid that Seth would slam the door and drive off.

Seeing Seth's expression—tight mouth, angry eyes —Emma decided he planned to do just that.

She laid her hand on his arm, felt the muscle tighten. He intended to be rude.

Emma didn't do rude, unless she knew why and generally not even then. The guy who'd called Seth seemed like an ordinary middle-aged man. He was almost as tall as Seth, but a lot thinner. His hair was gray and cut short. He didn't have a beard and was freshly shaved. He wore a respectable polo shirt, clean jeans and a dark brown hoodie. He didn't seem homeless or drunk or drugged out, and he didn't smell.

"Maybe you could introduce me to this pretty lady," the man said. His voice sounded scratchy, as though he didn't use it very often and had pickled it in cigarettes or alcohol. The smile he turned on her, however, was pure charm.

Emma noticed he stopped slightly beyond Seth's reach but close to the light from the open door of the car. In that instant, she knew who he was. Seth's father. "How do you do, Mr. Logan," she said, "I'm Emma French." She stuck her hand out to shake his.

Seth startled her by putting his hand on her forearm none too lightly, pulling it out of shaking range and holding it against his side, as if he was afraid of contagion. He didn't speak to the man.

"Nice to meet you, Miss Emma." Another flash of that killer smile. She'd never seen Seth smile like that.

"We have to go," Seth said. "Now." He dropped his hand and turned to walk around the car to the driver's side.

"Nice to meet you, too, Mr. Logan," she said. It *wasn't* nice, but being polite was imprinted in her. She climbed into the car, and Seth's father closed her door. He barely had time to step back before Seth turned on the ignition and laid rubber out of his parking spot, then narrowly avoided sideswiping a pickup that was driving peacefully down the street beside him.

"Hey, tiger, we'll get whiplash," Emma said.

Her attempt at lightening the atmosphere fell completely flat.

"Don't ever do that again," he whispered. Much scarier than if he'd shouted.

"Do what? Act like one polite human being to another?"

"He's not a human being. He forfeited that designation a long time ago."

"You don't mean that. He's still your father, whatever he did."

"He's a killer. Anyone who kills another human being—even worse, his own flesh and blood—is something other than a human being."

"You don't mean he actually *killed* somebody." But she remembered Barbara's rather vague comments about Seth's younger sister...

"He was responsible, whatever he tells himself. I don't want to discuss it."

"You say something like that and you expect me to ignore it?"

"Like I said, I don't want to talk about my father. I didn't know he was back in town. If I had, we'd have driven to Somerville for dinner."

"It's a small town. You can't live your life hiding from him."

"He needs to be the one doing the hiding. Anywhere else but around here."

At that moment his cell phone rang. Emma

jumped. Seth caught his breath and glanced at the display on the dashboard.

"Aren't you going to answer that?" she asked. "Could be poachers were spotted or something."

"I know who it is."

The phone stopped ringing and went to audio. "Seth, I know you're there. Call me right now. I mean it." A woman's voice.

"Well, pull over and call her," Emma said. Girlfriend? Ex-wife? She felt a stab of jealousy she had no business feeling.

The phone began to ring again. This time he picked up. "I know you're there," the voice said again. "Call me right this minute or I'll drive straight out to your house and snatch you bald-headed."

Not a girlfriend, then.

"It's my mother." He pulled over and parked, but left the truck running.

"Let me get out and give you some privacy," Emma said and reached for the door handle.

"No! Don't move. You might as well hear this." He punched the phone hard enough that Emma was afraid the button would snap. Of course, he would have his mother on speed dial. Obviously also synced for hands-free speaker, so he wouldn't have to stop if he got to call out.

"I'm here," he said through clenched teeth.

"I'm sitting by the side of the road, and I am not alone, as you no doubt already know. He must've called the minute we drove off. If you're trying to intercede for him, don't bother."

"Hello, whoever you are with my son," the disembodied voice said. "I hope I haven't spoiled your evening." The woman's voice was low and very Southern, not unlike some of Emma's friends' mothers.

"How do you do, ma'am," Emma said. She didn't protest that Seth's mother hadn't spoiled their evening, because obviously she had a hand in it.

"My son is being a jackass. He doesn't do that often, but makes a doggone good job of it when he does."

"Mother," Seth growled. "Why didn't you warn me he was back? He's not staying with you, is he?"

"Your father—and he *is* your father, however much you wish he wasn't—is staying in a room downtown somewhere. I do not know where. He's got a piddling little job selling hardware out by the expressway. Staying with me? The very idea!"

"Yeah, right."

"Now you just hush up and listen. He's sober,

Seth. Has been for over three years. He showed me his two-year Alcoholics Anonymous pin."

"Which he probably stole."

Heavy sigh down the line. "Now, you stop that. I've been tellin' you for years to let go of all that anger. It's hurtin' you a darned sight more than it's hurtin' him. He's trying to get his life straightened out."

"So you'll take him back?"

"Certainly not! But I don't hate him. He gave me you and Sarah…"

"Then he took her away."

"You don't have to take him out to dinner, but you could at least speak to him in the street," she said.

"You might let him get away scot-free with killing Sarah, but I can't. So far as I'm concerned, he gets a life sentence, no parole. Let Saint Peter decide after he dies whether he goes up or down. At that point, it's out of my hands." He clicked off the phone.

"You just hung up on your *mother*!" Emma squealed. "Call her back and apologize."

Seth started the truck and pulled into traffic. "I'll call her later."

"This is none of my business," Emma said. "I'm sorry if I made things worse with your father."

"Not your fault. You had no way of knowing

who he was when he waylaid us." He growled like a wounded grizzly bear. "I already told you I don't want to talk about it."

She was out of his truck and on her front porch before he could open the truck door for her. "Thank you for a lovely evening," she said in her coolest voice. "At least the first part." He stood at the foot of the porch stairs. His body language showed he was still angry. His voice said he was disappointed, as well.

"You're still coming tomorrow morning, aren't you? And doing the grilling?"

"Of course. Emma, I'm sorry you heard all that."

"Don't be. Don't people say that every family is more or less dysfunctional? We all drive each other nuts." She came back down the stairs, held out her arms and hugged him. It took him a second to react, then he nearly crushed her ribs.

She stepped away from him and was across the porch and into her house before he was in position for a good-night kiss. Which obviously she didn't want. He couldn't blame her. Maybe he *had* acted like a jackass, but that was simply the way it was, the way *he* was. The situation wasn't about to change until his father left town again. As he would. On his own. If he took too long, Seth would do it for him.

He walked back across the road. Emma was

right—he'd have to call his mother and apologize. She'd want to know all about Emma.

Yeah, he'd like to know all about Emma, too. Right now he wasn't sure where he stood with her or where he wanted to stand. All he knew was that he ached to hold her, make love to her—and the hell with everything else.

CHAPTER THIRTEEN

EMMA WAS UP at the crack of dawn to see to the skunks, but also to set up for the picnic. Maybe tablecloths and linen napkins was going a little overboard for hamburgers and hot dogs, but she wanted to show the people who were kind enough to help build her kennel that they were important to her.

She wasn't unused to getting up early. When a meeting started at nine in the morning, she always had the setup checked by eight. That meant leaving home at seven. The town house on Mud Island was no more than two miles from the office, but she still drove her SUV from one parking spot to another. If she left it at home, guaranteed she'd have to make a quick trip to see a client in Forrest City or the suburbs of Memphis. Today, however, she wouldn't be moving it from the side yard—the other side from where they were finishing the kennel. She was as jumpy as if she was doing a presentation for the CEOs of a dozen Fortune 500 companies.

At ten o'clock a giant silver crew cab pickup

pulled into the yard and parked. Before it had stopped moving, all four doors opened, and a pair of half-grown boys tumbled out of the back-seat while an attractive woman climbed out of the passenger side. She was carrying a big covered plastic bowl.

Earl came from the driver's side. "Hey, Emma, how's your foot?"

She'd prayed he wouldn't mention her catapult into the azaleas. At least he didn't go into big explanations for his wife.

"Fine, Earl. You do know how to wrap a sprain. Hey, you must be Janeen."

She'd been interested to see the woman Earl had married. No sense in putting out her hand. Janeen was using both to hold the potato salad above the boys' heads.

"Momma! This is the perfect tree!"

Emma turned as the smaller of the two boys grabbed his brother's shoulders and began to climb up him as though he were a ladder.

"Boys! Get down here this instant and come meet Miss Emma," Janeen said.

"Now!" Earl's voice got a reaction that Janeen's hadn't. The larger boy shrugged his brother off his back. He rolled on the ground and howled.

"Get over here!"

Grudgingly, the older boy—Earl Jr.?—reached

down and pulled his brother to his feet. "Aw, hush, Carl, you're not hurt."

Both boys raced over and jammed on their brakes one stride from their mother, who still held the potato salad over their heads. Emma almost reached for it, then dropped her hands. Grappling for possession would probably cause the whole thing to wind up on the ground.

"Hey, Miss Emma, I'm Earl Jr.," the taller boy said. "This here's Carl, squalling like a stuck hog. Shut up, Carl."

Amazingly, he did. In an instant his particular weather had morphed from storms to sunshine. Standing shoulder to shoulder, the boys each gave Emma a smile that was as glorious as her brother, Patrick's. They had wheat-blond hair like their father's, and blue eyes that came from both parents, although Janeen's hair was a suspicious strawberry blond, cut short and falling in waves around her heart-shaped face. The boys probably looked angelic asleep at night. The rest of the time—Emma remembered the cartoon character that moved so fast it was a blur.

"That's the right tree, isn't it, Daddy? Come on, let's put the rope up."

"Earl Jr., Miss Emma hasn't heard about the plan yet. She may not want you climbing her tree."

"But it's the right one, Dad! I can do it. I don't need Carl."

"Janeen, come on in the house, and let's get that potato salad in the refrigerator." Emma led the way while the discussion about the rightness or wrongness of the tree went on in the background. Why the argument, she had no idea.

"This is charming!" Janeen said as she walked into the great room, which gave a whole new meaning to shabby chic. "Just right for one person."

"It *will* be charming if I stay here long enough, which I probably won't. In any case I have to get it ready to rent when I leave. This is just a stop-gap between jobs. Here, let me have that bowl. It'll fit in the refrigerator, but I may need to do some rearranging." She moved around a couple of platters, slid in the bowl and closed the fridge door. "What's all this about my tree? They're not considering cutting it down, are they, because…"

Janeen laughed and sat on one of the stools at the counter. "Lord, no. It's supposed to be a surprise for you, but actually, it's more to keep the boys occupied and out of the way until the kennel's finished. As you can see, they tend to get above their raisin' when they're out in public. Entirely too much energy. That comes from Earl's side of the family."

"So the tree?"

"Earl and the boys brought all the stuff to put a bag swing on that tree. Only takes one rope, and a big burlap bag stuffed tight. You hang the rope…"

"Oh, I know! I had a bag swing on that very tree when I spent my summers here! I loved it. I wanted a swing made from an old tire, but Aunt Martha said I'd get filthy every time I swung on it, so we ended up using the bag instead."

"Well, I'm sure they'll have it up and swinging before everybody else gets here to work."

Emma started for the front door, but Janeen laid a hand on her arm. "I suggest we hide in here until the preliminaries are complete. I've heard that going to a rock concert can ruin your hearing, but probably not as much as Earl and my boys hashing out how to do *anything*. Besides, we wanted to give those two something that was far enough from the kennel that they wouldn't try to use the chain saw."

"Even *I* wouldn't use the chain saw," Emma said.

"You're not a boy," Janeen said. "Earl Jr. will try anything, and what he tries, Carl demands to try, as well. We've told them they are *not* to pick up a tool, power or otherwise, and to stay out from under everyone's feet. That doesn't mean they'll do it." She cocked her head. "It's too quiet. Come on."

They were just in time to see Earl Jr. shimmy up the trunk of the old water oak farthest from the kennel and slide out on the big branch that stretched straight and strong ten feet above the ground.

"That high?" Emma whispered while visions of her homeowner's liability insurance danced in her head. "Earl? Do they have to go so far up?"

"Hey, Emma. Don't you worry. We won't hang the bag more than four feet above the ground."

He tossed the end of a heavy rope up into the tree.

A skinny arm snaked out between the leaves and grabbed it. "Yes, sir, I got it. Want me to tie a bowline?"

"Now, what else would I want! Take a good bite around that limb."

"He's a Scout. He knows every knot in the seaman's instruction book," Janeen whispered.

Janeen seemed both calm and proud that her eleven-year-old son was ten feet in the air tying a bowline around a limb.

"That's good, son, now send the rabbit down the hole," Earl said. "Take your time. Make sure it's secure. Good. Come on down now."

Instead of repeating his shimmying, Earl Jr. flipped his feet loose and hung full-length. Emma gasped.

Earl Sr. grabbed his son around the legs and lowered him to the ground.

"Can I go up, Daddy? I can do it!" Carl danced around his father.

"Not today, son."

"Aw, how come Earl gets to do *everything*? I never get to do anything fun." He stomped away with his hands in the pockets of his shorts.

"Hey, shrimp, you can test the swing first," Earl said. "Break *your* neck instead of mine."

At that moment Barbara Carew's truck rolled in. She climbed out holding a giant cooler of iced tea floating with lemons and clinking with ice. "This is glass, I'm afraid. I'll go put it on the kitchen counter before we break it."

Within the next thirty minutes, four more of Seth's colleagues arrived—all big men, tanned and fit. Earl introduced Emma, and enlisted two of them to help hang the bag and test it.

"Shoot, if it'll take their weight, it'll sure as shooting hold a normal-size adult," Earl said.

Immediately everyone began to take turns swinging. Everyone except Emma. She smiled and applauded, but stayed on the porch. She didn't tell them that the last time she'd swung from this very limb in the final summer she'd spent here at Aunt Martha's, she'd lost her grip and fallen off.

She had that same old feeling of falling and not being able to save herself. This time she intended to avoid being the party klutz.

Thirty minutes later, Earl stopped waiting for Seth's SUV and organized the crews to stretch the wire and tack it up inside the kennel.

Where was Seth? He'd sworn he was coming. Surely he wouldn't stay away because they'd argued over his father?

On one hand, she wanted to ask Earl to call him. On the other, if he *had* decided not to show up, she had no intention of trying to trace him. That was one of Andrea's lessons that had taken root. *You do not call boys. You wait for them to call you.*

All right, that was old-fashioned. But there was something about being here, where she was the outsider, the newcomer. These people must all know that Seth was supposed to be heading up the crew. He'd asked them to come.

So where was he?

Stretching the wire went faster than anyone believed it would with all the adults working on it. They'd all be ready for Seth to cook the hamburgers and hot dogs before he showed up—if he showed up. Earl was already putting the final screws into the upright to hang the screen door. Then, all that needed doing was to fill the kiddie pool and put a couple of branches inside for the skunks to practice foraging for insects.

Fine. She'd dealt with catering disasters before. Even she could grill hamburgers. The rest of the food simply needed to be set out, so everyone could fix his or her own. She had to heat the grill. That would take some time.

Seth had already put the charcoal briquettes in the bed of the grill. The can of fire starter was sitting on the ground right beside it.

She could ask Earl to do it.

No, she couldn't. This was her party. Earl had done enough. Once he finished hanging the door to the kennel and helped straighten up, he could go play with his sons.

Barbara and Janeen seemed comfortable in the porch swing. She wouldn't bother them either.

As she turned toward the grill, which sat in the shade under the pin oak on the left side of the house, Earl tapped her on the shoulder. Behind him she could see Earl Jr. and Carl happily taking turns on the bag swing. They'd progressed from merely swinging to climbing onto a lower branch, standing on the bag, then swinging off in a broad arc. With accompanying yells and intermittent squabbles.

"I've called Seth," Earl whispered. "Just goes to voice mail." He shook his head. "He said he had to run into the office first thing, but then he was planning to come right on out."

Forcing her voice to sound cool, she said, "He probably had an emergency. We'll go ahead without him. I'm starting to heat the grill now."

Oh, heavens—charcoal and liquid fire starter and the igniter. Three of Emma's least favorite things. She never had to light the outdoor grill at home. Either her father or Patrick handled that chore. Theirs was state-of-the-art with a fancy built-in fire starter. This one looked as though Noah might have used it after the flood.

In any case, today it was her job.

At least Earl and the others thought it was. They were paying no attention to her. Seth had moved the old grill into the front yard in the shade.

Before her first horse show, her father had told her, "Ride like you know what you're doing." Andrea's corollary to that was, "If you're wrong, be wrong at the top of your voice." She agreed with both.

She picked up the gas fire lighter from the serving table, and the can of fire starter stuff she was supposed to spray to get the charcoal burning. She upended the can and sprayed the charcoal in a neat grid from side to side and front to back. Daddy always used a lot.

She checked around her. Everyone was otherwise occupied. So far, so good.

Holding the igniting device at arm's length, she flicked it on and touched it to the charcoal.

The whoosh of flame erupted two feet above her head.

Just as Seth's truck turned into his driveway.

She fell back on her bottom. Everyone came running. She'd set the tree afire and probably the entire forest.

Seth ran over, grabbed the hinged grill cover and slammed it shut. Then he took the can of liquid fire starter, closed it and tossed it to Earl, who was ten feet away. He slid his hands under Emma's shoulders and stood her up. Again. Just like the azaleas.

Over his shoulder, she was surprised to see that the fire under its cover was almost totally out. The immature leaves on the tree had flared and gone out, too. Fires needed air. Seth had shut the air supply off. Bingo, no flame.

"What were you thinking?" he snapped.

"That you weren't here when you said you'd be, and now I'm going to burn down the house."

"No, you aren't," Earl said quite calmly. "You have to let this kind of fire starter soak in for five or ten minutes before you light it." He patted her shoulder. "Otherwise you set the fumes on fire and don't light the charcoal."

"Great. Now you tell me." She shook off Seth's hand and ran for the house. She dived into the bathroom, slammed the door behind her and sank down on the toilet seat, trying to get her breathing under control.

She looked up when someone knocked on the

door. "Emma? Emma, it's Janeen. You okay in there?"

"No, I am not okay."

"Are you burned?"

"Not even warm." She felt her face. "Eyebrows all there. Eyelashes all there. Face still there."

"Open the door."

"Why? So everybody can laugh when I take my curtain call?"

"Nobody's going to laugh."

"Why not? I would. I'm probably the only person out there, including Earl Jr. and Carl, who doesn't know to let the fire starter set before you try to light it."

"Come on, Emma. Do I have to get Seth to pop the lock?"

"Lord, no!" She glanced at the lock. One of those childproof things that could be opened from the outside with a hairpin. She couldn't even hide properly. "Are you alone out there?"

"Yep."

"Okay, but if everybody's clustered around the door…"

When she opened the door, she found Janeen sitting on the floor of the hall holding out a diet soda.

"Here. Adrenaline makes you thirsty."

Emma sat across from her and drained the soda. "Now that Seth's finally here, he can cook the burgers. I intend to be halfway to Memphis before that grill heats up again."

"No, you won't. You have to serve and check out the kennel and move the skunks and clean up afterward. I'll help, but it's your house."

"Janeen, does the word *humiliation* mean anything to you?"

"Nothing bad actually happened. You've set up a beautiful party…"

"I should've booked Nero and his fiddle for the entertainment."

Janeen snickered.

"I can't do this," Emma continued and fought to keep the tears out of her voice. "No matter what I try to do to fit in, I blow it. I don't belong here. I belong where I can order takeout and use valet parking."

"The boys loved today. They'll talk about it for weeks."

"Janeen, you're not taking this seriously."

"Because it's not serious. If anything, Seth is the one who should be embarrassed. I'm used to guys not showing up on time. You're not. Come on. I'm starving, and those look like Angus burgers in the fridge." Janeen unfolded herself and reached her hand down to Emma. "Seth can probably relight the fire by now and start cooking in twenty minutes. Just enough time to set everything out."

"I can't."

"Sure you can. I promise you nobody will even mention it. Let's go."

Hand in hand, the two women walked into the living room. Earl sat in the club chair. Seth stood by the fireplace as though poised to flee.

"Emma, I thought you'd wait until I got here to start cooking," he said.

"I do not wait on people who break their promises," she said. "So where the hell were you that you couldn't call to say you'd be late?"

"I was chasing a four-hundred-pound Duroc sow and seven piglets down the middle of Highway 14 before somebody hit her and killed her—and themselves." He shrugged. "I didn't think it would take nearly as long as it did to get her corralled. She's done this before. She gets smarter every time. I planned to call you the minute we had them back in their pen. Before that, I had my phone on vibrate, so I wouldn't spook her any worse than she already was if it rang."

"Earl?" Janeen said. "Is he telling the truth?"

"Uh-huh."

"Took Marquette sheriff's deputies and the highway patrol before we finally got her and the piglets back in their pen."

"How long before she gets out again?" Earl asked.

"This time I gave Jim a citation for dangerous livestock on the road and told him to fix his damned fence this afternoon, or I'd be having barbecued ribs for lunch tomorrow."

"Why you?" Emma asked. "Weren't you off duty?"

"I got the call while I was in the office, so I went. She's a humongous pig. They grow until they die, and she's had half a dozen litters. Hitting her in a car would've been like hitting an office building. I couldn't take the chance, either on that or squashing one of the piglets. Emma, I'm sorry. I should have stopped and called, but I didn't want to lose sight of the piglets in somebody's field. They'd have disappeared in a heartbeat."

"Yeah, you should've stopped and called," Janeen said. "You both know better. Now, if they've finished putting the dawn-till-dark lights around the kennel after Mrs. O'Leary, here, tried to burn Chicago down, would you please go grill some hamburgers and hot dogs?"

CHAPTER FOURTEEN

EMMA HAD TO admit nobody so much as mentioned the fire at lunch. Not even Earl Jr. and Carl. Earl must've warned his sons to keep their mouths shut. Their eyes were wide, and they circled Emma as if to be certain she wasn't a cinder, but they waited quietly—well, quietly for them—for their hot dogs, then went over by the tree with the swing, hunkered down in the shade and ate. And ate.

Emma was glad she'd bought as much food as she had. After they washed the dirt off from building the kennel, the crew consumed massive amounts of hot dogs, hamburgers and iced tea while they congratulated themselves on the brilliance of their construction.

Emma sat on the porch steps with Barbara, and left the porch swing to Janeen.

Even the boys were winding down. The mid-May temperature was in the eighties, and everyone was ready for a nap. Emma certainly was.

She wasn't used to parties dividing themselves by sex. Maybe it was a country thing. The men were talking baseball, while the women automatically removed the remains of lunch, filled the tiny dishwasher for the first load and rinsed and stacked everything else for the next. They didn't ask whether they could help clean up; they simply organized themselves and did it.

They worked smoothly together as women almost always did when they handled logistics. They were trying to include her, but Emma felt she was on the edge of the group, not quite part of them. They moved around each other casually, never getting in one another's way, even in the tiny kitchen, while Emma found herself relegated to refolding the tablecloths and loading the dirty napkins in the washing machine.

"Momma!" came a boy's voice. "Momma, come see what we found."

Emma froze. What now? A six-foot rattlesnake?

Carl grabbed his mother's hand, dragged her through the living room, onto the front porch, down the steps and around the far side of the house. The other women followed.

Around the corner of the house, the men and the two boys clustered around something large on the ground.

"Lookee what we found!" Earl Jr. said.

"I found him, not you," Carl protested. "Can we keep him?"

"He's a big one, all right," Earl said. "And no, we can't keep him. Watch your fingers. He's fast when he wants to be."

Looking like an irate grandfather awakened from his afternoon nap, a snapping turtle the size of Earl's hubcap glared at the crowd around him.

"Aw, Daddy, we could keep him in our pond."

"We *both* found him," Earl Jr. said. He pulled a large poke sallet leaf and held it out to the turtle. Instantly, he withdrew his head into his shell, but a moment later he reached out, took the leaf delicately and began to munch with what probably passed for turtle gastronomic ecstasy.

"I said, watch your fingers," Earl told the boys.

"I forgot I said we might have time to move some turtles from Emma's pond this afternoon." Seth looked around. "But at this point, I don't think anyone's up for turtle trapping, are we? Anybody?"

Groans from everyone except the two boys.

"What do we do with him?" Emma asked. She stayed well back. She had no idea how fast he could move, but she wasn't about to find out. With her luck lately, he'd bite off her big toe.

"He's beautiful," Janeen said. "He seems friendly."

"He's a turtle. He is not friendly. He's after frogs," Barbara said. "Wandered away from the pond."

"Why *don't* you take him?" Emma suggested to Earl. "I certainly don't need him. I think I have enough at the pond to be able to spare one."

"Daddy, he wouldn't be any trouble. See, he likes the leaf. I'll feed him," Earl Jr. said. "We haven't had a turtle in the pond in years and years."

Earl gave his wife a "well?" look.

"Oh, why not," she said. "He is pretty, and he'll keep down the snails in the hosta. If you boys can get him braced in the truck bed so he won't slide around on the way home, then if Emma doesn't mind, we'll take him."

Emma did not mind. She was delighted. He was smaller than the behemoth she'd spotted on the way back from her trip to the pond, but apparently much more adventurous. She didn't want to step on him inadvertently and either get bitten or slide off his curved shell and break her ankle for real this time.

Everything she encountered seemed to be colluding to break some part of her. And she was helping.

Once the turtle was safely buttressed in the bed of Earl's truck, the party had reached its natural end. She thanked everyone for coming and for her wonderful kennel, then stood on the porch and waved as they drove off into the twilight. She was now plus one bag swing, plus one

kennel and minus one turtle. Not a bad score for
the afternoon.

She glanced across the street. Apparently, she
was also minus one Seth. He must have gone
home while she said her goodbyes to everyone
else. Obviously he didn't want to be alone with
her. The heck with him, then.

She'd hoped he'd help her move the babies to
their new home, but she could manage three little
baby skunks on her own. She wanted to watch
them explore their new digs. She'd wait until
tomorrow to clean up their old ones and return
Seth's playpen, scrubbed and clean. The night
was going to be perfect with a nearly full moon
and no hint of rain. A good time to introduce
them to night sounds and night foraging. Now
that the lights were set up to cover the kennel
after dark, she'd be able to check on them from
outside it.

But before that, she wanted to enjoy the perfect evening. She always felt the best time in any
party came after everyone except the most inti-
mate friends had left, fed and happy. This party
would definitely give rise to interesting conver-
sations in the cars and trucks on their way home.
They were probably already telling stories about
the crazy lady and the grill. At least they'd remember who she was.

Janeen was right to tell her to lighten up. If

Emma had gone overboard with the arrangements and tried to set the trees on fire, it wouldn't be the first time she'd had to deal with disaster. There were worse things than trying too hard. And since—as Janeen had said—nothing bad had actually happened, there were worse things than making a fool of herself.

She walked over to the bag swing and gave it a tentative push. Earl hadn't hung it that far from the ground, so it wasn't that perilous. Why not? Did she even remember how to climb aboard? She held on to the rope with both hands, straddled the bag, hopped up and wrapped her legs around it.

It was beautifully balanced. Too well balanced, actually. It seemed to have a mind of its own. She remembered everything about swinging on a bag swing except how to stop it and get off. She wrapped her legs tighter and clung to the rope above her head with both hands. Everyone who'd enjoyed swinging this afternoon had a partner to start the swing and stop it so the person swinging could slide off and stand up safely.

Without a partner controlling the action, however, it continued to swing. If anything, it moved faster with the motion of her body.

She was supposed to shove back at the moment it started on its downward swing and land on her feet. She'd done it a million times when she was twelve. She just didn't seem able to pick the right moment.

But then…there didn't seem to be one. She was going to wind up on her rump in the grass and add another bruise to the ones she'd already collected.

Here she'd gotten herself in another fine mess. Why did she never learn? At least nobody else was around to watch.

She squeaked when she felt strong arms encircle her waist and lift her free. She let go of the rope and leaned back against Seth. She knew it was Seth. He smelled like Seth and breathed like Seth and felt like Seth. Safe and warm and…maybe not safe.

"Need a little help dismounting?" he whispered.

"Where were you hiding?" She didn't move, but simply relished the feel of him against her back. "I thought you'd gone home."

"I was in your house getting some iced tea."

She began to tell him she didn't need his help. She would eventually have figured out how to get off without falling. Well…probably not. Besides, this was much more pleasant. "Thanks," she murmured.

"I'm sorry. I should've called this morning," he said, his arms still wrapped around her. He set her down and turned her to face him. He ran a finger down her cheek, looked at it in the dying light and shook his head. There was a distinct smear of dirt on the tip from in front of her ear, where she hadn't quite scrubbed herself clean.

"I..."

He took her face in his hands and very gently kissed her.

A jerk he might be—and that was debatable at this point—but a good kisser he definitely was. No other man she'd kissed elevated her pulse and her body temperature in an instant the way he did.

"I swear, woman," he said, "you need a bodyguard."

"You're hired," she whispered.

CHAPTER FIFTEEN

"DO WE HAVE to leave the babies outside all night their first time in their kennel?" Emma asked Seth. She was back in her usual place on the pantry floor with all three babies crawling over her lap. Seth sat backward on one of the chairs he'd brought in from the dining table.

"I promise you they won't escape," he answered. "They have their little wading pool for water..."

"They may drown if they fall in and can't get out."

"We'll watch them until we're sure they can."

"And they're used to having their meals delivered to them."

"Earl picked up a jar of night crawlers at the marina yesterday. The skunks should enjoy catching them and eating them. It's what they have to do in the wild. You won't be there to offer them dog food on a silver spoon."

"I know, and it's killing me. If this is what it's like to raise children, I'm not having any."

"Human babies are a lot more trouble and

take longer to raise," Seth said. "You get used to them."

"You have an answer for everything."

"Babies are wildlife. I'm supposed to know about stuff like that."

She smacked his knee. "Like you know so much. At least I helped raise my half siblings." She caught her breath. "Oh, I'm sorry. I didn't mean…"

"Emma, you can't tiptoe around Sarah's death. It happened. I was thirteen. I've had years to get used to not having her around."

"Do you ever forget her?"

"Do you ever forget your mother?" He stood. "Come on. Time to bite the bullet and see what happens."

He took the three babies from her and held them against his chest in the palm of one big hand. She scrambled to her feet and took Rose and Peony back. Sycamore had always seemed to prefer Seth—guys would be guys, even among skunks.

In the kennel, Emma set her two down on the rotten log Seth had found in the woods to give them something to explore for bugs. He put Sycamore down beside them.

Emma assumed they'd be hesitant in their new habitat. Rose, however, stuck her nose in the log, scrabbled with her claws and came up almost instantly with one end of a night crawler dangling from her jaws. She grabbed it between her front paws and began to stuff it in her mouth two-handed.

Peony made a swipe for the wriggly end, but in usual Peony fashion missed completely and fell off the log.

Sycamore turned his back, jumped off the log and went exploring.

It broke Emma's heart to watch Peony claw at Rose's log in hopes of finding at least a grub or a beetle, but when she reached for the night crawler jar to give Peony a little help, Seth shook his head at her.

"She'll catch on," he said. "She always does. Just takes her longer."

"But…"

"Don't help."

She subsided on the lawn that that made up the floor of the kennel. Rose climbed into her lap and, replete with night crawler, went to sleep.

Sycamore hove into view munching on a large caterpillar. Peony went for it and accidentally stepped on a beetle. She ate it in one gulp.

"Yes! I knew she could do it!" Emma said.

"Told you. Here, put her down and let's watch from outside."

The two of them leaned against the outside of the wire and watched the three grow less hesitant, more adventurous, until they'd all tried the kiddie pool that was filled with only a couple of inches of water. Even Peony managed to scramble out, march over to the log and climb up with four wet paws.

"Okay, we're going to leave them out here tonight," Seth said as he stood.

"Who died and made you general?"

"I'm the one with the badge. Come on. We can sit on the front porch and check them periodically."

"Then what?" Uh-oh. Wrong question. At least if Seth spent the night, he could keep checking on the babies. Unless he was otherwise occupied, which, if he stayed, he almost certainly would be.

Was she ready for that? They had chemistry together, but they barely knew each other, and they always seemed to butt heads. He seemed to consider himself her rescuer, because she kept needing to be rescued. Not the image she wanted to portray. Grown women who had responsible jobs—or used to have them, anyway—should be rescuers, not need to be rescued.

It would be simple to throw caution to the winds and jump into bed with Seth. He wouldn't hesitate, but then very few men would, given the invitation.

Couldn't do it. Not this soon after the train wreck with Trip.

Too many of her friends, both married and single, seemed to consider sex of no more importance than a kind of adult version of spin the bottle. Emma had never found sex anything to be casual about. She was too socially uptight to have participated in the hookup stage most of her friends went through. Trip was one of her few partners, and only after they became exclusive. Well, she'd thought they were exclusive. Trip obviously hadn't.

Sex with Trip had been pleasant, but not mind-blowing. What on earth had convinced her that everything would miraculously be paradise on their wedding night? Didn't most married couples have to learn over time the best ways to please each other? Another instance in which Emma had tried to organize the situational dynamic the way it ought to be and missed by a country mile. Or in this case a city mile.

Now she knew why. Her instincts had sensed that something in the relationship was off, even if her rational mind had not.

Unfortunately, the opposite was true with Seth. Every time he touched her—shoot, every time he *looked* at her—her body reacted in completely inappropriate ways. Nothing rational about how she felt.

Tonight should definitely not be the night. For one thing, she was so tired and so bruised that she was likely to fall sound asleep when she should be most awake. Talk about an ego downer for any male. If—and it was still *if*—she and Seth wound up in bed together, she wanted everything to be perfect.

Uh-oh! Lately the more perfect she tried to make things, the more chaotic they became. If her recent track record held, they'd end up making love on top of a beaver dam seeded with five sticks of TNT with the fuses lit.

If it was going to happen, it would. She made a vow that she wouldn't try to orchestrate the perfect tryst. She'd aim for solid friendship first, then see what developed.

She sank onto the porch swing beside him, pulled her feet under her and snuggled into Seth's shoulder. "Thank you for all you've done," she said.

He leaned his cheek against the top of her head. "Like nearly getting you incinerated?"

"My fault. I am so used to being responsible for everything's going smoothly, that when it doesn't, I jump in. I'm a natural fixer, except sometimes I make things worse. I should've told you I have a very, very limited repertoire in the cooking department."

"The spaghetti the other night was great."

"That's one. I also make a mean chef salad and halfway decent chili, but that's about my limit, except for breakfast stuff." She yawned hugely. "Sorry. It's been a very long day."

"Why don't you go to bed?" he asked. "I'll check on the skunks. I promise they'll survive the night without you."

She yawned again. "I need to unload the dishwasher, reload it and run a bunch of napkins through the washing machine."

"That can all wait until tomorrow. What if I pick you up about eleven? We can drive to the country store in Somerville for their Sunday brunch. It's quite a spread."

"You don't have to…"

"How about if I want to? To make up for letting you down today." He held up his hand. "Don't argue. Go brush your teeth and go to bed."

As pleasant as it was to cuddle against his warm body, bed without company sounded like a truly great idea. She half stumbled into the house. She'd never felt sufficiently comfortable in any male-female situation to let down her guard so totally, but somehow she trusted Seth, as she'd never trusted Trip.

"I'll lock the doors when I leave," he said to her retreating back.

She waved good-night and disappeared into her bedroom. In the last twenty minutes, every bit of energy in her body seemed to have drained out her toenails. Some kind of psychological avoidance of dealing with Seth as a man? Or her feelings for him?

If so, it had apparently worked. She brushed her teeth but didn't bother to take off her makeup. She sank onto the coverlet, pulled the quilt over herself without even taking off her clothes. Her last conscious thought was *Am I crazy or what?*

SHE WOKE AT two in the morning when her stomach reminded her that she hadn't eaten since her hamburger at lunch. She considered hunting up a couple of cold hot dogs from the leftovers in the refrigerator and going outside to check on the babies. Give them a little snack. They loved hot dogs. And she could always have some of Janeen's potato salad…

Then she remembered the giant turtle that had been roaming the yard. Earl and his family had taken that one, but the one she'd spotted back by the pond was three times larger. Better to trust that Seth had checked on the babies. She didn't think turtles ate baby skunks, but in any case, Seth swore the kennel was impregnable from any creature that might.

She got out of bed and, barefoot, tiptoed to her bedroom door. The floor was cold.

She saw that the lamp was still lit in the living room.

She hadn't left a blanket out, had she? Then

she saw one large, naked foot sticking out at the end of the couch. Seth hadn't gone home. He'd sacked out on her couch.

She retreated silently and climbed back into her own bed.

She'd put up with her hunger pangs to avoid waking him. He'd stayed over to check on the babies during the night, rather than going back and forth from his house to hers. What a sweet guy he was.

At least when it came to animals. Human beings, not so much.

Good thing was, he didn't snore.

When she stuck her head in the living room in the morning, the blanket was neatly folded over the back of the couch. She found a note on the kitchen island. "Pick you up at 10:45 to beat the crowd. Casual."

She'd nearly forgotten what it felt like to put on a dress. She planned to keep it that way for as long as possible. She cut slices of apple and rounds of hot dog for the skunks' breakfasts, and found all three waiting beside the kennel door with their front paws on the wire. "Breakfast is late, so sue me," she said. They were basically omnivores, and had fallen in love with apples the first time she'd offered them. They had progressed as far as the hot dogs from their dog food gruel faster than she'd dared hope. She tossed the fruit around the enclosure to make them hunt, but she didn't see a single insect or worm, from night crawler to lightning bug. If nothing else, they were thorough.

They were so close to being ready to go home to the woods. The only step left in their development was their ability to spray real scent. Not a step Emma was looking forward to. At this point they poofed when they were annoyed, but with no more than the faintest of odors. Still, they couldn't be released until they could protect themselves from predators like coyotes and bobcats. Their spray was their only defense.

She'd have to ask Barbara how to make that transition as painless as possible for the human beings. She'd always heard that the way to get the scent off was to scrub with tomato juice, but there must be something newer and more effective than gallons of tomato juice. There must be a test that didn't actually involve annoying three skunks enough to spray.

From outside their enclosure she watched them munch and stomp. The human momma had to cut her ties—not to mention her heartstrings.

She left them to clean up the few remaining bits of fruit and hot dog. She could scrub and depoop the kennel after lunch.

When she heard Seth's SUV, she'd already finished straightening the house and putting away everything she'd used for the party. She had taken Seth's advice about dressing casually, but she wore her best designer jeans and an elegant spring sweater in a soft peach that complemented her hair and gave her skin a glow. Since the morning was surprisingly chilly for May, she tossed a light jacket over her shoulders. The peach sweater reflected against her skin enough to impart a healthy tone it didn't deserve after the last few days.

"You can't have been comfortable sleeping on the couch last night," Emma said as she buckled her seat belt.

"Not bad, although I'm taller than the couch is long. A couple of places got prodded by loose springs, but it was more comfortable than traipsing across the road at two in the morning to check on the skunks."

Would've been a boost for his ego if she'd asked him to join her, he thought. She'd managed to shoehorn a king-size bed into that little bedroom.

But if she'd invited her to join him just to sleep, he would not have been trustworthy. He also wouldn't have gotten any sleep.

She glowed as though she hadn't missed a moment's rest. Her sweater wasn't tight, but it did fit what Earl would call a rack. With the exception of his mother, Seth didn't know any other woman—no matter her age—who wore elegance as casually as Emma did.

She was so far out of his league they weren't even in the same country.

She chattered on about the skunks and the party, while he wondered if she was still talking to Trip or her former boss. She hadn't mentioned setting up job interviews. The part-time gig with Barbara was only a stopgap. She obviously wasn't concentrating on finding a career-track job in the Williamston area. She still planned to leave, and soon.

"Here we are," he said as he pulled the SUV into the parking lot in front of the restaurant. "Prepare for your cultural experience of the day."

"What a wonderful building," Emma said as she climbed out onto the gravel parking lot. There were already half a dozen pickup trucks and SUVs, so they weren't too early.

"I'm starving," Emma said. "No dinner last night and no breakfast this morning."

"These folks will fill you up."

"This place is obviously old. What's its history? How did it become a restaurant?"

"It was built as a general store and to supply the railroad back in 1850 or so. Before the Civil War. After the railroad stopped running passenger trains along this line, the store closed about

1950 and stayed closed until ten years ago. It's a wonder it didn't fall down, but they built to last in those days. Then the McCabes bought the place and restored it. Serves breakfast and lunch all week and brunch on Sundays. It's too far from Williamston for Earl and me to drive over here every day. Besides, we'd wind up as fat as Tweedledum and Tweedledee if we did."

He held the front door for Emma and followed her through.

"Oh, this is wonderful!" Emma exclaimed. "All the trains!" A dozen feet up the brick wall, a balcony ran around the perimeter. On the balustrade an antique model train set chugged around and around.

The walls were hung with daguerreotypes in ornate frames, interspersed with antique plow-shares and saws as well as antique arms. Several modern skylights had been set into the roof to give the building natural lighting. The whole room had been stripped to the original handmade brick and turned into a time warp for country antiques.

At the far end, a broad table at least fifteen feet long was covered with hot and cold dishes. Another table set at right angles held desserts and drinks. Round tables of various sizes sat around the room.

People were already lining up for their first go-around of the buffet.

"Never know what they're going to serve," Seth said. He and Emma took possession of one of the two-seater tables. Emma left her handbag behind to hold the table without a moment's concern. A waitress who might be Velma's clone set mason jars of ice water at their places.

"What y'all want to drink, Seth?" she asked. Of course she knew him.

"Unsweet tea, lots of lemon," he said. Without a glance at Emma, she left.

"This *is* a tiny town," Emma whispered as they waited for the line to move forward so they could reach the food. "Where do their customers come from?"

"Folks drive forty, fifty miles sometimes," a lady in front of them with big hair dyed a suspicious shade of red volunteered. "We're from Memphis. It's a marvelous day for a drive. And look what you get at the end of it."

Emma gave up attempting to try even a small bite of all the dishes, from okra to chicken livers to pecan pie to oysters on the half shell to fried dill pickles to barbecued ribs. She couldn't begin to take it all in. She whispered to Seth, "I'm going to fill a giant syringe with cholesterol, open a vein and shoot all the fat straight to my heart."

"Plenty you can eat here that won't give you a heart attack," the woman with the suspicious hair said. From the size of her, she was working on having her heart attack sooner rather than later. "But once every few months won't hurt you. Much."

Emma, who watched her carbs and her fats as a general rule, decided to throw caution to the wind. She kept her portions selective and miniscule, but she enjoyed everything from the crab cakes to the hush puppies to the fudge pie.

"Do not ever do this to me again," she said to Seth. "I mean it. Is it like this every day at lunch?"

He grinned at her. "Lord, no. It's more like the café in Williamstown. They only put on this spread for Sunday brunch. It's safe the rest of the time. Except for the biscuits and sausage gravy at breakfast. And the country ham. And the sorghum syrup."

"You are a demon, Seth Logan," Emma said. "I'm going to have to run a marathon to counteract this. How do you do it?"

"First of all, I don't eat like this but once in a blue moon. Second, when you chase poachers you burn off calories. I just thought you needed to see another side of us is all."

"So yesterday, nobody cared whether there were cloth tablecloths or not," Emma said.

"Nope, but everybody appreciated the trouble you took."

"They were too busy noticing my arson trick to see how the napkins were folded."

He laid his hand over hers on the table. "People noticed that you took the time and effort to make them feel special for coming to help. They won't forget it. Neither will I."

Their eyes met. He continued to hold her hand, and she could feel the heat between them. *Thank God I'm wearing a good bra*, she thought. *Otherwise I'd look like I have BBs under my sweater.* Maybe this afternoon was the time to finish what they kept starting.

Seth's phone rang. "Damn, great timing," he said. "Give me a minute. It's too noisy in here."

He left her finishing her iced tea and walked out under the front portico away from the crowd.

She watched him through the glass doors. If his shoulders were any indication, he was not happy. It was Sunday afternoon, for heaven's sake. All the poachers must be napping or watching basketball in front of their TV sets. She hoped Seth wouldn't have to chase anybody after the meal they'd just eaten.

He flicked the phone shut and came back, was glowering. Obviously trouble.

He stopped at the cashier's desk at the front

of the restaurant, gave the woman a credit card and waited until he'd signed.

Emma collected her handbag. Whatever had happened, it signaled the end of their brunch.

As she started to get up, he held her chair for her and bent over to whisper, "Can you ride a horse?"

"Depends on the horse. Generally, yes, although I haven't for a while."

"Good. We'll need all the riders we can get."

She followed him out and had to trot to keep up with him.

"Riders? For what?"

"Search and rescue. We have a regular team of volunteer searchers, but it's not that easy to get them together on a Sunday afternoon."

"Can you drop me at my house on your way? You may have noticed I don't *have* a horse."

"Sonny brings a couple of extras."

"What about you?"

"I board my two quarter horses over at Earl's. He'll bring one of mine along with his. He also trains search-and-rescue dogs. I'm sorry, but your house is twenty miles in the other direction from where we have to start the search. If you can't ride with us, I'll try to find you a ride home once we get to the meeting point."

"Of course I'll help. Who is it? I've heard of

dementia patients wandering off, but don't they usually stay close to home?"

She watched the way his jaw worked. "This is a three-year-old child who's been missing for hours." He sounded grim. "It's already afternoon. We can't wait any longer to get into the woods."

He floored the truck. She kept silent and allowed him to concentrate on his driving. She wouldn't want to be chased by him—he drove like a cop. She held on and prayed the child would be found before they got to the rendezvous spot.

Half an hour later, Seth drove down a dirt road to a group of a dozen horse trailers and trucks parked on the overgrown shoulder. The entire operation looked chaotic, but they seemed to know what they were doing. Both men and women were tacking up horses, mounting and clustering around Earl and a big redbone hound sitting patiently beside one of the trailers.

"Come on, Emma," Seth said. "Sonny," he called to the mayor, "you got a horse for Emma?"

"Sure. I brought extra in case we picked up some more riders. I've got a bombproof walking horse mare. Already tacked up and ready to go. Come on, sweet thing." He patted Emma's arm, "Let's get you mounted. We about ready to start off. Just waiting for Seth." He pulled off his broad-brimmed straw hat that looked as though it had been through the last couple of world wars, stuck it on her head and walked toward the largest horse trailer on the road. Emma followed and hoped the horse Sonny rode could carry his bulk. When she saw his broad quarter horse, an equine tank, she decided the horse could probably carry two Sonnys if it had to.

The horse he offered her was a big bay mare with a kind eye. Sonny tightened the girth, shortened the stirrups and gave Emma a boost into the flat walking horse saddle. Then he pulled a small spray can out of his camouflage jacket pocket and sprayed her from her neck to her toes.

"Mosquitoes out here can chew up kittens," Sonny said. "You ought to have on some boots and some chaps, but the spray will help some in the brush. Try to stay away from the cockleburs. Seth can get the ticks off you when we come back."

"What am I actually supposed to do?"

Sonny swung himself into his saddle with the agility of a teenager—impressive for a man of his age and bulk. "Stick close to Seth. Main thing is to have as many eyes as we can get scouring the ground and hope that toddler is somewhere close to here and screaming his head off. So far, nobody's heard anything that sounds like a child."

There were only eight riders in the group. No wonder Seth had enlisted her. "This is all we could find to ride on Sunday afternoon," Sonny said. He led her and her mare over to Seth, then swung back to join another group.

Seth hadn't been fooling when he said he needed her along. In all these woods and underbrush, a small child could disappear under a lettuce leaf. She thought of the snakes and bugs and poisonous plants and shuddered.

"Don't *you* get lost," Seth told her as she came up to his horse's flank. "Last thing we need is *two* lost people to hunt."

"Why on earth would that child be way out in the woods?" Emma asked. "Where's his house?"

"Double-wide trailer a mile or so from here. The problem is he's been gone since before his mother got out of bed this morning—maybe before dawn. She looked for him, but she didn't call it in until noon. Apparently, he opened the door by himself and went out into the yard naked and barefoot. She found his pj's by the door."

Emma visualized the mother—stunned, hysterical, angry, terrified. Wanting to go out looking, but knowing she had to remain at home in case her son showed up on his own. "How old did you say he was?"

"Three, almost four."

"That small?" Boy, did that sound familiar. And terrifying. Little older than a baby. "I remember my half brother, Patrick, at that age.

He'd take off into the neighborhood stark naked if he could get away with it. But we lived on a cul-de-sac with sidewalks and no traffic. My parents finally installed dead bolts on all the doors, as well as chains too high for him to reach. My sister never ran off like that, but Patrick could eel out and be gone in an instant."

"*You* ever lose him? Like when you were baby-sitting? I assume you did from time to time."

Emma chuckled. "I caught him halfway down the driveway once. We lived on a quiet street, but still. I've never hit a child, but I swear, I wanted to blister his behind after I hugged him half to death. The phase didn't last more than six months or so, but he's never lost the wanderlust. Now that he's seventeen and driving, my father has a tracker on his phone and on his car. Patrick knows about them and agreed to them. If he doesn't report in and make it home for his curfew, he loses his texting privileges. *And* if he ever gets caught talking or texting while he's driving, his entire world falls in on him from a great height. So far, that seems to work." She knew she was running off at the mouth, but anything seemed better than silence and imagination.

The riders came to a wide place on the dirt road, where four smaller roads spoked off in different directions. Seth held up a hand. Instant quiet. The big hound Earl had brought sat down beside his horse and waited, too. So far he hadn't alerted on the boy's smell, but they might have to quarter the area and go deep into the woods before the dog picked up a scent.

"Split up," Seth said. "Two to a spoke. Everybody got a gun?"

Nods and assents.

"Uh, Seth, I don't have a gun," Emma whispered. "Why do I need one?"

"Find any sign of the boy, one shot. Find the boy alive—two shots." He didn't say anything about how many shots to fire if the child was *not* alive. No one was admitting that possibility. "Stay close behind me, Emma. Keep your eyes peeled for anything that looks unnatural. Usually we find fabric caught on branches. We won't this time, since he's naked. If you see *anything*, yell your head off. The rest of you, divide up, but stick close to one another. Sonny, you head one team. Earl, can you take the other? Pay attention. Don't want to walk over the kid without seeing him. He could be two feet away. He may well be hiding."

"Why would he be hiding?" one of the female riders asked.

"Shoot," Sonny said, "I can tell you that. He knows he's in trouble. He wants to go home, but he's scared his momma is going to blister his behind."

"And we might spank him, too," Earl added. "Besides, we're adults and we're strangers."

Oh, great, Emma thought. She was obviously as incompetent at this as she was at picnics. Ten yards up the little dirt road, Seth turned his horse into the brush that edged the road. Emma had no idea where he was going, but when she came to the spot where he'd turned, she realized there was some kind of animal trail—probably deer. A child would likely take the easy path, rather than climbing over bushes and fallen timber. If he was even in the vicinity…

"I'll check the right side, you take the left," he said. "Look at everything—broken branches, flattened grass—anything that looks the least bit unnatural. And don't worry that what you find isn't important. Just sing out. One of us will check what you find."

If she overlooked that child, she'd never forgive herself. She wished she had a stick to sweep the underbrush, but she'd probably spook her horse. She brushed a cloud of mosquitoes away from her face and spat out a fly that had attempted to climb into her mouth. By the time she got home, she'd be covered in chigger bites. That poor little child! No bug spray, no clothes. "Can we call out?" she asked Seth.

He nodded. "You call. Better for him to hear a woman's voice than mine. His father's been out of the picture for a while. I would guess his mother's brought home substitutes from time to time. Not surprising, but his mother says he's scared of men."

She heard the anger in his voice. Another unreliable father like his own. Another child at risk because of it. How *many* strange men did the mother bring into her house? How had they interacted with the boy? Was that why he'd run away? She prayed silently that the child would be found safe. "What's his name?"

"Bobby Joe."

She nodded, cupped one hand around her mouth and shouted his name.

Seth looked back over his shoulder with his eyebrows raised. "I suspect they heard you in Memphis."

"Sorry."

"I didn't mean that. It's good, but you keep that up, you'll lose your voice pretty quick."

"Small price to pay. Bobby Joe!" she shouted again.

They settled into a routine. Seth's quarter horse bulled his way through the underbrush with his broad shoulders. Emma followed the same path on her walking horse, shouting as she went. Her mare was apparently as bombproof as Sonny had promised. Many horses would've been irritated and grumpy with a stranger in the saddle yelling blue murder. Maybe the horse was deaf.

After no more than ten minutes yelling, she realized she was so thirsty she was what her father called "spitting cotton." Ahead, Seth pulled up under a giant oak. Without a word, he dug into his cantle bag and held a bottle of water out to her.

"Oh, thank you." She dropped her reins on the horse's neck, twisted off the cap and drank about half the water in one long pull. Then she handed it back.

"Finish it. I brought a bag of them."

She did, then asked, "What do I do with the empty? I can't just drop it."

"Give it here." He sidled his horse against hers, took the bottle, put it in his saddle bag, then leaned across and brushed the hair off her forehead. "How you holding up? You didn't sign on for this, but I'm glad you're here." A moment later he added, "To do the yelling and all." He wheeled away and walked his horse farther into the woods.

"I hope *you* know where we are," she called after him. "I've been lost since we started. Surely no three-year-old could have come this far."

"You'd be surprised. We'll give it another twenty minutes, then head back. They're sending down a heat-seeking chopper from Memphis after dark if we don't find him before then. It's going to be in the low sixties tonight. We leave that child out here, tomorrow we could be looking at recovery instead of rescue."

She held back a sob. A naked child on the damp ground would be dead of hypothermia before morning at sixty degrees. She began to yell again. There had been no gunshots, so no one else was having any better luck than they were.

Following Seth's horse, her mare tried to fit in between two saplings. The mare knew how wide *she* was, but she hadn't allowed for Emma's extra width. The tree raked Emma's thigh. She raised her leg quickly, but not fast enough to avoid what would no doubt be a bad scrape. She started to say "ow!" then bit the inside of her cheek instead.

She would show Seth she was no weakling. Not just some prissy city girl who didn't even know how to throw a picnic.

He stopped, held up a hand and whispered, "Shut up."

Well, all righty. He should make up his mind.

Suddenly she heard it, too. Or thought she did. It sounded like a mockingbird. They could imitate anything. Then it came again. Too soft to be a mockingbird. The sound hadn't changed position either. She searched the trees for the bird just in case.

"Here," Seth said, handed her his reins and slid to the ground. "Don't move."

She'd heard all the stories about trackers who moved soundlessly through the woods. She'd always figured it was nonsense.

Not anymore. Seth didn't so much as snap a twig as he crept toward the sound. After what seemed to Emma like a millennium, he parted the branches of a small sapling, then disappeared from view as he dropped to his haunches. "Hey, Bobby Joe," he said so quietly and gently that even a lost child wouldn't be frightened.

But this one was. He howled. A moment later Emma heard crashing through the brush. She was off her horse instantly. "Seth? Let me." She took the time to wrap both sets of reins around the nearest limb, then called softly, "Bobby Joe? Honey? It's okay. You're not in trouble." She found Seth, crouching, and touched his shoulder. "Where is he?" she whispered.

He indicated a spot several feet in front of them. "Where?" She couldn't see anything that resembled a child. Then the failing light reflected off a pair of pale eyes.

She pulled a bottle of water out of Seth's backpack, undid the cap, lifted it to her mouth and took a swallow. "Mmm! That tastes *so* good." She held the bottle out to where the child was still hidden. "I'll bet you're thirsty, aren't you, baby?" She took a step.

"Not a baby," said an angry little voice. She must be looking right at him. Then a small head crowned with a cap of spiky white-blond hair rose out of the honeysuckle straight in front of her.

She held out the bottle again. "Here you are, Bobby Joe." A filthy little paw reached out toward her. She moved carefully, as though he were a wild animal. Which, in a sense, he was...

He grabbed the bottle, and the arm retreated. She heard glug, glug sounds and moved closer.

He stood up, and she caught her breath. No wonder the searchers were looking foot by foot. He was encrusted with mud and festooned with honeysuckle. If he'd closed his eyes and stayed still, she might have stepped on him without seeing him. She sank to her knees. "I'll bet you're real hungry, too, aren't you?"

The blond head nodded. She could see him squarely now. His eyes were almost colorless blue.

She slipped off the light jacket she'd worn over her sweater. The head disappeared. "It's okay. Bet you're cold. It's cold out here." She offered him her jacket, without reaching to touch him.

He ran forward two steps, snatched the jacket and retreated a step. She dropped to her knees and held out her arms. Suddenly, he dived straight at her with enough force to knock her onto her rear end. He locked his legs around her waist and buried his face against her shoulder. She enfolded both of them in her jacket.

He smelled of dirt and urine and fear. But he was alive and still clutching the empty plastic water bottle. "Come on, buddy, let's go find you some food. What do you say? You hungry?"

"My mommy's mad."

"She won't be mad when we get you home. I promise. We have to show her you're all right, so she won't be scared anymore." She struggled to get to her feet. He was only three, but obviously a muscular little boy, and he clung to her like a limpet.

She felt Seth's arms around her, and he stood her and Bobby Joe up in one smooth motion. The child shrank from him, but refused to let go of Emma.

"This is Seth," she said. "He's been looking for you, too. He helped me find you. He's going to take us back to your mommy. Is that okay?"

"Uh-huh."

Seth led them to where the horses were contentedly nibbling honeysuckle drooping from the branch Emma had wrapped their reins around.

Bobby Joe whimpered when Emma tried to unhook him long enough to mount her horse.

She settled him on her hip until Seth was able to boost him into her saddle. She mounted behind him, took her reins and waited while Seth mounted his horse and started leading them back toward the road.

Emma kept an arm around Bobby Joe so he couldn't suddenly catapult off the horse and run back into the brush. Obviously he'd been on a horse before. He acted as though this was his usual mode of transport. Out here, it might well be.

She felt him begin to tremble and heard his sniffly voice. *Okay, here we go*, she thought. He'd reached his limit. Now that he was safe, it was time for the meltdown.

"Hungry!" This was a wail, a very healthy wail. "Want my mommy!"

She rolled up her jacket sleeves, worked his short arms into them and held out a hand to Seth. "Another water, please, sir. Without the cap."

The child huddled against her while he slurped down the entire bottle of water. She realized he probably wasn't all that toilet trained in these circumstances. Oh, well. These jeans were toast anyway.

Now remounted, Seth held his arms out to take the child onto his horse from hers.

"No!" Bobby Joe wasn't having it. *"Her."*

Emma shrugged and gripped the child more

securely. "Seth, aren't you forgetting something?" She nodded toward his sidearm.

"You're right. Now, young'un, I got to fire off this pistol so your momma will know we found you safe and sound. You put your hands over your ears and don't be scared."

Bobby Joe's eyes went huge. He put his small hands in their overlong sleeves over his ears.

Seth pointed his pistol above his head and pulled the trigger twice. Neither horse so much as flicked an ear. But then both were used to gunfire from field dog trials.

"Can you hang on to him the whole way back?" Seth asked.

"You sit quietly and hold on to the pommel—the front part of the saddle, Mr. Bobby Joe," she said into his ear. "The faster we go, the faster you'll get some lunch, but you mustn't fall off. Can you hang on for me?"

"Yes'm. I'm hungry."

Seth was leading them back through the brush to the road. As usual in such treks, the way back took less time than coming in. When they finally reached the road, all the other riders were cantering toward them. Bobby Joe squeaked and huddled back against Emma.

"You found him!" Sonny said.

"It's okay, Bobby Joe. They're just going to take us back to your mommy," Emma whispered.

"Let's get on back to the trailers. His momma's waiting up there."

"I'll never be able to hold him at anything faster than a walk," Emma said. "He's as slippery as an eel."

"Well, shoot, Seth can hold him. Give him the boy. You can follow along at your leisure."

"No! Her!" howled Bobby Joe, grasping Emma around the neck so tightly that she choked.

"Well, well, nothing wrong with this young scamp's lungs! All righty, we'll walk. But a good running walk, Miss Emma. Can you manage that?"

Emma nodded. "But if I say stop, Mr. Mayor, I mean stop. Got that?"

"Nothing wrong with *her* lungs either," Seth said. "Let's go."

Emma had ridden very few walking horses and never one at a full-out running walk, but the ride was so smooth that she had no difficulty holding on to Bobby Joe. They'd come to a fork in the road and started back toward the trailers, when Emma heard a woman shout, "Bobby Joe! Baby!"

"Mommy!"

She was tall and thin with precious little meat on her bones, but she could run. She raced up to Emma, took Bobby Joe as he slid out of Emma's arms and dived at his mother, then crushed him to her and sobbed. "Thank y'all so much!" She narrowed her eyes at her son. "Here you are, buck nekkid with half the county out looking for you! And those chigger bites. If you ever do something like this again I'll—well, I don't know what I'll do because it will never, *ever* happen again. Do you understand me, Bobby Joe?"

"Yes'm. I'm hungry."

Even Seth laughed.

By the time the horses were loaded and Bobby Joe and his mother were cuddled in Earl's truck on their way home, Emma's chigger bites had begun to itch and turn into small red bumps. She'd picked two swollen ticks off her ankle. She was covered in mud, but Bobby Joe had not wet her jeans. Where her mare had run her into a tree, however, her jeans were split and her bruised and scraped thigh was oozing blood. Underneath Sonny's hat, her hair was flattened and sweaty. She couldn't smell herself, but she suspected everyone else could, including Seth. They wouldn't be smelling roses. Her thighs and stomach muscles—her riding muscles—were protesting that she hadn't used them for a couple of years.

Her stomach rumbled. And she really needed to go to the bathroom, but she had no intention of using the underbrush. She'd probably get snake-bit. Heaven only knew how she looked. Seth's truck had no mirror on the passenger side, and she never carried a compact, so she'd have to imagine until she got home and into a hot shower.

What an afternoon. It could so easily have ended in tragedy instead of backslapping and congratulations. There wasn't even any beer. None of the riders had made a pit stop on the way to the meeting place. Seth shared his water, no longer cold. Nobody minded.

In the final analysis, she was sore, itchy, dirty, sweaty and probably smelled.

She'd never felt more alive in her life.

When she finally slid into bed hours later, she was daubed all over with pale pink anti-itch ointment. She glared at herself in the mirror. "I look like I have the measles. I used to be really put together—eyeliner and everything. Now look at me. I think the Australians call it 'going bush.'"

As she drifted off to sleep, she sat bolt upright. "I'm supposed to work for Barbara tomorrow morning. I'll never make it."

CHAPTER SIXTEEN

BUT OF COURSE she did. She'd been correct about her riding muscles. The first thing out of whack, when she gave up wearing sneakers and riding boots to wear high heels every day instead, was that her calf muscles tightened. Now, after no more than a week of wearing nothing but flats, her muscles were protesting that she wasn't being fair to expect them to spring back like rubber bands.

Barbara had told her that Monday morning at the clinic was usually busy.

Judging by the trucks and SUVs parked in the clinic lot, the customers had arrived well before the hour the clinic was supposed to open. And she was expected to organize.

She had no idea how to triage animals. She figured she'd start the way the media did its stories—if it bled, it led. Any animal that was bleeding, therefore, went to the front of the line. After that, she hoped Barbara would give her guidance. She suspected, however, that she was on her own.

Barbara had warned about the lame goose called Mabel. The goose didn't bother the customers with their dogs on leashes and their cats and other critters in cages. It seemed, however, to take a dislike to Emma and flew at her with wings and beak extended. She took a deep breath and shooed it out of her way and off the path to the front door. Like a lot of bullies, it just needed someone to call its bluff.

Mabel seemed to know who didn't belong; maybe having an animal was the goose's version of a ticket to pass.

Emma smiled and slipped through the clients to open the front door. It was unlocked, but no one had walked in without being invited. She checked the clock over the registration desk. Two minutes before the eight-thirty opening time. In city shopping malls, even one minute past opening would have resulted in shoving and pushing.

She slipped behind the desk, turned on the computer and smiled at the first person in line. "Yes, ma'am?"

"Pooky threw up all night. I'm scared to death somebody's tried to poison him." The woman's face was ashen. She was attached to a leash, but whatever was at the end of it didn't show up over the counter.

Emma stood up and peered over the edge. Pooky was some sort of Chihuahua cross. At the moment his ears drooped. He looked pretty miserable. No doubt he was about to throw up. And guess who'd be mopping the floor? Emma quickly took the woman to the closest exam room, and met Barbara coming down the hall toward her. She updated the vet as fast as possible. "Oh—I didn't even ask her name."

"There are appointment forms in the top drawer. Hand them out. They can fill them in while they wait."

"She thinks Pooky was poisoned."

"He was, by half a fried chicken and mashed potatoes and gravy. She gives him what she calls Sunday dinner. He's in here nearly every Monday throwing up. It's a miracle he doesn't have pancreatitis." She disappeared into the exam room.

After a few false starts, Emma began to get into the swing. It helped that after the first rush, the number of clients and the severity of their problems tapered off.

Although most of the clients had dogs and cats, Barbara also had to drain a foot abscess on a very pregnant nanny goat that arrived standing on the backseat of the owner's BMW sedan.

"Mignon just hates the truck," the large lady chauffeuring the goat said. "She rides fine in the BMW. Pregnant as she is, I hate to make her any unhappier."

At ten minutes after twelve, Barbara locked the front door.

"Can you do that?" Emma asked. "What if somebody shows up late?"

"Then they'll have to come back. If I didn't lock the door, neither one of us would get so much as a cracker for lunch. So, how was your first morning?"

"Harder than I thought it would be."

"But definitely easier for me. It's pretty clear you have your hands full with the clients. I'll have to get Betty to clean cages and mop the floor when she comes in after school this afternoon. You couldn't possibly stay until five thirty, could you?"

Emma felt her heart sink. There went the résumés and the cold calls. "How on earth have you managed? How long since you had somebody in the office?"

"Never full-time, but I had a darling girl going to school in Jackson. She graduated in January and went off to graduate school in March. I haven't had time to look for anyone full-time since she left. Come on, let's have some lunch."

"I didn't bring anything. Where's the closest grocery that fixes sandwiches?"

"In town. Don't worry, I brought lunch for both of us. I heard you had a busy day yesterday."

Of course Barbara knew about the rescue.

Might as well run a continual news feed on a blimp over the county. If she'd gone to bed with Seth, everybody would be discussing it before either of them woke up from postcoital bliss.

Another good reason to avoid even the semblance of an affair.

After lunch Barbara introduced her to the animals being rehabilitated. "I think the fawns can all be released Thursday morning," Barbara said. "You couldn't by any chance come early, could you? Seth's coming to help load, but I could use another person."

"How early?"

"Say—six thirty?"

And then work her regular hours at the computer. Did these people *ever* slow down? It was worse than the last days before a new marketing campaign went up when she and the rest of Nathan's team worked most of the night.

"Then can I leave a little early if it slows down?"

Barbara nodded, closed her eyes and breathed a sigh of relief.

This might work as a stopgap Joe job, but she needed her career back, her house back, her family and friends back, and working for Barbara wasn't the way to get them.

She noted that the squirrels were gone from the big cage, replaced by baby raccoons that seemed to be growing as she watched them. They spent more time climbing the wire than they did on the ground.

"My next major construction is a flight cage for raptors. I don't know what I'd do if I got a screech owl that needed to exercise a broken wing. They have to be able to dive onto their prey. I get bags of frozen mice to teach them. It's not as good as actual live mice, but although they're bred as raptor food, I can't let them loose to be killed. I know that's stupid. My friends who are trained as raptor rehabilitators laugh at me when I drag frozen mice along the perches to convince an owl to eat them, even if they aren't alive."

"How do you train as a raptor rehabilitator?" Emma asked.

"You have to train to be a licensed rehabilitator first," Barbara said. "Pretty strict rules and training. And then you get much more training. Among other things, you have to raise your own bird and train him. You work with a licensed raptor rehabilitator until he says you're ready. The fish and wildlife people—Seth's people—run classes in Williamston. A good deal of it is common sense, but there's also bookwork on various anatomical differences among animals. For example, in the vet business, if I shoot a syringe full of penicillin into a horse's artery, he'll likely die before I can get the needle out. Vein is fine. Artery—a no-no. You can't give aspirin to a cat. Nor, by extension, a bobcat or a panther. Then, if people would only leave fawns they find curled up in the brush alone, nine times out of ten the mother will return to pick up her baby, usually when she's through foraging. And raccoons like to dip their food in water before they eat it. Oh, and beavers poop in water, not on land. You like this stuff, don't you?"

"I have to admit I do like it. I could never get all of it straight."

"That's why we all work together. There's always another rehabilitator to give you advice or come and help you. Why don't you take a class? The wildlife people run introductory courses all the time. Then you can see if you really do enjoy this stuff."

"But I couldn't do it back in Memphis. The raccoons are quite a plague in the city. If I rescued any, my neighbors would go ballistic."

"So, you're still planning on going back to Memphis."

Emma felt her face flush. "There are no decent jobs in the country, Barbara. I have a career. Or I did have. I liked it. I made a really good living. I have a mortgage to pay. I've pretty much showed I haven't got a clue how to fit in out here. I mean——everybody thought my ironed linen napkins were way over the top."

"But we appreciated them."

Emma patted Barbara's hand. "Of course you did."

THE FIRST THING Emma did when she got home from the clinic was to clean up after the skunks. She brought Seth's playpen into the yard and sprayed it with the outside faucet, then scrubbed it with disinfectant. After that, she scrubbed the pantry the same way. Still no lingering odor of skunk. So no release into the wild yet.

She knew she had to keep going with her chores until she finished. If she sat down, she'd fall asleep where she sat and not wake up until morning. At which point she'd be covered with mosquito bites to match her fading chigger bites.

She spread the remaining night crawlers, along with carrot pennies, apple slices and hot dog rounds, in the skunks' kennel. They pounced as though they hadn't been fed for days. Then she cleaned their little kiddie pool. Did they eat minnows? If so, Barbara was bound to know where to get some. If they ate them in the wild, they needed to learn to chase them and catch them before they departed for the woods.

Finally, she scrubbed all the combined odors she'd encountered off her body and out of her hair. She put on Bermuda shorts and a long-sleeved work shirt, combed her hair but left it wet, cropped bits and all. Then she fetched a glass of white wine, sprayed herself with mosquito repellant and sank into the front porch swing.

The grill sat in the front yard under the water oak. She really didn't care when, if ever, it made its way back to the rear porch.

She gave a longing look at the bag swing, which swayed gently in the evening breeze. She couldn't count on Seth to rescue her again, so no bag swing.

Seth's SUV wasn't in his driveway. Working late? Or a hot date?

Now, that presented an interesting situation. Did he already have a steady girlfriend? Nobody—probably not even Barbara—would feel the necessity to clue her in if he did. So far as anyone knew, they were simply neighbors. No one would consider that she would want to have that information. She and Seth were simply acquaintances.

Did Seth think that's all they were? Did she? Okay, so they'd spent some time together, but they'd barely even kissed. As good at kissing as he was, he'd obviously had plenty of practice.

Barbara said his wife had left him. Why? According to Barbara, the ex didn't like the country and was currently married to a city dentist.

Was that the whole story? Seth was an attractive man. Possibly one of the most attractive around here. What to say his wife hadn't left him because she got tired of his playing around. He didn't seem like the type, but then Trip hadn't seemed like the type either.

Until he was.

What was Emma to Seth? A couple of peculiar dates, but no pressure to take it to the next level. Emma's stepmother had said that in her day, men all wanted you to go to bed with them. But she said, "They didn't actually expect you to do it."

Emma had found that in too many instances, most of the men she'd gone out with *did* expect you to go to bed with them. It infuriated her. Like every single woman she knew, she'd had to fight her way out of situations that verged on rape. The wine was vintage, the food was French, so sex was the expected end of the evening.

She and Seth had enjoyed brunch—Lucullan, but still during the day. Would he have pushed for a little post-prandial delight if not for Bobby Joe's rescue?

But he hadn't pushed after he'd hauled her off the bag swing. That would've been the obvious opportunity.

Or maybe he wasn't pushy because he wasn't that interested? Talk about a downer.

Because, dammit, she *was* interested. When she dreamed at night, there was no other face in her dreams—erotic or otherwise.

Before long, if he didn't do something, she might have to. And she never in her life had before. She'd always been pursued. She didn't have a clue how to pursue.

CHAPTER SEVENTEEN

BY TUESDAY AFTERNOON, Emma felt comfortable running reception for Barbara. The cases had been pretty routine—a couple of spay and neuters, some gashes that needed stitches, the usual horses needing shots. Unlike many vets, Barbara tried to avoid taking outside calls as much as possible; she simply didn't have time to travel. So even the large animals generally came to the clinic. She did have one call out to a cow that was having difficulty calving, but the call was close by, and the calf came relatively easily after she'd managed to straighten its twisted foot.

Still, Emma was glad to leave after her shift finished. She'd never realized how difficult being tied to a desk at someone else's beck and call could be. She decided to send the secretaries at Nathan's office a big box of Dinstuhl's chocolates to thank them for putting up with her.

For the second night, Seth's SUV wasn't in his driveway. Where was he? He certainly had no reason to report to her, but he seemed to be avoiding her. Drawing away from her? So it would seem. She wasn't going to sit behind drawn curtains waiting for him to come home—alone or otherwise. He was sleeping somewhere, in someone's bed, just not his own. Or hers. Avoiding her, so she wouldn't ask questions about his father? Afraid that if he came home, she'd go bang on his door and demand an explanation? She would never do such a thing. She had no right to burrow into his life.

Maybe it was time for her to return to Memphis. Not like she was going great guns here.

That evening when she called home, her father answered. She made the story of the Saturday party and Sunday rescue sound very funny and not nearly as critical as not finding Bobby Joe would have been. "Is Trip still calling you?" she asked.

"Not as often. I'm sending him straight to voice mail. He's beginning to get the idea. Is he calling you?"

"Not in several days."

"Now, however, Nathan Savage is calling. He wants to know when you're coming home. I think he may want to offer you your job back."

"Well, hooray for him," she said drily.

"Are you still interested?"

"Of course I am, Dad. But not under the same rules. I'm happy with the salary for now, but I want more autonomy, more trust, less meeting planning and more design responsibilities. I'm actually enjoying living up here at Aunt Martha's. I think after I come home, I'll rehab it with Andrea's help, and we can use it as a weekend getaway."

"As if your siblings want to spend weekends away from their friends. You remember what you were like at that age."

"Then maybe just for you and Andrea and me," Emma said.

"And miss golf? Good try, Emma, but you're going to have to come home to us, and that's all there is to it."

By the time she went to bed, Seth's SUV still wasn't in his driveway.

Nor was it there when she climbed out of bed to feed the skunks. Wherever he was, it was serious. If he wasn't with another woman, what about the disasters that could be keeping him away? Drugs or poaching or road accidents or hunts for criminals or more lost children. She had no right to expect him to call her to check in, but she wished he would.

She had just put the clean dishes away when she heard a car in her gravel driveway. Her heart turned over. Seth! At last! She was going to kiss him and then she was going to kill him—or maybe vice versa. She ran to the front door and yanked it open.

Standing on the stoop with his hand raised to knock was Nathan. "You won't take my calls, so I drove up." He gave her a hug.

"Well, if you ain't the sexiest Ma Kettle in the wilderness." He kissed both cheeks. "Give me to drink, dear lady, before I die of thirst."

"Beer, wine, lemonade or iced tea—unsweetened."

"Lemonade homemade?"

"But of course."

He nodded. "Then I want that. Who's the cage for? Installed your own Tarzan, have you?"

That was entirely too close to the truth, so she only smiled and ushered him in. "This is fondly known as The Hovel," she said.

"Actually, it would benefit from your stepmother's fine decorating hand, but it does have good bones. Andrea could turn it from a sow's ear to a Gucci handbag. I was afraid it was a log cabin. You do have indoor plumbing, don't you?"

She nodded and raised her eyebrows. "Heating and air-conditioning, too. At least I think they work. Hasn't been hot or cold enough to test out yet."

He wandered around the living room while she fixed the tumblers of lemonade and brought him one.

"Since you don't have to worry about Andrea's allergies, I expected you'd have adopted at least a cat or dog or two," he said, "But I didn't get attacked when I got out of the car, so no dog as yet, am I right? You haven't deteriorated into the local cat lady yet?"

"No cats. No dogs. Skunks."

He spat his mouthful of lemonade straight across the room. "Say what?" He whirled around looking at his feet. "Guard skunks? Am I about to get hosed?"

"It's called 'being skunked.' They're orphan babies, Nathan. They don't make scent yet. Want to see?"

"I'm more the labradoodle type, but if you're sure these trousers are safe from attack..."

They walked outside and around the corner of the house to the kennel. Having finished their breakfast, the babies were all curled up sound asleep in their quilted dog bed beside the tree limb.

"Ooooh!" He dropped to one knee. "A-dorable!"

"Hush. You'll wake them up," Emma whispered.

He leaned against the fence, made cooing noises, then let her drag him back into the living room. As she shut the door behind them, he clasped his hands. "I should've known you'd make beluga caviar out of dead fish eggs. Emma, I can think of two ad campaigns right this minute that would top the charts using those little sweeties. How soon can you bring them to Memphis so we can shoot lots of footage of them?" He glanced at the door. "You weren't kidding about their not 'skunking' yet?"

"Hold on, Nathan, just hold on. The only place they're going is back to the woods as soon as they're weaned. Nobody's supposed to know I even have them. It's against the law in Tennessee. You must not tell *anyone*. I mean it. I know how you get when you have an idea. We could all wind up in jail."

"Surely not!"

"Surely yes. That Tarzan you mentioned is a game warden and he lives right there across the street. I don't dare let anyone find out about them. Promise."

He sighed. "Very well. But I can bring my crew up here and film them in their cage outside, can't I? Nobody would have to know where I got the shots."

"I knew I shouldn't have mentioned them. My friend Barbara, a vet who lives down the road, rehabilitates orphan animals. At the moment, she has a goose with a lame foot, several orphan fawns, a couple of raccoon babies…"

"Baby deer? Yes, yes, yes. Let's go see them!"

"Nathan, you're such a baby yourself when you get an idea."

"Because I have such good ones. I still want the skunks, but I'll settle for the fawns in the meantime." He set his now-empty lemonade glass on the kitchen counter. "Grab your purse and let's go."

"She may not be available. I should call first."

The phone at the clinic rang until it went to voice mail. Emma started to speak, when what sounded like a very frazzled Barbara picked up. "This is Barbara. This better be an emergency... Emma? You're not supposed to be here today. God, I wish you were."

"One quick question. My former boss drove up here and wants to come see the fawns before you release them. Is that possible?"

"Um... Okay, but remember you're coming to load and release them tomorrow."

"We won't even go into the clinic. I'll take him straight to the barn." She dropped her voice to a whisper. "Although I may sic Mabel on him. That goose would scare the emperor of a third-world country."

"Okay. Sorry, got to go."

"Well?" Nathan asked.

"We don't bother Barbara, we don't try to touch any of them, and you don't scream."

"All right, all right. Let's take my car. Yours, as usual, is covered with mud."

"Around here, mud is a badge of honor. Come on. You buy me lunch afterward."

"Where? The ditch beside the road? Do we have to snare a rabbit?"

"Nathan, do we—I mean you—have a client who sells trucks?" She climbed into the BMW and fastened her seat belt.

"Two clients, as a matter of fact. What's your point?"

She directed him to Barbara's clinic. He pulled into the parking lot. As Emma climbed out, she waved a hand at Nathan. "Well, check these out, podna. This is what pickups look like in the real world and not in the ads we write for them." The pickups ran the gamut from elderly farm trucks held together by rust to big special-edition diesels hauling stock trailers. With the exception of a single bright red pickup that still had a dealer's drive-out tag in the back window, every one of the trucks was dusty or downright dirty. "If you wash your truck, you do it on Saturday morning while the kids are watching cartoons and before the golf matches are telecast in the afternoon. Or, if it's winter, before you head for the woods to get your deer or your doves."

"By 'get' you mean?"

Emma nodded. "Exactly. Come on. Now let's go look at the fawns." She started around the building, as Mabel the goose rounded it from the other direction in full attack mode—wings flapping, neck stretched forward like a cobra's, lame foot dragging but not slowing her down.

"My God, what's that?" Nathan slid behind Emma.

"A goose. Mabel, go away. She's harmless. She protects the place from strangers. You, Nathan, count as strange."

"And you don't? Ha!"

Emma ducked into the stock barn and walked to the stall at the far end.

"Okay, Nathan, fawns as requested." She picked up half a dozen thin carrots from the basket hanging on the hasp of the door lock, broke them into short pieces and handed a couple to Nathan.

"These aren't babies," he whispered. "They're full-grown deer."

"That's why Barbara is releasing them tomorrow."

"To where?"

"The deep woods. She has a friend who keeps a big hunting preserve where he no longer allows hunting. They'll be a ready-made herd." She held out a carrot, avoided getting bitten in the ensuing rush for the goodies, then took Nathan's offerings and handed those out, as well.

"They're not very big, are they?"

"Nathan, these are Southern deer. They're not elk or moose. They run small. They come in either gray or beige, and I think they are beautiful."

"Yeah, but they won't do for a marketing campaign, I'm afraid. Now, about your skunks…"

EMMA PICKED UP her own SUV to lead Nathan into town for lunch. She had errands to run after he left, and her house was in the opposite direction from the route he'd be taking back to Memphis. No sense asking him to bring her home.

More to the point, drive time without his chattering to her held off any offers to return to her old job. So far he hadn't actually offered. She'd be crazy not to want it. Nothing held her here now that her babies were going to the woods. She had no impact on Seth's life. Barbara would find someone to take her place at the clinic.

They were at the café early enough to get a parking space. "What kind of restaurant is this?" Nathan asked as he slid into the banquette at the back of the café. With luck they'd avoid running into Seth, but if they did, they did. She couldn't live her life avoiding him.

"Maker of the best steak burgers this side of the Tennessee River," Emma said. "Morning, Velma, what's the special?"

Velma stared at Nathan as though he had three noses. "Uh, chicken fried steak, corn on the cob and O'Brien potatoes."

"Oh, goody," Nathan whispered and then actually smacked his lips. "There goes my waistline."

"We can do you a chef salad," Velma said. "Diet dressing and all." She didn't sound pleased.

"Woman, are you mad? Of course I want the special! I am a child of the South. Fiddle-dee-dee, I'll diet tomorrow."

Velma went to put their orders in. As she moved away, a shadow that was all too familiar fell across their table.

The hair on Emma's arms stood straight up and her stomach tightened. She'd felt him when he walked in the door. She also saw Nathan's eyes widen as Seth's shadow loomed over their booth. She looked up to say hello.

He was not alone. The woman with him was nearly as tall as Emma and every bit as slim. Her hair was short, cut in layers and completely white. No tinge of faded yellow or old-lady lavender. Since her unlined skin didn't match the silvery hair, the hair must be prematurely white. She wore a long-sleeved jewel green silk shirt over black dress jeans that fit as though they'd been tailored for her.

Emma suddenly felt underdressed. And country. She wished she hadn't missed her haircut last month, and that chopped-off bits and pieces didn't continue to resist taming after her attack with the Swiss knife. She wished she'd put eye shadow on and redone her manicure. At least she'd gotten the ratty polish off.

The woman looked older than Seth, but not by that much. Maybe she was a colleague in town for a couple of days. Better than thinking she might be a girlfriend. Maybe they'd been off touring duck blinds or something. Or maybe he simply didn't feel he owed Emma a telephone call. One dinner did not spell *commitment*. She was used to guys who swore they'd call and didn't, but she hated for Seth to turn out to be one of them.

"Emma," he said. He spoke to her, but his eyes were on Nathan. So were everyone else's in the restaurant. It was like an old B Western. She expected him to say, "This town ain't big enough for both of us." Except he probably didn't care.

He stepped aside. "This is Emma French, the new neighbor I've been telling you about."

Then he turned to Emma. "This is my mother, Laila Logan."

Emma let out her breath. "How wonderful to meet you," she said. "This is my ex-boss, Nathan Savage. He drove up to visit. We've been to see Barbara's fawns. Seth, you know you're supposed to help us free them tomorrow?" *Shut up! You're babbling!* "Please, won't you join us? We just ordered."

"We wouldn't want to interrupt," Mrs. Logan

said. But she slid into the booth beside Nathan and turned a million-watt smile on him that would probably enslave him for the rest of his life.

Seth slid into the other end of the booth so that Nathan was effectively sandwiched between mother and son.

"Sorry I didn't call to check on the babies," Seth said. "I figured you were busy at Barbara's and didn't need any interruptions."

"And I figured that if you were dead in a ditch somewhere, I'd find out sooner or later." She studiously kept her voice low and casual. Men! Why did they think they were asserting their masculinity if they didn't check in and keep their friends and families from worrying about them?

Velma miraculously reappeared with four jars of iced tea that no one had ordered, but apparently didn't have to. Emma suspected she'd been peering around the edge of the kitchen waiting for the fireworks. Of course she'd know Laila Logan, but she couldn't have a clue where Nathan fit into the picture. Emma was sitting with her back to the room and suspected that every eye in the place was once more checking them out. "I'd love to come to see your babies," Mrs. Logan said to Emma. "Seth tells me they're nearly ready to leave home. But if there's any danger of getting sprayed…"

"Not yet, but any day," Emma said. "They're

almost completely independent now. I still have to provide the food, because their hunting preserve is only as big as the kennel, but what I give them, they discover and scarf up. You're welcome anytime. I'm working for Barbara Carew tomorrow morning, but I should be there after two in the afternoon."

"Are you sure you don't mind?" Laila asked.

"I love showing off my babies. I don't have much longer to do that. I might even run to a glass of wine."

"Sounds wonderful, but won't you be exhausted? I know what that clinic is like. Barbara absolutely has to hire some people and find a partner to take up some of the slack. Since her husband died, she's been essentially trying to do everything herself and work with the rehabilitators, too. I've helped out a time or two at the clinic, but frankly, I don't have the stamina." She squeezed lemon into her tea. "I'm retired and intend to stay that way."

Neither Laila nor Seth had given Velma an order for lunch. Again, apparently they didn't have to.

Laila took the lead in the conversation by eliciting Nathan's life history. Seth watched the exchange in silence. Then Laila said to Emma, "Seth's been staying with me the last couple of days." She pulled up the sleeve of her silk shirt to reveal a bandaged wrist. "I fell off a ladder." She laughed and held up her unbandaged hand. "A very short ladder, but I hit the edge of the counter. I wasn't really hurt, but I needed a couple of stitches, and some pain meds the first night. Seth decided to stay over until I was back in my right mind."

"You shouldn't have been on that ladder, Mom," Seth said. "Those people at the condos are supposed to change lightbulbs."

"They will, but not necessarily the first day you call them. I'm not totally helpless, dear. With your schedule, I certainly do not need you to come over to change a lightbulb."

Seth glanced at Emma and shook his head. "See, she won't wait for me to help *her* either. Must be genetic."

"Emma and I don't share genes, darling," Laila said. "Only gender. If you want to look after us, I'm afraid you're going to have to do it on our schedule, not when you get around to it. You and I both seem to have a sense of urgency, don't we, Emma?"

"He's been wonderfully helpful to me," Emma said. "But you're right. I hate to rely on anyone. Did he tell you about yanking me out of the azaleas?"

Velma, obviously all ears, delivered their food just then.

"I can vouch for Emma's sense of urgency," Nathan said. "She wants everything done, checked and rechecked well ahead of time. It's one of the reasons I value her." He tucked into his lunch with happy whimpering sounds.

Emma found her appetite had deserted her. Looking across the table at Seth, she saw he was only pushing food around on his plate.

Sounded as though Nathan was making noises to explore rehiring her. She had loved working with Nathan, but now, instead of the relief and joy she should be feeling, Emma felt a sense of loss so deep she nearly burst into tears. She wanted to stay here, but there was no real place for her. Even though this cougar was his mother, there might be a dozen other women in Seth's life. She'd never be told. She was an outsider. Nobody would surreptitiously let her know if he was dating half the town. Velma, for one, would never say.

In the parking lot after lunch, Laila made an appointment to view the babies Thursday afternoon about four. They said their goodbyes and walked to their respective cars. "I like your Emma," Laila said to Seth. "Charming. Seems to have her head on straight."

"Damnation, Mom, she is not *my* Emma. She never will be."

"You're stomping," Laila said. "Leave some gravel on the parking lot. And I wouldn't be too sure of that. The way you avoided looking at each other was pure farce. Right out of a bad French play. I've never known you to pay for a lunch you barely touched." Laila giggled.

"She never planned to stay up here. It was always a stopgap, a place to lick her wounds. That Nathan guy fired her. He obviously came up here because he wants her back. There's nothing to hold her here."

"There's you."

"Fasten your seat belt. I'll drop you at your condo. I have to go back to work. I've got a mountain of paperwork to do, then Earl and I have to check some fishing licenses. Whoopee. An exciting afternoon."

"Sarcasm does not become you. If you get down to the far end of the lake, would you go see that the cabin's all right? I had the cleaning team in a couple of weeks ago to get ready for the summer, but I haven't checked it out myself."

"Sure, although I may not get that far south." Seth parked in the visitors' spot outside his mother's cottage inside the complex, then went around and opened her door.

"Thank you, dear, I did teach you good manners." She kissed him and started up the walk to her front door. Halfway there, she stopped and turned. "The two of you are obviously what we used to call 'smitten.' About time you sealed the deal. It's harder to leave a lover than it is a casual beau. Remember that." Then she was gone.

Leaving him gawking. His mother had just suggested—strongly suggested—that he take Emma to bed. That was what he wanted, too, but to hear it from his *mother*?

CHAPTER EIGHTEEN

EMMA AND SETH both rolled into Barbara's parking lot at seven in the morning. Barbara had already hooked her stock trailer to her big truck and backed it up into the aisle of the little barn. The fawns watched from their stall, curious, apprehensive, aware that something different was happening in their lives. All six of them clustered together as though to take comfort from one another.

Barbara had spread a deep bed of hay in the trailer. "Right on time," she told Seth and Emma.

"How on earth do we get them to go in that trailer?" Emma asked.

"The first thing you learn about deer is to be sneaky. I built this barn to make it easier. When we open the back trailer doors, they just fit in the center aisle and close it off. Seth, help me pull the doors back against the wall and brace them open. No escape route out the front of the barn."

The rear door of the barn was closed, so no exit that way either.

"The only way out will be into the trailer."

"Or back into their stall," Seth said.

"You stand in there and block them," Barbara told him.

She opened the door to their stall. "All righty, then, here we go."

For several seconds, the deer merely stood inside as though they had no plans to leave. Then one of the young stags put a tentative hoof into the aisle. The other five followed carefully, ready to bolt.

One young doe came over to Emma and butted noses with her. So far everyone was calm.

The young stag, the obvious leader, stepped onto the ramp leading into the trailer. And backed out, snorting. He then backed into one of the does and she backed up into another doe. From one second to the next, calm collapsed into chaos. Seth kept them from running into their sanctuary. After a minute or so, they settled back to milling in the aisle. Emma took refuge behind the door of the stall across from theirs.

"Okay," Barbara said. "Now to the old tried-and-true paper-sack loader." She handed Emma a wadded-up paper sack tied onto the end of a long riding crop. "Whatever you do, don't hit anybody. Just shake it behind them. It makes a racket that they hate. We want them to think the inside of that trailer is sanctuary."

It worked. And quickly. After a couple of forays to try to go across Seth and back into their stall, they all walked straight up into the trailer. Seth and Barbara closed the doors and latched them. Once inside the dark trailer, the little deer settled immediately. The stag even began to nibble the hay at his feet.

"Let's head out," Barbara said. "We can all ride together. I'll bring you back after we set them free. See? Easy."

THE TRIP TOOK most of an hour, before they came to six bar gates heavily posted with Privacy and no-hunting signs. Emma noticed one that said, "All hunters will be stuffed and used for target practice."

There was no sign of any building, but the land was beautiful, a perfect mixture of woods and rolling fields. Half a dozen deer grazed in lush spring grass on the edge of hardwood forests. They didn't even lift their heads when the truck rolled by. As soon as the perimeter fence was out of sight, the land looked as it might have before the first trappers showed up in the nineteenth century.

Barbara pulled into a gravel turnaround large enough to turn the trailer without backing. "Now, we open the doors and stand behind them so we don't get run over. We wait until the deer discover they're free. Then we watch until they disappear into the trees, which should take about a minute. God, I love this part."

Emma watched around the edge of the door as the little stag, the leader as usual, took one step down the ramp, then jumped to land on the grass. He peered around on full alert, perhaps to spot the trick in letting them go. A minute later, all six were taking off into the trees, the white tips on their tails marking their progress.

Another minute and they were gone.

Seth shouted, a pure rebel yell. Emma jumped up and down, and Barbara punched the air and echoed Seth's yell.

They closed the doors to the trailer and climbed back in the truck.

"Will they be all right?" Emma asked.

"That is no longer in our hands," Barbara said. "We've done our best to let them go in a safe place. Would they be all right if they'd never been raised by human beings? If they'd been left on the road beside their dead mothers? Humans are so dangerous. I hope they're still afraid of us. I think they will be. But it's their world, now, not mine or yours or Seth's. Or even the man who owns this property."

"Who is he?"

"Our good friend Mr. Anonymous. He lives in Memphis, but he's dedicated this whole property as his own private preserve protected by a trust.

It's safe from development for a hundred years." She put the truck in gear. "In a hundred years, who knows if there'll be any animals at all, let alone human beings. Come on, y'all. Emma and I have patients waiting at the clinic."

They did. A dozen clients with dogs on leashes and cats in carriers waited in the parking lot.

"Thank you, Seth," Barbara said as he walked to his SUV.

"You really didn't need me."

"Yeah, but I would have if anything had gone wrong. You're the designated rescuer."

"Your mother's coming by to look at my babies this afternoon," Emma called to him. "If you get off in time, you're welcome to a glass of wine."

"Can I have beer instead?"

"Sure."

He nodded and drove away. Emma headed for the clinic and the madhouse she was walking into.

Would she feel the same sense of joy when she turned her babies loose?

Just so long as she didn't dissolve in tears of grief and loss. Or have hysterics with Seth watching. Men did not deal with hysterics well.

Around the corner of the building came a flash of wings and a loud squawk. "Oh, Mabel, knock it off." She shoved by the big Canada goose. "You're worse than a Rottweiler."

She still hadn't figured out how Mabel knew the difference between staff, whom she felt free to terrorize, nonclients, ditto, and clients. She never terrorized clients. Maybe she terrorized anyone who didn't show up with an animal or smelling of an animal. Emma would have to ask Barbara.

CHAPTER NINETEEN

"Thank you for inviting me," Mrs. Logan said. "I haven't been in this house since Martha died, but I did help her when she redid the downstairs. The ceiling was sagging. They had to put in a steel beam to carry the weight of the house. If it was built to any sort of code, it was a hundred years out of date." She patted the back of the old leather recliner beside the brick fireplace.

"It's a good house," Emma said. "I'm sorry I didn't visit more often after I became a teenager. I got caught up in other things. Right now it's been a godsend having someplace to get away from my family. My father's bound and determined to find me a job whether it's one I want or not. Red or white?"

"White, please." Mrs. Logan accepted a glass of Chardonnay. "Fathers are like that." She took a sip of the wine. "The older I get, the less I like really acidic wines with masses of tannins," she said. "Merlot puckers my mouth. This is lovely."

"Are you a connoisseur?" Emma asked. "I'm not, but I do try to listen to the guy who owns the shop in Memphis where I buy my wine. Then I get credit for being knowledgeable."

"I'm happy if it doesn't come in a box," Mrs. Logan said. "When can I see the babies? Seth says that's what you call them."

"Right now. Bring your glass."

Emma picked up a bag of apple slices and led Mrs. Logan around the house to the kennel. In late afternoon and after their nap, the little skunks were searching for an overlooked caterpillar or beetle and trundled happily around their enclosure. Peony fell into the wading pool and had to squirm herself out.

Mrs. Logan laughed. "They are precious! I've never been this close to a skunk before, but I've heard people make pets of them."

"After they've been neutered and had their scent glands removed," Emma said. "I don't think you'd want one in your house otherwise. But these, at least, are very loving to the people they know."

"Of whom I am not one. Am I standing too close?"

"Not yet. They're very straightforward about warning people away. First they bounce on their front paws and threaten you. If that doesn't clue you in, they turn around and spray. Of course, they aren't spraying yet, so you're good however close you are. For the time being, at least. Here, toss them a few apple slices." She held the door to the kennel open while Mrs. Logan tossed slices in. The skunks were off on the hunt immediately.

"Seth says they're supposed to be a secret," Mrs. Logan said. "I'm surprised the news hasn't leaked. He's usually such a stickler for rules, but he's always a pushover when it comes to the little ones. I never knew what I'd find in the carport or the kitchen when I got home from school in the afternoons." She paused. "I used to be a teacher before I retired."

Barbara had mentioned this. Emma nodded, as Mrs. Logan threw the remaining apple slices into the kennel, far enough out so the skunks would have to chase them. The two women meandered back toward Emma's front porch.

"I finally had to draw the line when Seth came home after school and put a couple of water snakes in his wading pool. I do not like snakes, poisonous or nonpoisonous." She sat on the porch swing, while Emma took one of the chairs across from her.

"You have no idea how startling it is to discover a baby beaver in your bathtub at six in the morning. They can only poop in water. That's when I changed to showers, although Seth was very good about scrubbing up after his menagerie." She walked her feet back and forth so the swing moved gently.

Emma wasn't certain what she'd imagined Seth's mother would be like. Her hair in a bun, glasses on a chain. Perhaps a little dumpling person in sensible shoes. Stereotype. Emma knew better than to expect stereotypes. Mrs. Logan's startling white hair set off her blue eyes. Bluer than Seth's, which were almost gray. She wore flat leather shoes, and her French manicure was immaculate. She made Emma as feel dowdy as she had at the café.

"More wine, Mrs. Logan? I'm afraid I didn't have time to bake any goodies, but I do have some bought'en Scotch shortbread."

"Yes to the wine, although this had better be my last glass. Having his mother up on DUI charges wouldn't help Seth's career. And I don't usually eat between meals. I have never been able to understand how the British can stuff themselves with sugar at afternoon tea. Oh, and please call me Laila. Isn't that the most awful name? Right out of the 1920s. It was my grandmother's name, so I got stuck with it." She wrinkled her nose. "Laila Logan. I've always hated it. Emma is a good, straightforward name."

"Also my grandmother's name," Emma said.

She topped up Mrs. Logan's wine. "I would've preferred something fancier. Sounds too Jane Austen."

"Bite your tongue. Nothing wrong with Jane Austen."

"You taught English?"

"I taught eighth grade, which means I taught everything. Eighth-graders still tend to like their teachers, usually the last year they do. The school I taught in does not put up with rudeness or bad manners. Our students have to do the work or they don't make the grades. We generally top the list in SAT scores in this area. It's difficult to tell at that age which children will graduate, but three-quarters of mine went on to college." She shrugged. "Half of them stayed to graduate from junior college at least, which is better than average. And, like Seth, a good many of them got free rides. He had both an academic scholarship and several offers of athletic scholarships."

"To play football?"

Laila laughed. "He's so big that coaches would take one look at him and try to turn him into a linebacker. Then they discovered he hated hitting people."

"So he went the academic route?"

"He always planned to go into veterinary medicine after he graduated. He'd already been accepted to the vet school at the University of Tennessee." She shook her head. "Unfortunately, he got married instead. Making a living had to take precedence. I hoped he'd go back to it, but I think he really likes his job now."

Uh-oh. So Mrs. Logan had not approved of Seth's marriage. Because the ex was the wrong woman, or because any woman who stood between Seth and what Laila wanted for him was the wrong woman? Andrea had warned her a long time ago that mothers of sons could be peculiar when it came to the women their sons married. "With luck I'll like Patrick's wife," Andrea had said. "Or I'll learn to suck it up and put up with her for the sake of the grandchildren they had better give me."

"Patrick, my half brother, has never been serious about any girl," Emma said. "He's seventeen and so handsome and sweet-natured they chase him constantly. Thank goodness he doesn't have a clue. We all pray he'll finish college and get a decent job before he falls in love."

"Doesn't necessarily happen that way, I'm afraid. Not that I think those two were ever truly in love. Clare was in love with the idea of being married to Seth. He was the best prospect around. I have always wondered if she convinced Seth she was pregnant. He would've done the gentlemanly thing. They had a very small wedding—not what

Clare envisioned at all. When she married that dentist in Nashville, she wore the big white dress and everything. Tacky for a second wedding, but she must've felt she'd missed out with Seth and decided to remedy the situation."

"So she wasn't pregnant?"

"Apparently not, thank God. There was no sign she'd had a miscarriage. At least after they married they put off having children. I have always believed in divorcing young, if you're going to divorce at all. No property to argue over, no children to cause nasty custody battles. Both partners can get on with their lives." She drained her wineglass. "Clare certainly has."

So as much as Laila wanted grandchildren, she was willing to forgo them if they had Clare for their mother.

"Tell me about *your* family, dear," Laila said.

Uh-oh, here it comes. Emma had her family statistics down pat after all the social interrogations she'd endured. She delivered them expertly.

"You've never married?" Laila asked.

"Not yet," Emma said.

"But you do want a husband and children?"

"If possible. I have—had—a job I liked. I hope I can get another that's just as good." She tried to keep the challenge out of her voice.

"I spent thirty years in the school system before I retired. I believe that every woman should have her own career and her own money. Women should never rely totally on a man." Laila ran her fingers through her white hair. "For one thing, you can't. Most of them don't seem to be reliable. My husband, Everett, certainly wasn't."

"We ran into Everett after dinner the other night," Emma said. *And speaking of unreliable husbands, how's that for an unfortunate segue?* Laila didn't seem to notice.

"That was the night Seth hung up on me." Laila laughed, but there was no amusement in it. "Poor man."

"Seth or your ex-husband?"

"Both. You know that old saw about emotion turning your hair white? It happens. I had auburn hair until my daughter drowned. Six months later it was white. I colored it for years, but when I retired I decided I'd let it go natural."

"It's beautiful."

"Makes me look old, but then, I am old. Well, oldish. I keep hoping Seth will forgive his father."

"You seem to have."

"I had help. Years of grief counseling. Seth would never talk to a counselor, never go to any of the grief groups. He said he wanted to forget it, but of course you can't, can you? If he could forgive himself, he might be able to at least tolerate his father. He refuses to admit Everett suffered, too."

"Guilt that he survived? That wasn't Seth's fault."

"Seth was supposed to go fishing with Everett and Sarah that morning. He was thirteen. That was the last thing he wanted to do on a Saturday. He took his bike and snuck off to town to play video games with his friends, but Everett made Sarah go. Because he was angry at Seth for avoiding him, I suspect. Everett tended to throw his weight around.

"Seth is certain that if he'd been there, Sarah would be alive today. There's no way of knowing, of course, but it's what bedevils him. He thinks he has to hate Everett. Otherwise, he'd have to acknowledge that he feels responsible for Sarah's death."

"You seem to have a good handle on the situation."

"I had professional help. Lots of it. I could talk about my own guilt. Sometimes it seemed that's all I did over and over—talk about my guilt."

"What could you possibly feel guilty about?"

"I knew Everett drank. We fought about it constantly. I knew he was demanding and controlling and wanted his own way. It was easier to do what he wanted and ignore the rest. I spent my time with my teaching, or trying to stand between the children and their father.

"That morning I had shopping to do. I always

did after teaching all week. I left before Everett discovered Seth was nowhere to be found. All I knew when I left the house was that the three of them were going fishing in our little lake. Everett promised he'd never drink in the bass boat. I've never known to this day whether he was drinking that morning or not, but he did admit he stashed the life jackets in the locker in the cockpit. Sarah was a good swimmer, but she knew she was supposed to wear a life jacket any time she was on the boat.

"That morning, she was so annoyed at being forced to go with her father that she didn't put one on. The lake was calm. Why bother?

"That lake is treacherous. It's small, but it drains into the Tennessee River. When the wind comes up, you can get whitecaps and straight-line winds and bad thunderstorms in ten minutes. You have to pay attention. Apparently Everett wanted to drive the boat down to one of his favorite fishing spots close to where the lake drains into the river. Several witnesses said he was driving the boat too fast for the conditions. When the storm came up, he didn't slow down. Then someone cut across his path. He swerved just as Sarah started down into the little cuddy cabin for a soda. She lost her balance and fell overboard. Everett swears he tossed her a life jacket, but by then she was gone. All the boats searched for her, but she never surfaced. When they found her body two days later, she had a gash on her forehead. The medical examiner thought she must have hit her head on her way over the side and knocked herself out long enough for her lungs to fill with water."

Emma saw that the hand holding Laila's wineglass was threatening to break the stem. She gently took it out of Laila's fingers.

"Oh, sorry," Laila said in surprise. "I've told that story so many times it's become a kind of myth. I think my grief is so deeply hidden now I can't actually touch it. I've walled it off. Otherwise, I don't think I could go on living, counselors or no counselors. Having Seth helps, of course. If only I could help him. I doubt he'll ever be free until he can deal with his feelings about his father. Deep down he either loves him, or he wishes there was something there to love but knows there isn't."

"How soon did you get a divorce?" Emma asked.

"The marriage was doomed the day Sarah drowned, but we held on for almost six months. Everett told me he'd stopped drinking, but I discovered he'd secretly started again. When I confronted him, he said he needed the alcohol to dull the pain." She shrugged. "The rest of us were in pain, too, but Everett only thought of his own.

Statistics say that most marriages don't survive the death of a child. Each parent thinks the other parent isn't grieving as much, doesn't miss the child as much, doesn't hurt as badly. Kind of an I'm-sadder-than-you thing. When Everett went back to drinking, I kicked him out. He's been trying to get back in ever since."

"Seth is worried it might happen," Emma said.

"He needn't be. I feel sorry for Everett, and I can be civil in a social situation, but I still can't stand to be in the same room with him for more than ten minutes at a time."

"Even though he says he's been sober for two years?"

"There is such a thing as a dry drunk," Laila said. "I think that's what Everett is, until and unless he can admit his responsibility for Sarah's death. He's always blamed the storm, or her lack of balance, or any other excuse he can come up with, including that it was all Seth's fault for not coming along."

"You're kidding."

"I wish I were. I warned him that if he ever so much as hinted anything like that, I'd make his life hell." She glanced down. "Oh, look at the time! I'm so sorry to have dumped all this on you. Seth said you were a good listener."

Emma followed her to her car.

Laila turned on her ignition, then lowered the

window. "Best of luck with your babies. Let me know when you release them."

Emma watched as she drove away. That was an interesting encounter. There was no reason Laila should have opened up that way unless she was asking for Emma's help.

Maybe it was time for Emma to be the rescuer. Could she be the "fixer" that would broker a truce between Seth and his father?

SETH FOUND EMMA scrubbing her pantry with disinfectant and spraying it with air freshener.

"You missed your mother by ten minutes," she said. She rocked back on her heels and brushed her damp hair out of her eyes.

"I stopped her on the road. She said she had a good visit."

"She's a lovely lady. With her white hair, she's like Martha Washington in jeans."

He laughed. "I'll tell her you said that. How are the skunks?"

"Digging anywhere they even dream there might be something to eat."

"They're pretty self-sufficient. We should be able to release them in a couple of days."

She came to her feet. "But they don't skunk yet."

"Close. Unless you want to pay someone to fumigate your house."

"Not if I can help it. How far does their spray reach?"

"Far enough. There are some great new shampoos that get rid of the odor on dogs. They work on humans, too. Better than tomato juice, which used to be the standard treatment for a skunked dog. That kind of shampoo isn't the kind of stuff you get at your local hair salon. Barbara keeps it in stock, but you don't want to use it unless you have to. Which reminds me, how's your job going at the clinic?"

"It's crazy, but I enjoy it. She's a good vet. She badly needs a partner, though. It's too much for one person. There's a new class graduating from UT vet school in June. She's going to set up some interviews to find a newly fledged vet to work with her. I've persuaded her to put an ad in the 'help wanted' section of the paper for a full-time vet tech. The girl she has coming in to clean in the afternoons can't give her any more hours, and I can't afford to work full-time for her. I have to concentrate on getting a real job that will pay my bills." She scrubbed the pantry door. "There, that should do it," she said.

That was as close as Emma had ever come to talking about her finances. She'd obviously been well paid in Memphis. Seth couldn't think of any jobs in Williamston or the surrounding towns that would come close. If she wanted to maintain her lifestyle, which no doubt she did, she'd look farther afield. Farther away from her little house. From him.

So why didn't he simply sweep her up in his arms and carry her off like in one of those old Westerns? Or *The Taming of the Shrew*? The problem with that particular play was that if the audience didn't know instantly that these two people were nuts about each other, it became a play about spousal abuse. He knew he was nuts about *her*, but he still didn't know how she felt.

There ought to be some way to get them both away from the continual demands that seemed to intrude every time they were alone.

Maybe tonight over Chinese food.

What he'd just said in his mind, he would never have said out loud. Not an option.

Watching Emma put away her cleaning supplies, he wondered what she'd do if he ran away with her. He chortled at the very thought.

"What?" she asked as she brushed her hair off her forehead. It was a gesture he'd grown fond of. He was fond of everything about her.

"Just picturing you as a Sabine woman."

"Where on earth did that come from? I can tell you right now, I would have removed the head from whoever was trying to abscond with me, and I'd have made his life hell until he took me home to my parents."

"I'll bet you would. How about if I bribe you instead? I picked up Chinese food on my way home."

"Goody. I never seem to get to the grocery store since I started working for Barbara. But I can't continue to rely on you to feed me."

"You can rely on me for anything you like." He'd feed her for the rest of their lives if she'd be a part of his. He'd faced down an angry black bear sow without turning a hair, but he couldn't tell this woman how he felt about her.

There were still the same problems. Emma was no less on the rebound. He was no better able to give her the life she deserved up here in the woods. Skunks were all well and good, but the symphony ball would appeal to her more. He didn't even own a tux, and he didn't think the rental places carried tuxes big enough for him.

"My favorites!" Emma said as she opened the cartons he'd brought. "Moo shu and lo mein and dumplings. How did you know?"

"Instinct. My favorites, too."

Her cell phone rang as she was getting out plates and chopsticks. "Drat!" she said. "It's my father. I have to take it. I'll be quick. You mind pouring the wine?"

She walked into the bedroom and shut the door. What was she saying to her father that she didn't want him to hear? Was the man arranging job interviews for her? Telling her how much Trip was suffering without her? Nothing good. He'd never met Mr. French, but he considered him a threat, seducing her back to his world and away from Seth's.

"Looks wonderful," Emma said as she slid into her chair a few minutes later. No mention of her conversation.

"How's your family?"

She ate a crab puff and drank some of the white wine Seth had found in her refrigerator. "They're fine. Daddy wants me to come for the weekend. He says someone wants to rent my town house. It's only for six months… Actually, my former fiancé, Trip, wants to rent it for his new girlfriend."

"How do you feel about that?"

"I said not just no, but *hell* no. She's some fancy new weather girl at one of the TV stations. I guess she wants to be certain the station plans to keep her before she buys a house, but I don't want her using my stuff while she's having a hot-and-heavy fling with my ex-fiancé." She put down her chopsticks and broke into laughter. When she finally calmed down, she said, "Now that's just creepy."

Not five minutes later, Seth's cell phone rang. He let it ring until Emma asked, "You going to answer that?"

He closed his eyes and sighed. "I'd really rather not." But he had to. They both knew it. "Excuse me," he said, then did what Emma had done and walked into the bedroom. The ID said the call was from the civilian night-duty clerk at the office. "Hello, Patsy, what's up?" Nothing good. Not at this hour.

"Just got a call from one of the cottages on the lake. There's somebody driving an ATV all over their property shooting off a shotgun."

Seth bet he knew exactly who that was. Good ol' Tyrell. So his wife hadn't managed to shut him down. This time he'd definitely be taken into custody if they could catch him. Patsy said she'd send the relevant info to his cell phone the minute she hung up. He waited until he had the address, then he dialed Earl and explained the situation.

"I'm helping Earl Jr. with his math homework."

"Okay, I'll handle it by myself."

"No, you won't. Drunks, ATVs and shotguns do not mix. I'll pick you up in twenty minutes. Hey, at least it gets me out of trying to help Earl. I don't remember any of that stuff."

CHAPTER TWENTY

TONIGHT, RIDING ON a high of lo mein and dumplings, Seth had hoped he could finally get some uninterrupted time with Emma. As usual, that wasn't going to happen. He explained to her only that there was a problem he and Earl had to handle. Might take a while. She walked him to the door.

"Thank you for dinner," she said.

He pulled her into his arms. She moved closer and wrapped her arms around his neck. He was hard as a rock and knew she could feel him against her. At the rate they were going, that was as close to sealing the deal as they were likely to get.

He hoped Mr. ATV came along peacefully. If the man resisted arrest, he might find himself with a black eye. Seth was not in the mood to forgive.

ALONE AGAIN, EMMA turned on her computer and started surfing the career opportunity websites, but the only jobs that sounded interesting were in places like Tulsa.

The problem was that she liked her previous job. But she also liked being here in her little house. If Seth were with her, it would be well-nigh perfect, small and decrepit as it was.

So much of her time in Memphis was spent on the professional part of her life. How many friends did she actually have who weren't part of that world? Most of the people she'd gone to school with were married with children. Right now Emma didn't fit in with them.

She and her friends at work talked almost exclusively about work, rather than their personal lives. They might go out for a drink occasionally, but not that often. And these days, maybe because they didn't want to be associated with someone who'd gotten fired, they certainly hadn't been heating up her internet with updates and gossip and asking how she was.

Still, she couldn't stay here, much as she might—in certain ways—want to. For one thing, she couldn't afford it.

She didn't want to walk away from Seth. Not that she saw him all that often. Every time they settled down, one or the other of them had to leave.

She finished cleaning up the kitchen, checked

on the babies and gave them some grapes, then went to bed. Alone again.

SETH WAS NO happier than Emma. When he climbed into the cruiser with Earl, he said, "I could learn to hate this guy."

"Hot date with Emma, huh?"

"Might have gotten hot. Didn't get a chance to find out."

Earl snickered. "You're crazy about her, aren't you?"

"*Crazy* is the word for it. Why couldn't I fall for some farmer's daughter who knows how to drive a combine and milk a Jersey cow?"

"She'd have bored you spitless. Now, Emma is something else, even if she does wind up in the azaleas."

"When she's playing with the skunks, she's not just beautiful, she's luminous. I wish she'd look at me the same way. My rivals are skunks?" He ran his hand down his face. "She's intimated that she needs a job soon. From what I saw at lunch, that Nathan guy would take her back if she wanted him to. Then there's her dear old daddy. Knows everybody who counts and wants her back in Memphis. I don't imagine he'd see me as son-in-law material."

Earl turned away from watching the road to gape at Seth. "We've gone from wanting to get

Emma into bed to marriage in one easy step? Hell, no, he doesn't see you as a possible son-in-law. I don't either. You know you're in line for a big promotion, but that would mean more time riding a desk. You'd hate it."

"Yeah, I would. I love the woods and the lakes and the animals. But if I took the promotion and a desk job, I could work in Memphis. That would solve one of my problems."

"I can just see you duded up in a tux at some fancy party."

"Hey, I'd look good in a tux. If I can rent one big enough."

"That Trip guy would eat you up and spit you out." Earl slowed down and cut his lights. "I think I hear our friendly neighborhood ATV."

Two *krumps* came from the woods to their right.

"Yep. That's a shotgun. Think he's shooting at us?" Earl asked.

"Put your vest on," Seth said.

"Aw, Seth…"

"I've already got mine on. Do it, Earl. Janeen would kill me if I got you killed."

"And Emma would kill me if I got *you* shot. Okay, let's see if Tyrell will come in peaceably. I'm gonna tell him that's what his wife wants. *I'd* stop what I was doing if she told me to. Hand me the loud-hailer."

In the end, their old friend Tyrell drove his ATV up to them. He had slung his shotgun down his back and seemed to be in high spirits. And very drunk.

"Hey, y'all," he said cheerfully. "I ain't doin' one thing wrong. No, siree. I got my legal deer in the freezer. Just blowin' off a little steam. I done paid my fines. Got me a new registration and all. Y'all want a drink?"

"Blowin' off a little shotgun is more like it," Earl said. "Folks do not like to have you digging ruts in their yards and shooting off guns in the middle of the night…"

"Aw, it ain't no middle of the night and I'm shootin' up in the air. But, hey, I'll quit. Don't want to upset folks." He nodded cheerfully and started to climb back onto his vehicle.

Seth stopped him. "Tyrell, how about you borrow my phone and call your wife. Tell her where you've parked this thing and then you'll take a ride into town with us. Tell her she can come get it and you tomorrow morning."

"I'm kinda tired. I'll just go on home and get me some sleep."

Earl raised his eyebrows. "I believe you'd better come with us, Tyrell. You can sleep in the car driving into town. Here, call your wife."

When his call was finished, Tyrell had sobered up considerably. He rolled his ATV onto the grass verge and climbed into the backseat of Earl's cruiser. Before the two men had taken their places in the front, Tyrell could be heard snoring softly.

By the time the paperwork was completed at the Williamston jail and Earl dropped Seth back at his house, there were no lights at Emma's.

His final thought before he dropped off to sleep was that the only way he'd ever get some alone time with her was if he kidnapped her.

CHAPTER TWENTY-ONE

THE STORM THAT had been predicted hit as he ate his breakfast. No tornadoes forecast, but six inches of rain and some strong wind with a warm woman. He had the perfect candidate, but her car was already gone from her driveway. The rain and wind were projected to continue all day and into the night. At least the poachers would be home. Nobody would enjoy hunting in this. Even the animals hunkered down.

His mother called on his cell to remind him to check on her cabin by the lake. "It shouldn't flood, high up as it sits," she said. "But I'd appreciate if you'd make sure nothing's leaking and there aren't any trees down."

"Not supposed to be that much wind," he said. "I'll check and let you know." He pulled on his rain gear on his way out the door. As he climbed into his SUV, he took a hard look at the kennel. The skunks should be safe, if miserable.

But six inches of rain was a lot of rain. He walked across the street, found the playpen on Emma's back porch, opened it, then set up food and water inside. He made three trips to carry the skunks under the porch roof and out of the rain. Bedraggled as they were, they seemed grateful. He zipped up the top of the playpen so they couldn't climb out and, satisfied that they'd be safe, left for his mother's cabin.

He drove past Barbara's clinic on his way to the lake. This must be one of Emma's days. Her car sat at the side of the lot to give the clients as much room as possible. Rain or no rain, the lot was already half-filled. He should call to tell her he'd moved the skunks, but he had plenty of time to do that before she got home.

The cabin was several miles past the clinic off the same road. At several points along the road, he could peer through the woods to glimpse the little lake the cabin sat beside. It didn't look happy either.

Sarah drowned in another small lake only a bit larger than this one.

Because it was small and shallow, it could kick up whitecaps fast. He turned his head so that he wasn't continually aware of it. Too many memories. He hadn't set foot in a swimming pool again until he'd been forced to swim laps in college as part of his athletic classes.

He found the cabin clean and dry. Lights worked, refrigerator was stocked with beer, wine and soft drinks. No mildew smell even in the bedroom. The sheets smelled fresh. He locked up, estimated that the waves were lapping well below the little bluff the cabin sat on and drove away.

That was what he and Emma needed. A private place where no one could find them. Now he just had to figure out how to manage it.

At noon he pulled up in front of the clinic. As he started to climb out of the SUV, the front door opened. Barbara and Emma walked out together. They must be driving into town for lunch.

He leaned across, opened the driver's side door and called out, "Barbara, you mind if I borrow Emma for a while?"

"Not at all."

"Now wait a minute," Emma said. "Barbara and I are going to lunch. Then we're shutting down the clinic for the rest of the day until the storm blows over."

"I'd rather stay here, open a can of soup and do paperwork. Go on. Enjoy," Barbara said.

"But..."

"Emma, please get in." He leaned across from the driver's side and shoved the passenger door wide. Emma braced herself against the door as the wind threatened to slam it.

"If we're going to lunch, why can't Barbara come?"

"Emma, for once in your life, would you please do as I ask?"

HE WAS STARING out the windshield, not even looking at her. Something bad had happened. Had to be. She slipped into the passenger seat, shut the door and fastened her seat belt. Outside, the first blast of rain hit the SUV so hard it rocked.

He turned right out of the parking lot—away from home, away from Williamston.

"Is somebody hurt? Your mother? Your father? Oh, Seth…" If not his family, then hers. She closed her eyes against whatever disaster was to come.

"Nobody's hurt."

"Thank God. Wait—my babies. I have to go take care of them! They could drown outside in all this rain."

"They're fine. I brought them up on the back porch out of the rain and put them back in the playpen with plenty of food and water."

"They'll climb out the top."

"No, they won't. I zipped it up. Emma, I promise you, they'll be dry and happy."

"Thank you for looking after them. But *something's* wrong. Why are you upset?"

He slowed down long enough to glance over at her. "I'm not upset at *you*. I'm mad at me, and it's about time I did something about it. Walking in on your lunch with that Nathan showed me that."

"You don't have to kidnap me. All you have to do is ask me to go with you."

"It was either kidnap you or go crazy. I'm crazy enough already."

"What is all this about? Talk to me."

He slowed down again. The steady whack of the windshield wipers on their highest setting wasn't as fast as her heartbeat. Even when she'd almost blown up the oak tree, he hadn't been angry. He hadn't laughed either. He accepted her fears and simply stepped in to help. He took her seriously, so this was serious. That was one of the things she loved about him.

Where did that come from? Neither one of them had ever mentioned *love*. Nobody fell in love in a week. And at this rate they weren't likely to. Suddenly, he wasn't the only angry one. "If there isn't any disaster, you have no right to snap like a bear with a sore toe. You say you're not mad at me, but I'm the only other person in this car, Seth. Talk to me, or I'll unkidnap myself and walk home in the rain."

"Assuming you could get out of a moving car without breaking your beautiful neck, you'd fall in a ditch and I'd have to drag you out. I promise I'll explain, once I figure out how to do it. I hope you'll forgive me, or at least cut me some slack in the meantime."

He kept his eyes forward and concentrated on

his driving. He was right about walking home and drowning on the way. So far they hadn't run into any truly flooded stretches on the road, but he'd slowed down to avoid hydroplaning.

They drove for twenty more minutes in silence. She didn't take her eyes off him, but his jaw seemed to relax the farther they drove from the clinic. Was that it? Something bad about the clinic?

Then he turned left, crossed a one-lane bridge and drove down a gravel road into a thick stand of loblolly pines. Ahead, the normally placid lake roiled with whitecaps. On a bluff a dozen feet above the lake stood an A-frame cabin all by itself among the trees that swayed, whipped in the wind and threatened to come crashing down on it.

Seth stopped the SUV but left the keys in the ignition where she could reach them if she chose.

"I knew this was a bad idea," he said. He rested his forearms on the steering wheel. "I don't know where my head was. I'm sorry. I'll take you back home right now."

"In this storm?" Emma asked. "Just tell me where we are and why you're doing this. Whatever it is, we'll work it out. My father always tells me I can't screw anything up so badly that we can't unscrew it. We'll unscrew it together."

He gave a short bark of laughter. "Little does

your father know. Okay, if you're still game, come on."

He climbed out of the SUV, ran down the flag-stone path, up three steps to the front door, un-locked it and held it open for her. "Sorry," he called, "I don't carry an umbrella."

"Now you tell me." She ran after him, followed him inside and leaned back against the door after he'd closed it. "We're wet," she said.

"You think?" For the first time he smiled. It was tentative. He was apparently still not certain of his reception. "I'll light the fire."

"In May? We won't melt if we dry off natu-rally. Got any towels handy?"

He disappeared through what was obviously a bedroom door and emerged with a big armload of towels. She grabbed one and went to work on her hair.

When it was semidry, she looked around, tak-ing in her surroundings. The main area was an open room furnished with comfortably shabby furniture, the kind of furniture that had outlived its first life, but could endure sand and damp and not complain too much.

The entire back wall, the one facing the storm and the lake, was entirely made of windows. A river-stone chimney and fireplace covered most of the wall that backed up to the pinewoods. An unlit log fire was already laid.

"This is charming," she said. "What is this place? Who does it belong to?"

"My mother. Actually, it belongs to me, too, but I never use it. She spends almost every weekend here with her friends playing bridge and swimming when the weather's too hot to breathe in town."

"I hope she's not driving out here alone in this storm."

He shook his head and toweled off his head and arms. "Nobody else is coming." He tossed the damp towel over the counter that divided the great room from a small galley kitchen.

"This is laid out a lot like The Hovel," Emma said.

"It should be. Martha borrowed the layout when she redid her living room. There's a master bedroom and bath in there." He pointed behind Emma. "And a loft upstairs that sleeps six. My mother had it built after she moved from the house I grew up in to her condo. She said she had to have someplace away from town where she could be alone. Sounded like a good idea, so we did it. I lived here after Clare and I separated, but it's really too far from town for easy commuting, so I moved into the house across the street from you."

"I love this place." She turned and walked over

to him. "But why all the subterfuge? Why not just tell me you wanted to drive out here?"

He ran his index finger gently down her cheek. "I wanted someplace different, perfect. With nobody else around."

She caught her breath, felt her heart speed up. "We don't seem to do perfect too well, do we?"

"At least I got the nobody-else-around part right." He slid his arms down to encircle her waist. "Whatever happens, out here we won't get phone calls we don't make, visitors we didn't invite, emergencies we have to drop everything for…"

"But aren't you on call?"

"I am officially off duty. Only Earl knows how to get me."

"Can you do that?"

"More often than I do. Mostly I don't mind when I get called out. The others have families. Not so easy for them to go out at four in the morning to chase some idiot jacklighting deer. Usually I don't have anything better to do. Tonight Earl can handle problems." He held her away from him. "The other day when I found you having lunch with your old boss, I had a sudden desire to toss him out of the café and boot him and his fancy car back to Memphis."

"You were jealous of Nathan? That's silly. He's my boss—*was* my boss—not even truly a friend.

If he was a friend, he wouldn't have fired me the way he did."

"He's important to you. He's everything you're used to. Everything I can't touch in your life. I worried all night. Finally I decided I had to get us away." He brushed his hand across her forehead. "You are so beautiful."

"I look like a drowned rat."

"Wet or dry doesn't matter. When you banged on my door that first night, you looked worse than a drowned rat and sounded meaner than a junkyard dog, but I knew I was a goner right that minute. Makes no difference how hard I try to deny the way I feel, I'm stuck with it, and it keeps getting worse. I thought if I got us away somewhere without people and animals and responsibilities, I could tell you..."

"What took you so long?" she whispered.

She melted into his arms. Didn't matter that they were wet to the skin—everywhere their bodies touched, they generated their own heat. He lifted her up, kicked the bedroom door open, carried her inside and set her back on her feet.

"This is going to happen, isn't it?" she whispered. Their eyes met and held.

"Only if you want it to. Do you?"

In answer, she peeled off her wet sweater and dropped it on the floor, then began to unbutton his wet shirt. After the first two buttons, he yanked it over his head and flung it beside Emma's sweater.

She unfastened her bra and added it to the collection of wet clothes. "I'm cold. Maybe you should've lit that fire," she whispered.

He slid his lips down her throat to her breast. She shivered at the touch of his tongue on her nipple.

"Too late now," he whispered. "We'll have to create our own."

The rest of their clothes came off in a tangle until at last they lay naked, side by side.

The storm seemed to grow with their passion, their hunger to explore with tongues and fingers. When he moved away from her, she whimpered, until she saw him take a condom from the drawer of the bedside table. When he came back to her, driving her farther to that precipice, she clung to him as he slid into her.

Their bodies seemed to know without learning how to fit together, to pleasure, to savor. She matched him thrust for thrust, and when at last they came, they came together.

Emma felt as though she'd never breathe again. Seth moved beside her and gathered her into his arms, where her head fit into the hollow of his shoulder. She could feel his heartbeat slow as his muscles relaxed. She drew her hand down his chest to his stomach and below, simply to enjoy touching him, holding him.

"Oh, my," she whispered against his throat. "I don't think I can stand up."

"Then don't. Stay here. I'd offer to carry you, but I'm not sure I have the strength. I'd drop you."

"I'm not exactly a virgin. I thought I knew about sex," Emma said, "But what we just did is a whole other thing entirely—at least for me." She rose up on one elbow. "I want to do it again soon."

"Not without a couple of rare sirloins first," he said. "And maybe a couple fingers of Scotch."

"I hope you brought the steaks, because no way am I getting out of this bed to go to the grocery."

He curled a strand of her still-damp hair around his finger. "You're in luck. I brought a cooler in the back of the SUV with steaks and fixins, and Mom stocks a full bar for her bridge club." He reached down to the foot of the bed and pulled a thick down comforter over them.

"Ooh, lovely," said Emma. She cuddled against his side with her arm across his chest.

He felt rather than heard her laugh, and propped himself up on one elbow so he could look down at her. "What's funny?"

"I can't believe you actually kidnapped me," Emma said.

"Let's say I invited you."

"Forcefully, without telling me where we were going."

"If you'd hesitated, I'd have taken you home. I figured I could talk you out of having me arrested if everything worked out."

"And if I'd said no?"

"Then, like I said, I would've taken you home. I thought this was what we both wanted, but every time we got close, either someone would show up at your front door or the skunks would need you or I'd get called out to arrest somebody."

"Or I'd wind up in the azaleas."

"That, too. When that Nathan guy showed up at lunch with you at the café, it was all I could do to be civil to him."

"He's a nice man."

"He's a part of your life I can't share."

"Not *can't*. Don't. Just as I don't share how you chase poachers. Most people share only bits and pieces of their lives with each other. My stepmother and father are close, but there's plenty she doesn't know about his legal cases, and plenty he doesn't know about her volunteer work at the children's hospital. They love each other dearly, but they're very different." She paused. "I don't want anyone to try to absorb me, either."

He chuckled and kissed the top of her head. "Good luck to anyone who tries. One thing you learn working with wild animals—a fox may seem tame, but he's still a fox, just as your skunks are still skunks. Push their buttons hard enough, and they'll skunk you."

"Now I'm a skunk?"

"Parts of you are pure skunk, lady."

She slipped out of his arms, piled up the pillows that had landed on the floor behind her and leaned against them. "I never thought of it that way, but that's what Trip tried to do—make me into what *he* wanted, never mind what *I* wanted."

"You should've skunked him."

"Not a bad idea. You know," she said, "you and I had Sunday evening alone after we found Bobby Joe. Nobody interrupted us then. I still ended up going to bed alone."

"I would gladly have made love to you while we were both covered in chigger bites and anti-itch lotion—well, maybe not gladly—but somehow the romance was missing."

She hit him with a pillow. A moment later they

were rolling around on the bed laughing. Until the laughter stopped. "Kiss me," Emma whispered.

He smiled down at her. "The heck with the steaks."

CHAPTER TWENTY-TWO

By MIDNIGHT THE storm had blown itself out, but left a chill in the air more like early April than mid-May. Seth lit the fire. He kept several changes of clothes in the loft, so he didn't have to wear his damp ones. Emma borrowed one of his sweatshirts that hung to her knees. She laid their damp clothes over a couple of rocking chairs in front of the fire. They'd be dry by morning.

They microwaved a couple of potatoes while Seth pan-broiled the two steaks. Emma set up a picnic in front of the fire.

"You do know this was a crazy thing to do," Emma said. "Whatever possessed you?"

"You possessed me," he said and slid his fingers down her back. "You ought to realize by now that I don't handle frustration well. But you'd just walked out of another relationship, and I didn't want to take advantage while you were vulnerable."

"Shoot, getting fired was worse than discovering Trip's infidelity. I'm usually smarter than that." She took their empty plates to the sink, rinsed them and stacked them in the dishwasher. She walked over to the window wall. "Look, Seth. After all that rain and wind, the clouds are gone. We've got most of a moon."

He joined her, wrapped his arms around her. She leaned back against him with her hands clasped across his arms to hold him close. "You can kidnap me anytime," she whispered.

IN THE MORNING, he dropped her at the clinic to pick up her car, then followed her home. The babies were snuggled together in a corner of the playpen, but tried to climb out when they saw Emma and Seth. Emma filled their food and water dishes in the kennel and Seth helped her return everyone there. The ground was wet, but their elevated nest box was almost dry. The minute they were set back inside, they began patrolling to see if anything had changed.

"I have to dress and get back to the clinic," Emma said.

"I'm going to be late for work if I don't do the same." He took her in his arms and kissed her—the mind-blowing variety. "If I take you into town for dinner, can we have a sleepover at your house tonight?"

"Don't bother to bring your jammies," she said, and sent him off.

Barbara was the soul of discretion. She didn't

ask for an explanation of Emma's sudden disappearance. Emma didn't give her one. She did, however, find herself singing a love song to a bloodhound that came in for his rabies shot. Until the bloodhound decided to join her in song. The whole waiting room broke into laughter, then applause. Emma blushed to the roots of her hair.

It was her day to bring lunch. In Barbara's office she laid out bowls of gazpacho, which didn't have to be heated, added ham-and-cheese baguettes. As they sat down, Barbara said, "Pleasant evening?"

"Very, thank you." She glanced out Barbara's window. "Look!" In the wading pool in the backyard Mabel paddled proudly ahead of six fat goslings.

"I always said Mabel had the morals of a goose," Barbara said. "Come on." They pulled on their Wellington boots and slipped out the back door.

Mabel squawked, hopped out of the pool and led the goslings back to her nest box, where they burrowed under her.

"Oh, shoot, we'll have to lock them up at night," Barbara said. "Or the coyotes will get them sure as this world. She can't protect them all. All right, old lady, we'll look after your babies." She tossed a handful of corn into the feeder. Mabel attempted to keep her goslings under control while she scarfed up the food. "I wonder who the daddy is," Barbara said. "Got to watch out for those traveling men. Get you in trouble every time."

"I thought geese mated for life," Emma said.

"He may come back. Or he may be in somebody's freezer."

"Barbara! Bite your tongue."

"That's why we do what we do to protect the little ones. When are you planning to release yours?"

"Seth says in a couple of days. I'm going to worry myself to death."

"They can protect themselves better than most."

"I wish I knew what I was doing," Emma said. "I want to learn. You don't have time to teach, and I don't know any of the other rehabilitators."

"Take the classes."

"What if I go back home before I'm finished?"

"Then finish at home. There are classes at the zoo among other places. Plenty of things you can do. Even specialized things like working with raptors—although that's a whole other licensing process."

"Where do I find classes locally?"

"The fish and game people run classes at Saint Andrews Church parish hall in Williamston. Go to an orientation. See if you like it. While you're working here and deciding what you want to do, I think you'll find it interesting. Somewhere on my desk I have a schedule of classes. Seth and Earl often teach at least the first couple of nights, although I don't think it's fair for you to seduce the instructor to improve your grade."

"I would never seduce Earl."

"Janeen will be thrilled to hear that. But there's another instructor."

"He's fair game."

That evening Emma took a chair out to the yard to sit beside the skunks. She had so few moments left with them. They already paid very little attention to her, but they made no threatening moves. After all, she was still delivering their food. While she was enjoying them, she called home. This time Catherine answered. "Emma! When are you coming home? We haven't seen you for *ages*."

"A couple of weeks isn't ages. How are you and Patrick?"

"He's driving me crazy. He's got a dozen girls calling him every night. And they all want me to tell him how wonderful they are. OMG! The girls are supposed to get the beauty in the family. All I got is brains. He's got brains *and* beauty."

"You're beautiful."

"I'm not popular. You know what that's like."

"You *are* popular."

"I play chess. I'm a geek. You weren't popular either. Oh, sorry…"

Emma laughed. "I wasn't popular in high school, but I caught up in college. Don't sweat it, baby sister. As to when I'm coming home, who knows? Maybe never. I really, really like it here. I like the people and the informality and not having to dress up all the time. I have not put on a pair of panty hose since I got here."

"I'll bet there's a guy, isn't there? Who is he, Emma? What does he do? Is he big and gorgeous? You and I are too tall to mess with short guys."

"Yes, there is a guy. He's my neighbor across the street. Yes, he is big and gorgeous. He's a game warden."

"A what? You're not serious. Daddy will have kittens. He is such a snob."

"It's not serious. Yet. Maybe never. Remember, Daddy endorsed Trip the first time I brought him to dinner. Some track record *he's* got."

"Trip tried to hit on me once."

"Catherine, are you sure that's what it was?"

"Of course I am. Not hard. Big-time flirty. I'm almost sixteen and taller than you. I shut him down."

"Don't tell Daddy. He'll kill him."

"Duh. Can Patrick and I come up in a couple of weeks when school is out?"

"One of you will have to sleep on the couch or bring a sleeping bag. Besides, I may be back home by then. For a visit anyway."

"For real? Oh, I got a call on the other line." She dropped her voice to a whisper. "It's a boy. Bye."

Emma clicked off the phone. Had she made an error confiding in her sister about Seth? Catherine tended to tell Andrea everything. What Andrea knew, Daddy knew.

David French didn't realize he was a snob, but everyone else did. Well, he could just suck it up. Seth was a truly fine man—smart, kind, compassionate. He did what he liked and was good at it. About time her father started recommending guys based on merit rather than Dun & Bradstreet ratings.

CHAPTER TWENTY-THREE

DAVID FRENCH CALLED at eight thirty the next morning to tell her all too casually that he was driving up to see her and asked that she make a reservation for lunch at a nice restaurant.

When Emma stopped laughing, she said, "I'll fix sandwiches for lunch. Reservations not required."

"Why don't you invite your neighbor to join us?"

"I doubt he'd be available."

"I always enjoy meeting your friends. What's his name?"

"I didn't tell Catherine, did I? So you don't know."

"Why didn't you tell me you were seeing someone local? And his name is?"

"First, because it's none of your business who lives across the street from me. Second, his name is Seth Logan. He's a game warden, as I'm sure you heard."

"Ah, yes. Interesting job, I'm sure. I would enjoy meeting him."

"I'll see what I can do."

Or not. She called Seth, told him her father was coming and said that if he wanted to drop by for a drink midafternoon, he was welcome. She didn't offer lunch. It wasn't that she was ashamed of what Seth did. She was proud of him and his job; he was the finest man she knew. He was also, unlike Trip, a gentleman.

She simply didn't want him to endure a whole lunch of "What are your career plans?" "Do you always intend to live in Williamston?" Blah, blah, blah. And the life Emma lived in town and her town house and her job and her friends and blah, blah, blah. Not doing it.

Not getting the linen napkins out either. Paper was fine.

Daddy arrived at one. He always preferred a late lunch. Emma had been snacking since eleven thirty. She took up some time by showing him Peony, Rose and Sycamore, although he chose not to toss them any treats.

"My dear girl, what have you been up to?" He laughed. "You can't seriously consider trying to live on the salary from this Joe job at a veterinary clinic and raising skunks. I'm sure it's fascinating, but..."

Emma loved her father and knew he loved her. She knew he wanted what was best for her. The difficulty arose when what he thought was best wasn't what Emma thought was best. If she'd been a different sort of person she'd have accepted his suggestions. She wanted to live up to his expectations, but she couldn't. The time since she'd come to The Hovel was the happiest and freest of her life. And now there was Seth, the most wonderful, caring man she'd ever known.

As she poured the coffee, she heard Seth's SUV pull into her driveway. The car door slammed and a moment later he was at the front door.

"God, he's immense," her father whispered.

Actually, the two men seemed to take to one another. Daddy was seriously interested in what Seth did. They shared golfing and fishing and boating and basketball. Emma was reduced to waitressing, keeping the coffee topped up and filling Seth with shortbread cookies. He handled Mr. French's questions with aplomb.

When Seth left to go check out a problem at one of the marinas, the two men shook hands.

"He seems like a nice young man," he said as they watched Seth drive away.

"Don't patronize either of us, Daddy."

He draped his arm around her shoulder. "Emma, are you pregnant? If that's what all this is about, you have choices. You do not have to marry this man."

She blinked. "Pregnant?" She burst out laughing. "No, Daddy, I am not pregnant. And who said anything about marriage?"

"He's crazy about you. You are certainly a catch in every respect. If he doesn't want to marry you, he's a fool, and I don't think he's any kind of a fool."

"So what would happen if we were to get married? You'd disown me?"

"Don't be silly, Emma, of course not. I would do everything in my power to move him into a career that was worthy of him. He wanted to become a veterinarian, didn't he? Or there's always law school."

"A job worthy of *you*, you mean. Watch it, Daddy, I'm getting close to tossing you out of my house."

"Be sensible. What sort of life would you have with him? He seems like a decent, competent man. He obviously cares for you. I like him. But liking a man doesn't make him right for my daughter. You can do better. I know Trip disappointed you…"

"You might say that."

"But he offered you the life you're used to with people you've known for years. If you marry Seth, you're looking at maybe fifty years or more of living in the middle of nowhere with a man who may or may not come home on time or at all. A man who's in danger a good deal of the time. What do you share when he's at home? Great sex? You've heard the old story about the jar of beans."

"One of your lawyer jokes?" Emma asked.

He patted her arm. "The day you get married, you start putting a bean in the jar for every time you make love throughout the year. The next year and forever after, you remove one bean from the jar for every time you make love. Most people die without ever emptying the jar."

"Who do *you* think would be right for me, Daddy? The CEO of a Fortune 500 company? We marry, he cheats during our honeymoon, then six months later the company goes bankrupt and he has a stroke that leaves him paralyzed. And impotent."

"Hardly likely. CEOs have good doctors."

"That isn't funny, Daddy. I want to marry a man I'd still love and want to be with if all those things happened. After Momma died, did you think, 'I wish I'd never met her'?"

"Of course not! I'm grateful for every moment we had together, just as I'm grateful for every moment Andrea and I have. Nobody knows what's coming down the pike. All I'm saying is that you have to play the odds. Start as you mean to go on. This—" he waved a hand at the little farmhouse "—is no way to start."

"I don't think I've been truly happy since

Momma died. I kept feeling it was my fault that she left us, Daddy."

"I have heard that's a fairly standard reaction among children who lose a parent early either to death or divorce. You know now that isn't true, don't you?"

"That was then. I couldn't figure out who I was without her. I wanted to be who you wanted me to be so you wouldn't miss her so much. I was scared all the time that I wasn't good enough, that I was letting you down. I kept going because I was afraid not to. When I'm with Seth, I *do* know who I am. I'm not scared I have to be somebody else. He sees me and loves me anyway, just as I love him."

He put his hands on her shoulders, began to speak, but she shook her head to stop him.

"I can't be that person I was, not anymore. I'm happy living where I'm living, doing what I'm doing, and doing it with Seth."

"What about money?"

"If we need money, I'll go make some. I still can, you know. That skill hasn't gone away because I fell in love with Seth. I'm happy with my small life with my small animals and my large lover. Whose babies I really *do* want to have. I've lived my life scared. For the first time in what seems like forever, I'm not scared."

"And if something happens to your pipe dream?"

"Then we'll do something else. Together."

He enfolded her in a hug. "Let me go say good-bye to your funny little babies and I'll go home to Memphis. Whatever happens, I love you."

"I'll put the dirty dishes in the dishwasher and then I'll join you. Here, toss them some grapes. They love grapes."

She finished wiping the kitchen counter and hung the dish towel up to dry when her father yelled, "Emma! Help!"

Oh, Lord, he's had a heart attack. I knew I shouldn't have upset him.

She jumped off the porch and raced around the house. And into a miasma of skunk scent so powerful her eyes closed of their own volition. She wadded up her shirt and covered her mouth and nose. "Oh, God! You've been skunked!"

He had fallen back on the grass. Emma grabbed him under the arms and dragged him out of the odor zone. Their eyes were streaming. Emma got the garden hose, turned it on and held the spray so she could wash her eyes, then gave it to her father. He coughed, pulled his immaculate linen handkerchief from the pocket of his chinos, wet it and held it against his eyes and nose.

"Get farther back in the yard." Emma flew into the house, picked her cell phone off the kitchen counter and called Seth. "I don't know how it happened, but Daddy's been skunked. We need help."

"Ambulance?"

"He's not hurt, he's skunked. What on earth should I do?"

"I'll be there in ten minutes."

CHAPTER TWENTY-FOUR

"DADDY, WHAT DID you do?" Emma held her hand across her nose and mouth. Not that it did much good. The entire yard, porch and kennel smelled like skunk.

"Nothing, I swear. Stay away from me. They only got my bottom half, but I have to get out of these trousers right now." He wrinkled his nose. "And burn them. But I can't drive back to Memphis in my undershorts."

Seth pulled into her driveway, jammed on his brakes and flew over to her father. "Sir, are you all right? Do you need an ambulance?"

"Young man," he asked Seth, "do you have any sweats you could lend me? I don't guarantee to return them in wearable condition."

"Sure. I'll be right back. How about some socks? Can you drive in socks? I don't think you'll want to spend a couple of hours in your car wearing those tennis shoes. My shoes would be too big. Your clothes need to be double-wrapped in garbage bags and stuffed into your trunk until you can dispose of them somewhere they won't stink up the neighborhood."

"My leather upholstery will never be the same."

Seth started across the street. "Emma, I'll call Barbara, tell her we need all the de-skunk shampoo she has. I'll bring some sweats, then I'll go pick up the shampoo from the clinic." As he ran across the road, he was dialing his cell phone.

"Those little devils," David French said. "Look at them over there. Butter wouldn't melt in their mouths."

Emma walked around the house and sat on the porch step. When her father started to join her, she warned him off. "No, you don't. You stay out in the yard. Daddy, what did you do to annoy them?"

"It was only the one with the two stripes down its back," he said.

"That's Sycamore, the male."

"I was just kind of chatting to them when I saw an apple slice on the ground outside the cage door. I picked it up and started pushing it through the mesh. All of a sudden the one with two stripes was bouncing up and down on his front paws. I thought he was thrilled to get an extra treat. And then he swings around, up comes his tail and *pow*! He lets fly. I thought I was going to suffocate."

"You're lucky he didn't give you a direct shot to the eyes."

"I never thought I'd be grateful for bifocals. I dropped the apple slice, of course, on my side of the fence. I don't think that made him any happier. By that time the other two were headed in my direction with their tails in the air, so I slid back on my butt."

"Daddy, that bouncing thing they do on their front feet—that's skunk talk for 'go away or I'll l get you.' You didn't, so he did. Poor Daddy." She snickered.

"Will I be able to go home tonight? How long will I smell like this?"

"The shampoo should take care of it. Maybe not a hundred percent, but close enough so Andrea won't make you move into a motel. I have a guest room. It's not much, but it's yours if you want to stay tonight and go home tomorrow."

"Let's see how this skunk shampoo works before I decide. Thank heaven you were able to get Seth back. Look, can I please sit down? Bring me that chair from the porch. Phew! I can smell it in my hair. The little dickens didn't even get my hair. How come I can smell it?"

Emma brought him the chair, and he sank into it. He stayed six feet away from her.

"It's pervasive," Emma said.

"I would certainly agree. No doubt handy to have a man like that available."

"A man like that?"

"I see the way he looks at you. Be careful, Emma. You've had a bad few weeks, losing your job and Trip all at the same time. You may see Seth as a stopgap, someone to salve your wounded ego. I doubt he sees you that way."

"Please back off, Daddy. I don't run from someone like Trip to someone like Seth simply because he's close. He is a very, very good man. I could do a lot worse."

"Than this?" Her father sounded incredulous. He waved his hand to take in everything from Seth's house to Martha's. "This is not your world, Emma. You might as well move to Alaska and live in an igloo."

"I could never eat whale blubber. Don't get so uptight, Daddy. I like this life, but I'm not tied to it. This is the first vacation I've had since I graduated from college."

"It's not supposed to be a vacation, and I hardly think those stinky little hooligans add to the ambience. Now Andrea tells me you have some part-time minimum-wage job at a veterinary clinic. How could you tell Andrea that and not me?"

"Because I knew you'd go ballistic. I was right. Here you are, trying to save me from myself. I *am* sending out résumés." Thinking about how few she'd actually sent, Emma crossed her fingers and swore to do better. "It's not you. I didn't want to talk to *anyone* but Andrea."

"Obviously."

Seth came trotting across the street and stopped beside her father. "These are the smallest sweats and socks I have. They'll still be too big, but they shouldn't fall off on your way home. Don't go running into some convenience store without holding them up."

"He stinks. Don't give them to *him*!" Emma said. "I'll take them until you get back with the shampoo. Thanks, Seth."

"All part of the service. See you in a few." He trotted back across the road to his SUV, then off toward Barbara's clinic.

By the time Seth delivered the shampoo and Mr. French was totally fumigated and scrubbed, Emma's whole house carried a mild scent of skunk.

"I've called Andrea to warn her," Mr. French said. "So I think I will attempt to drive home. May I take a bottle of that shampoo with me to use again after I get home? My garage can pick up my car at the house tomorrow to detail it. Assuming it can be done. Emma, Seth, I've had an…interesting afternoon."

The minute he drove around the corner of the road, Emma clung to Seth.

"Right here in the front yard?" he said and propped his chin on top of her head.

"Daddy was planning to go commando if you hadn't gotten back from Barbara's with the shampoo fast enough."

"You do realize what this means, don't you?"

She took a deep breath. "Their scent glands are functional."

"And they know how to use them. That means we can release them tomorrow before you go to work at the clinic."

"Do we have to?"

"You know we do. It'll be all right. I promise."

"Do you have someplace to let them go?"

He nodded. "All scoped out."

CHAPTER TWENTY-FIVE

FOR THE FIRST TIME, Emma spent the night in Seth's bed in Seth's house. He was pretty neat for a male living alone, and his house didn't smell even vaguely of skunk.

The morning dawned misty and foggy. Seth kissed Emma awake. She groaned. "Before you ask," Seth said, "this is good weather for the release. Plenty of smells close to the ground, plenty of edible creatures wandering around easy to catch."

"I don't think I can stand it," she said. "Let's do it far away, so there's no chance they'll find their way back home."

"I promise. You take a shower first."

"How big is your shower?"

"Big enough for two, but you're not going to con me. Go take your shower alone. I'll make coffee and toast a couple of English muffins so we'll have something in our stomachs."

"Which I may throw up," Emma said.

"If you do, you do. I know this is hard, but it has to be done."

"I know. Showering first."

CONVINCING THE THREE skunks to leave their familiar kennel for the big wire crate Seth had prepared for them took some doing. But sliced apples, their favorite treat, finally convinced Peony, the least adventurous, to climb into the crate. Sycamore and Rose followed.

None of them even patted a toe, much less raised a threatening tail.

"What if they get upset in your SUV?" Emma asked.

"It's smelled worse. Keep your fingers crossed."

"Are we going to the same place we released Barbara's deer?" Emma asked.

"Closer to Mother's cabin, but not so close that they'll make a nest under the front porch or the deck. I promise you, they won't look back, and if they do, they won't recognize us."

"You guarantee?"

"Absolutely."

Seth drove farther down the road, past the drive to the little A-frame. Emma had a lovely sense of nostalgia. What a beautiful night to remember. Maybe they could return in the summer and make love on the tiny beach.

Seth drove what seemed to Emma like a long distance before he turned off on another dirt road that led deep into a stand of mixed hardwoods and pines. When he pulled over, Emma's heart sank. This was it.

Seth carried the crate to the edge of the woods, a place where a small stream meandered toward the lake. "See? Plenty of water, lots of rotten logs. A good place."

"I suppose."

"You do the honors. They're your babies."

"Do I have to?"

"Yes, Emma, I think you do. Don't you?" He aimed the front of the crate toward the small stream.

Fighting tears, Emma undid the latch on the cage and opened the door. Just like the fawns, at first the skunks seemed not to want to leave home, and it was Peony, the one Emma thought was slow, who took the first tentative steps out of the crate and into the grass.

Rose and Sycamore rushed the door and followed Peony. At first they turned toward Emma. She climbed into the truck and shut the door—possibly the hardest thing she'd ever done.

Seth joined her. They sat in the truck while the little skunks gamboled and rolled around in the grass. Then, as if at a signal too high-pitched for humans to hear, they trotted off into the woods.

"They're gone," she said. "Will they come back looking for us?"

"Probably not, but if they do, we don't need to be here." Seth climbed out of the truck, shut the carrier and stashed it in the back.

He drove one-handed while he held Emma's hand. "You did fine," he said.

"Then why am I leaking all these tears?"

"Because you're human. Human beings are self-aware. We understand loss and remember to grieve. Most animals accept loss. The skunks do. I hate to say this, but what you need is a new foundling."

"No, I don't. I don't know what I'm doing. I'm no rehabilitator and I have no idea how to become one."

"You take classes, work with licensed rehabilitators like Barbara, and eventually you get your own license." He didn't say, *That's if you stay around long enough for it to matter.* "Earl and I are teaching an orientation class on Thursday evening. You'll have to drive your own car. Earl and I will have to stay afterward to go through the paperwork. Then I guess I'd better come by your house and check your letters of recommendation."

"I have to have recommendations?"

"In your case, I'm recommending you, so I guess you qualify."

THE ORIENTATION CLASS consisted largely of filling out paperwork and listening to Earl and Seth talk about how much work it took to become a licensed rehabilitator. The talk was probably intended to limit participants to people who were serious and not simply dilettantes looking for an alternative to bridge night. Earl and Seth treated Emma like any other prospective pupil. She kept her head down and gave no sign that she knew either of the instructors. Finally, everyone left completed registration forms on the desk at the front of the parish hall and filed out into the parking lot. Emma knew that if he could, Seth would come to her when he finished.

The parking lot was half-full and well lit. There was a man standing under one of the lights. As she got closer she recognized him.

It was Everett Logan.

She considered walking by him as though she hadn't seen him, but that would be rude. She did, however, keep walking and nodded to him as she passed. "Good evening, Mr. Logan."

"Everett, please." He gave her a big smile and fell into step beside her. Oh, great. Just what she needed, to land in the middle of the family feud when Seth might walk out of the building at any moment. If he found her consorting with Everett, he'd have a fit.

She watched Everett turn up his charm, but it didn't touch her. He seemed surprised by her lack of reaction. She dealt with people who were experts at charm. Everett wasn't even in the top ten.

"Were you waiting for me?" She walked toward her car, which was in a well-lit corner of the lot. They weren't alone, but she didn't feel comfortable talking to this man in public or anywhere else.

"Not exactly waiting for you, although Laila told me you were going to the orientation class. She said Seth was leading it tonight."

"You've spoken to Laila? About me?"

"Oh, Laila and I talk most days."

God, he sounded glib. She would've believed him, if she hadn't known how much Seth doubted his veracity. "I wasn't aware that you talked so often."

He chortled. Again, very charming, completely natural. But somehow off-putting. A performance for her benefit. One that he obviously hoped would be reported to Seth to prove that he and Emma were friends.

"Laila doesn't tell Seth we talk, of course. He's still carrying around a great big load of guilt. Laila keeps telling him it isn't good for him. But when you're as close as Laila and I have been for so many years…"

"I really must go, Mr. Logan." She turned and walked quickly to her car.

Behind her, he said, "Nice to see you, Emma. Come into the store sometime. I'll take you out for coffee."

She slid into her car, shut the door and hit the

ignition. Coffee? With Everett Logan? Alone? Not in this lifetime.

But hadn't she just been thinking about brokering a truce between Seth and his father? The nerve of the man talking about Seth's guilt with no mention of his own!

She wondered if he was drinking again. The AA pin meant he'd been sober for two years before he received it, but she had no idea how long he'd been sober since it was awarded to him. She didn't smell alcohol on his breath, but that meant nothing. He *seemed* stone-cold sober, but that meant nothing either. Plenty of people in her world could be one step shy of knee-walking, yet act completely sober.

She was coloring her Everett encounter with everything she had heard about Sarah's death from Laila and Barbara and Seth himself. Not from Everett, however. His view of life had very little to do with the facts as she'd been told them. She could usually tell the difference between fact and convenient fiction. But not always. She'd bought Trip's stories. Buying a colleague's stories got her fired.

What was there about Everett that struck her as creepy?

He was too clean. His clothes were too sharp. Suit and tie in Williamston? To work in a hardware store? He'd obviously shaved twice today

and used expensive aftershave. She hated aftershave. Seth smelled like soap. Even Trip hadn't
used perfumey aftershave.

Everett was too aware of her. Watching her
reaction to what he said as though he were reading a script and seeing if she'd recite the lines
he expected back at him. She hoped she hadn't.

She'd worked with clients like that and always
found them difficult. They tended to lie or stretch
the truth, often when the truth would have served
them better.

Where did Everett's money come from? Surely
not a sales job in a hardware store. Was Laila
giving him money? Seth would hit the ceiling
if and when he discovered that. Should Emma
suggest it? And tell him about her meeting with
Everett?

She shrank from telling Seth. Not her business. But if she neglected to tell him and he
found out...

She loved Seth. No way could she allow him
to be taken advantage of. Or Laila either.

Maybe she *would* stop in at the hardware store.
She wouldn't go so far as to have coffee with
Everett, though. But she would call Laila to see
if she really did speak to Everett almost every
day. Seth might see even that as a betrayal. After
all, his mother hadn't told him. Why? What was
Laila afraid of?

Or maybe Emma didn't want to know. If she didn't know, she wouldn't have to decide whether or not to tell Seth.

Emma drove home alone and went to bed alone. The house no longer held the faintest scent of skunk. But it felt very empty without Seth.

She still missed her babies. Seth was right. She needed another foundling. Would she actually sign up for the animal rehabilitator class? It wouldn't be fair to start the course, take a place that might have gone to someone who was totally committed and lived in the area, then give the whole thing up if she decided to go home to Memphis.

Seth had never said he loved her, never asked her to stay, never asked whether she even wanted to stay. The old-fashioned romantic ideal should have morphed from a leisurely courtship with mind-blowing sex while she found a great job in Williamston at the same salary she'd had in Memphis or close to it. Something with a career path to status in the company. Something as much fun as working for Nathan had been—most of the time.

Eventually after she and Seth knew each other well, they'd marry. She could redo Martha's house and rent it out. Maybe enlarge Seth's house. Restore the overgrown pasture, clean the little pond and replace the roof on the barn. They could rent out that land. Wouldn't bring a great deal of income, but then she didn't need a closet full of evening dresses up here.

And she could do her own nails.

Over lunch with Barbara the next day, she decided to tell her about running into Everett. "He was waiting for me," she said.

"What did he want?"

"To ingratiate himself with me. I have no idea why."

"He knows about you and Seth."

"What about me and Seth? Yes, we spend a lot of time together, but nobody's mentioned anything formal. Neither one of us is…"

"Bull. If this 'uncommitted' relationship were to break up, which one of you would have to move? Could you keep living across the street from Seth? How would you feel if he brought another woman home?"

"He has every right to do that."

"If you brought another man home, he'd probably break down your door and toss the poor guy into the pond. And feed him to the turtles. Based on what I heard from Velma, he considered doing it to your friend Nathan."

Since Seth had admitted he'd been jealous of Nathan, Emma couldn't contradict her.

"He wants you to stay, Emma. He won't pressure you. You're going to have to tell him, not the other way around."

"My father keeps saying I need to look at this logically. So, logically, Seth wouldn't be up-rooting his life, or giving up anything—not his friends, his career or even his house. I would be giving up everything I've worked for. I'd have to sell my town house instead of renting it, and not see my friends or my family as often. And Seth definitely hasn't asked me to stay, or even asked whether I'm thinking of staying. It's the big pink elephant in the room."

"What do *you* want?"

"Time. Time I don't have. I thought I was in love with someone else very recently. I wasn't. He certainly wasn't in love with me. How can I be sure that what I feel for Seth is love? And how does that fit with the reality of living in a world where I have to make a *living*? Hate to tell you, Barbara, but this job, as much as I appreciate it, won't pay my bills for long."

"Oh, for Pete's sake, stop overanalyzing! What do you *feel*?"

"That I don't know how *he* feels."

"Ask him."

"'Hey, Seth, are you in love with me and what do you want to do about it?' I couldn't get up the nerve to do that on my best day."

"What's the worst that can happen?"

"Okay, how's this? 'Gee, Emma, we have great sex, but I'm not interested in anything else. So long. I'll give you a call the next time I'm in Memphis. Maybe we can hook up.'"

Barbara laughed so hard she choked on her coffee. "I'll be darned if you're not insecure. When I met you I thought you were the most together woman I'd met in ages. And here I find you're every bit as scared as the rest of us."

"I try not to let the bastards see me sweat, okay? But, yes, I am insecure. That happens when a kid loses a parent early, the way I lost my mother. I do not trust life. Better not to expect permanence."

"Seth lost his sister. Does that mean he has the same permanence issues?" Barbara asked. "If so, you both have to get over it, or I'll never be a godmother."

The next day was one of Emma's at the clinic. Spring rain sluiced down so hard that even Mabel stayed in her goose house warming her goslings. So far, motherhood had not improved her temperament.

In the few quiet moments when she was working at the clinic as she was today, Emma had streamlined the clinic's computer system to organize appointments and keep up with billing clients. After she sent an orange tabby back to surgery to be spayed, she was free to answer the clinic phone on the first ring, the way she preferred. It wasn't always possible.

"Good morning, Carew Veterinary Clinic," she said.

"Emma, good morning! Beautiful day for ducks, isn't it?"

Everett Logan. Damn. Several times in the last few days his name had come up on her call log. She'd ignored the calls. This time he'd blocked the caller ID. Sneaky. "Mr. Logan, how can I help you?" Not just cool, but cold.

"You recognized my voice! How about that. I'm flattered. We're having a slow day at the store. I wondered if you'd join me for lunch."

"What? Where? In town?" She wanted to shout, "Are you crazy?" She took a deep breath and said with what she hoped was aplomb, "I'm sorry. That's not possible."

"You don't have to worry that we'd run into Seth. I happen to know he's in Nashville in a budget meeting all day and maybe tomorrow. Didn't he tell you he'd be gone?"

"Nashville is hardly 'gone,' Mr. Logan." She wanted to say, *Don't you play gotcha games with me. I've won against the best.* "Nonetheless, Mr. Logan…"

"Please, call me Everett. I'm not that much older than you are, you know." He chuckled.

She wanted to tell him, *You darned well are.*

This was becoming a multilayered conversation. She didn't like any of the layers. "We never leave the clinic at lunch, Mr. Logan." That was a lie. Both she and Barbara did leave from time to time. Everett Logan didn't need to know that, although somebody had probably told him.

She'd taken Nathan to lunch at the café, for example. But she hadn't actually been on the clinic schedule to work the day Nathan showed up.

"I could pick up some sandwiches and come to you."

"Why would you want to drive all the way out here to have lunch with me?"

He actually chortled. Did he think he'd won?

"I want to get to know you. After all, if things keep going the way they are, you and I will be kin."

What a horrible thought. "No. Do not come out here, do not pick up sandwiches. For future reference, this is a business phone for the use of our clients, not for personal calls."

"We have a cat at the store. Maybe I can borrow her." Again, he chortled.

She sighed. Okay, no more Ms. Nice Guy. "Mr. Logan, do not borrow a cat, do not bring sandwiches, don't call here on this phone. I intend to continue to call you Mr. Logan, and unless you get off this phone, I will hang up on you."

"Come on, honey, lighten up. I'm well aware that you and my son are…shall we say, close.

Laila says you're good for him. It's not good for a man to live alone. I'm on your side. I'm really a very nice person."

Oh, Lord, he was drinking. She heard it in the precise way he spoke. She didn't get angry often. She usually didn't get mad about injuries to herself, only to her family and friends. Although the last time she'd been angry was when she discovered Trip's infidelity. But this man was trying to injure the man she loved, to interfere with his peace of mind and to take advantage of Seth's mother, who she hoped would grow to be her friend.

Since there were still three clients in the waiting room with their animals, Emma dropped her voice. "First of all, Mr. Logan, go find an AA meeting. And take off your sobriety pin. I can hear over the phone that you don't deserve it."

"I don't know what you mean."

"Of course you do. I am completely serious. Do not attempt to get in touch with me, or I'll tell Laila and Seth that you're drinking again at eleven in the morning. How can you do this to Laila? She wants you and Seth to at least be polite to each other, but that's not possible so long as you don't acknowledge your responsibility for your own child's death."

He started to break in. "Listen—"

"No. *You* listen. *You* broke the rules, not Seth

or Laila or even Sarah. As a parent you were responsible for *obeying* the rules. Your daughter was a child. Seth was a child. Sarah had to do what you said, even if it cost her life. You were drunk and driving crazy and sitting on your life jackets. No wonder Seth believes in rules. You break them because you think you can get away with anything if you smile big enough. Well, you can't."

"I have an illness…"

"You're the only one who can fix that, and I don't see you giving it much of a shot. Mr. Logan, go to a meeting." She narrowly avoided slamming down the phone. She sat there trying to keep from hyperventilating. Her hands were shaking.

The two cats and one dog waiting with their owners didn't eavesdrop, but Emma knew their owners certainly did. They studiously avoided looking at Emma. And wouldn't that little exchange make the rounds before nightfall?

She shouldn't have spoken to Everett like that, but she couldn't help herself. Everett would call Laila before Emma could. Lord only knew what Seth would say, because Laila would tell him Everett's version of their conversation.

Emma had no intention of calling Laila. And if Everett showed up at the clinic with sandwiches and a borrowed cat, she'd set the police on him.

While she and Barbara were eating lunch together, as they now did most of the days Emma worked at the clinic, Emma's cell phone rang. Her heart turned over when she saw that Seth was calling. Then she realized she was listening to a voice message and not to Seth. Well, better than nothing, although she'd have preferred to talk to hm.

"Hey," he said. "I'm in a meeting in Nashville. We're going into a working lunch, so I don't have time to talk. I'm sorry I didn't say anything earlier, but this came up at the last minute. I had to come home and pack after you left for the clinic. I got Mother on my way out of town, but I missed you.

"I doubt I'll get back tonight. We'll probably work late." His voice dropped to a whisper. "This is not the way I planned to spend the evening and definitely not the night. What's the sense of having a king-size bed if *you* aren't in it? Sorry, got to go. I love you." He rang off.

Emma stared at her phone. So that was the way Everett had discovered Seth was out of town. He must have talked to Laila.

What really mattered was that Seth had actually said, "I love you." Easy to do on the phone. He'd never said it live, not even when they were making love. Or afterward when he was feeling very mellow. Was it just something to say to finish the conversation, or did he mean it? She wanted him to mean it, because she did.

Whatever Daddy thought, this was not a rebound. She'd never felt anything like it with Trip or any of the other men she'd known. Love came out of the woodwork and smacked you when you were least expecting it.

CHAPTER TWENTY-SIX

SETH DOODLED THROUGH the budget meeting. It was deeply boring. He'd give anything to be out on the lake or beating through the brush, even if he was checking hunting and fishing licenses.

He hadn't worried about his salary or his career path since his marriage broke up. He'd received appropriate promotions and raises since he'd joined the warden service—enough to support his single lifestyle. He wanted to stay out in the field, not move paperwork sitting behind a desk. But families cost money.

He was beginning to have hope that Emma cared for him at least a tenth as much as he loved her, so he'd put up with budget meetings and actively work toward promotion. He didn't particularly like administration, but he was good at it.

He called Emma the minute he pulled out of the Nashville government parking lot, but got only her voice mail. You didn't ask a woman to marry you on a cell phone. He'd stop in Williamston and pick up a dozen roses to take with him. Be waiting with champagne when she came home from the clinic. *Home* was no longer a dirty word since Emma was there. She'd find a job within commuting distance of Williamston. Maybe go to work for Barbara full-time, until she found something she liked better. Neither one of them was a kid. With luck she'd get pregnant. As long as they were together, they'd make whatever they chose to do work.

Was he crazy to build all these castles in the air? To believe he could make her happy in his world? He'd failed miserably with Clare.

His cell phone rang. He had it on hands-free and assumed Emma was calling him back. Not Emma. His mother. "Hey, Mom, what's up?"

"Where are you?"

"Halfway between Nashville and Williamston. If there's a problem…"

"Oh, dear. I think you'd better pull over."

He went cold and pulled over onto the shoulder. "Mom, are you all right? Is it Emma?"

"I'm not even sure I should tell you. It's about your father."

He rubbed his jaw with one hand. He already could use a shave. "What's he done now?"

"Please don't be angry. I know she's trying to help. She's such a dear girl."

"Mom, what is it?"

"I should've told you earlier, but I know how you get. Everett has been calling me every day since he's been back in town. He says he wants to make amends. It's one of those twelve-step things he does. He's also been talking to Emma, asking her to set up a meeting with you. Maybe have lunch."

"He *what*?"

"She's worried that you'll be angry with her."

"She's got that right. Thanks for telling me, Mom. I'll take care of it."

How long had this been going on? How often did Everett call her? Did he actually meet with her? She should've told him after the first call.

What kind of man did she think he was? Did she think he could hurt his father? His hands were cold on the steering wheel. She *was* afraid to tell him. Afraid of what he'd say, or worse, do.

He'd warned her off the first time they met his father. Yes, he'd been angry, but he thought he'd gotten his point across. Stay away from the man. But she hadn't. Instead she tried to intervene, to fix things between them. He didn't want them fixed, and he couldn't accept her interference. He'd grown up with secrets. He couldn't live with them the rest of his life. If she'd lie about this, what else had she hidden from him? Or would in the future? For his own good? What gave her the right to make that decision for him?

By the time he turned down his road he was

mad at both his parents and the woman he loved. She had betrayed him with the man he hated.

Emma's car was parked in her driveway. Instead of going into his own house, he headed for hers.

She flung open her front door and threw her arms around him. "I missed you," she whispered and kissed him.

He held her away from him. "How often have you seen my father?"

"What?"

"Mom told me he's been calling you, coming by to see you..."

"Only calling. And in the parking lot after the rehab class. He *wanted* to come by the clinic, but I told him no."

"Why didn't you tell me?"

"He's asking to see me, not you. I knew you wouldn't like it. He's trying to be nice."

"So he's been in contact with you, and you're willing to help him hide his attempts from me. Not your concern. Nobody asked you to intercede."

"He did. I thought—"

"Well, don't. Keep your hands off my life. Leave my family to me. It's not your family, it's mine."

The wounded look in Emma's eyes told him he'd gone too far.

"Fine. As of this minute I'm out." She shut the door in his face.

"Emma! Emma!" He slammed his fist against the old oak.

"Get out of my yard and out of *my* life!"

He considered breaking the pier glass in the door. No, he had to cool off and give her time to cool off, as well. Their first real fight, and it was a doozy. Going to take more than roses to smooth this one out. If he *could*. He turned on his heel, stormed across the street and slammed his front door. He'd go over later to make up. If she *would*. She'd expect an apology he couldn't give.

What if she was serious about getting out of her life? She'd done it before with Trip.

"EMMA, DO YOU KNOW what time it is?" Nathan asked. "I was in bed watching the news."

"You're not asleep, then. Nathan, can I have my job back?"

"Say what? Are you serious?"

"Dead serious. I don't belong up here."

"Of course I want you back. Same money, same job description."

"More money, more responsibility. I'm worth it."

"This is not a conversation to have over the phone. When can you come to Memphis?"

"Tomorrow morning."

"Can you get to my office by ten?"

"Barring car trouble or a flat tire."

"See you then. Oh, and Emma...welcome back."

She called Andrea and asked for her old room for the night. "My town house is too dusty to sleep in."

"Sure. We'd all love to see you. Are you coming alone, or is your hunk coming with you?"

"Alone. Definitely alone. I'll be there in two hours."

"It's late. Be careful driving. You know those semis are lunatics in the middle of the night."

Emma tossed toiletries and a change of clothes into her duffel. She had plenty of business clothes at her town house. She could stop by and dress there for her meeting with Nathan. If she left now, she could even get a few hours' sleep before her appointment. As much as she liked her town house, she was in no mood to put fresh sheets on the bed and knock the top layer of dust off the kitchen counters before she went to sleep. For once she needed the feeling of being home where she grew up, in her own bed. Seth had made it perfectly clear that she was still an outsider in his life. That she wasn't good enough. He was willing to let her in so far and no farther. Parts of him were always going to be off-limits.

Seth's house was completely dark when she drove out. Apparently he didn't need her in bed with him to sleep soundly. She might never sleep again. She would not cry. She loved the man! Thought he loved her. How wrong could she be?

She slowed down to exactly the speed limit. All she needed was a wreck or a speeding ticket.

In Memphis in her parents' house she found a note on her bedroom door from Andrea. "Go to bed. We'll talk tomorrow if you want to. Love."

She thought she'd lie awake most of the night. Instead she was out the instant she pulled the familiar duvet over her.

The next morning she avoided explaining anything either to Andrea or her father by taking a mug of coffee and a couple of sweet rolls with her and driving away before either of them intercepted her. She stopped by her town house on the way downtown to change into business clothes. She'd always been proud of the decorating she and Andrea had managed in a minimum of space, but now the little house seemed like a bad stage set and carried the dusty odor of unoccupied and unloved homes. She couldn't wait to get away.

She still had her parking pass for the garage at Nathan's office, but after nine o'clock the lower floors were filled. She drove round and round searching for a place. She'd forgotten how tiring it was to fight traffic, fight to park, fight to drive out to an appointment during the day and fight for a parking place all over again when she got back.

She'd also forgotten how much she hated four-inch heels, panty hose and skirts. Small annoyances, but still annoyances. The traffic noise seemed louder and more incessant, as well. Made the barking dogs and yowling cats at the clinic seem almost pleasant.

Time to think positive. She'd loved the craziness of her job, her city life. She'd be happy to plunge back into the long nights, the endless sodas and coffee. Her friends. Her team. She'd be back in the swing in two days, tops. Or so she told herself.

She arrived at the office for her meeting with Nathan ten minutes early. Her office mates might have avoided calling her while she was in Williamston, but they seemed delighted to see her back. Instead of the office pariah, she'd become the office hero. Nathan even came out of his office to hug her.

"Grab some coffee and let's go talk," he said. He leaned against the receptionist's desk. "Then I'll take you to lunch at The Peabody."

At that moment Seth shoved through the glass doors from the foyer and strode over to Emma. He was wearing his full dress uniform.

"What are you doing here?" she asked. Every woman in the room went instantly on point. In his uniform, he looked so good, so strong—but still angry. Had he tracked her down here to yell at her some more?

"Why didn't you leave me a message to say where you were going?" he snapped. "Barbara was birthing a foal. She didn't tell me you'd driven back to Memphis until this morning. When I couldn't find you, I was one step away from putting out an APB on your car."

"It's none of your business if I drive home to see my family. You made it quite clear yesterday that you don't care whether you ever see my face again."

"Not see your face again? Why would I not want to see your face again? I love your face."

"*Keep your hands off my life* doesn't sound like a mating call. It sounds like *we're over, we're through and you leave me alone for the rest of our lives.*"

"I was mad. Okay, I was furious. The only way I've been able to deal with Sarah's death was by ignoring it—digging down deep and burying it. You stuck your cute little hook in my soul and dragged it all to the surface where I had to stare at it."

"I didn't mean to cause you pain." She tried to sound very cool, but her voice was trembling. Everyone in the office was standing in doorways or sitting at their desks listening to the whole thing.

Oh, who cared. Let 'em listen. They might learn how to lose a good man in ten easy steps. Or less.

"Well, you did. Big-time pain. When I cooled off, I started thinking maybe you hadn't done such a bad thing, after all. Like sticking a hot poker on a wound to cauterize it. Hurts like hell, but you don't die of gangrene."

"How nice to know I've saved you from gangrene. Just what every woman wants to hear."

"You want this job back?" he asked. "Go back to being a city mouse?"

"I'm good at it. I'm lousy in your world. I keep messing up your life and everyone else's."

"Fine. If that's what you want, then I better start trying to find a desk job in Memphis or close enough to commute. God only knows what I'll do for a living, but I'll have to be a city mouse, if that's what you're going to be."

For the first time she smiled. "You're too big to be a city mouse. More like a city *rat*."

"Whatever. I have some connections with the local government people. Money might even be better, if I work it right. Maybe go with one of the security firms."

"You'd hate it. Why would you do that?"

"Because I love you, you mutton-headed chump. I want to marry you, and if you want town, I'll take town, so long as I get you with it."

"Even though I messed around in your relationship with your father?"

"That's what families do. It's one of the problems you'll have to deal with if you take me on."

"Sort of like skunks?"

This time he grinned. "Exactly like skunks."

"Can I be a country mouse instead?"

"So you'll marry me?"

The office erupted around her, male and female. Above the din, Ashley, one of the assistants who'd worked closely with Emma before she lost her job, called from her office door, "Marry him, Emma! He's gorgeous!"

EPILOGUE

"WEDDINGS ARE SUPPOSED to be insane," Andrea said. "That's so the bride and groom will be so glad it's over they'll have a blissful honeymoon away from it."

"That's one I've never heard," Emma said. "Isn't there supposed to be a limit to the madness?"

"This has actually been relatively calm. Most weddings take up to a year to plan. We've done this one in two months."

"Only because you're amazing. I haven't been much help. I'm juggling the wedding with my part-time job with Barbara and the rehabilitation classes and Nathan's projects. Somewhere in there Seth and I have to find time for each other."

"You've done everything I asked you to do," Andrea said. "Thank heaven for cell phones and the internet. Now we can relax."

"This is relaxing?" Emma laughed. "Barbara is off collecting a hawk with a broken leg and probably won't be here. Earl and Janeen almost didn't find an overnight babysitter for their monsters. They're good kids, but they don't belong at the ceremony. Nor, heaven help us, at the reception. It would not have been fun if Earl and Janeen had been forced to bring them. The steeple on top of the church might not have survived. We have no idea whether Seth's father, Everett, will turn up, and if so, what state he'll be in. Laila swears he's sober again, but that could change with one drink. Catherine is having a meltdown because she hates the way the salon did her hair. Patrick wants to wear jeans to the ceremony—not going to happen."

"I'm still sane," Andrea said, "although I can't vouch for your father. I don't think I've ever seen him as nervous, not even at *our* wedding."

"I hated you at first, you know," Emma said. "I wanted to run away from home so Daddy would be sorry he married you."

"I knew that. I didn't like you either." Andrea slipped off her celadon satin pumps. "That jeans thing of Patrick's seems like a great idea after thirty minutes in these shoes."

"You do know I love you now, don't you?" Emma asked.

"Likewise. If you and I could get to this point, there's at least a faint chance that someday Everett Logan may shape up enough so he and Seth will be able to tolerate each other."

"I doubt that, but it would make Laila so

happy. Seth just wishes his father would move to the Mojave Desert or American Samoa."

"Speaking of which, where are you going on your honeymoon?"

"To Laila's cabin. We can't take time off right now. Seth has summertime crazy people to save, rescue or arrest, and Nathan wants me on call to drive into town for meetings at least once a week."

"So you *are* going to keep working for him?"

"Under contract for special projects only. I can do most everything from home on my computer, except meet clients face-to-face. The money he's offering is too good to pass up. Besides, I loved my job, and I want to keep my hand in.

"Plus we have to clear out my town house to sell, and find some way to integrate Seth's household goods with mine. Not that he has much. Clare took most of it. I still think it would've been easier just to cohabit, but Daddy would have keeled over in horror. He kept worrying that I'm pregnant. I'm not."

"Yet," Andrea said. They both jumped when someone knocked on the vestry door.

"Emma, Andrea, it's time." Laila stuck her head in. She wore a teal silk suit that contrasted beautifully with her white hair. "Oh, Emma, you look lovely! I'm so glad you decided to have a real wedding, even if it is the middle of July."

"And a reception in air-conditioned comfort in

the parish hall," Andrea added. "I've never believed in weddings and receptions out of doors. Too many miserable things can happen."

"Emma," Laila said, "I brought you something. It's a very old tradition. A sixpence to put in your shoe for good luck. Maybe if I'd used one, Everett and I would have made a better marriage. Oh, dear, I'm going to cry."

She patted Emma on the shoulder of her white silk gown. Andrea winked at Emma and slipped out into the narthex of the little church. She waited to walk down the aisle and take her place up front as Emma's matron of honor. In the meantime she attempted to calm David French's jitters before he walked down the aisle with his daughter.

"I'm so glad you're marrying Seth," Laila said with a sniffle. "I knew it was the wrong bride the last time. I know it's the right one this time."

Emma hugged her. "Thank you. Now, let's do this thing."

Emma had nixed the twelve bridesmaids and dozen groomsmen, although Seth's warden buddies would have enjoyed showing up in their dress uniforms. They came in civilian clothes as guests instead. Emma's simple, classic white silk gown didn't have a train or ruffles or a hoop, nor was her veil French lace. She'd never been a ruffles kind of woman.

As the organ began playing the Purcell wedding music, Laila walked down the aisle on Patrick's arm. He was already taller than his father.

"We can still call this off," David French whispered as Emma took his arm. "It's not too late."

"It was too late the first time Seth opened his front door and found me on his doorstep."

"If you're sure…"

"Sure and unafraid. That's a first for me."

The doors opened. Standing in a ray of sunlight by the altar was Earl, handsome in his gray morning suit, dwarfed by Seth, who stood beside him looking *incredibly* handsome. How could she ever have thought he wasn't?

Andrea walked to the front and took her place as matron of honor.

After Andrea was seated, Emma held her father's arm and went joyously to her beloved.

She had a crazy thought as she took her first step. Could she and Seth possibly find where her babies were nesting? They'd adore the wedding cake.

* * * * *

Look for the next book in the
WILLIAMSTON WILDLIFE RESCUE *series,*
available from
Harlequin Heartwarming Fall 2018!